INSTANT DARKNESS

EMP CRISIS SERIES: BOOK 1

MARK J. RUSSELL
J.J. HOLDEN

Copyright © 2019 by JJ Holden & Mark J. Russell

All rights reserved.

No part of this book may be reproduced in any form or by any electronic or mechanical means, including information storage and retrieval systems, without written permission from the author, except for the use of brief quotations in a book review.

This is a work of fiction. Names, places, characters, and incidents are either the product of the author's imagination or are used fictitiously, and any resemblance to any actual persons, living or dead, organizations, events or locales is entirely coincidental.

1

THE SHORTWAVE RADIO SQUAWKED AGAIN, and Abram Patterson whipped his head toward the workbench. The voice cut through the static: "This is Delta Whiskey Seven Tango, do you have your ears on, Abe?"

Abram picked up the microphone, repeating his call sign and frequency. "Danny, you're going to get fined by the IARU if you don't use protocol. What do you need?" he asked, booming voice echoing through the cavernous basement of his home in Manchester, New Hampshire.

"Yeah, yeah. Need to be sure you know about the event," Danny said through the static.

Abram keyed his microphone and ran thick fingers through his dark hair. "The CME?"

"Yeah."

"I heard this solar storm is nothing to be worried about. Only expecting low-level fields coming at us."

"Negative, Abe. The Feds are cautioning the news outlets about creating a panic. I've seen the images of the sun; this is not a low-level occurrence. I'd say we have less than three days to a major event."

"Are you sure about this?"

"Dead sure, man. I'm on my way out of town. I recommend you do the same, if you can."

Abram's lips flat-lined as a floorboard creaked overhead. His wife, Shelly, was probably setting the dining room table, though he only heard one pair of shoes plodding about. Their teenaged daughter, Emma, was likely somewhere else in their two-story colonial. Both Shelly and Emma were unaware of the life-changing event that was coming—soon, they would learn that their world would be turned upside-down.

Taking a deep breath, Abram could practically taste the musty air. He'd spent way too much time stocking the metal utility shelves that lined the far end of the basement, and less time worrying about the aroma of the dingy space. Abram exhaled slowly as his finger moved to key the mic again, but before he could reply, the man's voice interrupted him: "Listen, Abe, time's running out. Gotta go. D-Dog out."

The channel went silent except for the low buzz of static, and Abram stood, thinking. Then he hurried to his laptop that was also on his workbench, the sweat on his brow chilled by the cool air. He pulled up some images on his computer—not government images, but pictures of the sun that scientists he respected had posted. Scientists who, like him, believed in being prepared for catastrophic events. He shook his head at what he saw and felt sweat forming on his forehead.

"Damn," he said, his throat feeling dry as burnt paper.

He rushed across the cement floor toward some of his supplies, held in a Faraday cage he'd constructed years ago, when he first started preparing for such an event. He'd long held the belief that most of the things that needed to be kept in a Faraday cage in the case of an electromagnetic pulse, either natural or manmade, would be useless in the long run, but he'd recently changed his mind. Or rather, his wife, Shelly, had changed his mind. She had explained there were certain items that could come in handy—even before the power grid had been restored—and that would make his teen daughter's life more bearable, and thus make Emma easier to live with, so he had decided to build a Faraday cage out of a steel garbage can.

He opened the can and peered into it. He'd lined the can with cardboard, padded it with some old towels his wife wouldn't miss, and added a desiccant to absorb moisture and additional electronics he'd purchased for this purpose. Also in the can were a second-hand ham radio, a laptop (mostly for Emma), a solar charger, and extra batteries, which probably didn't need to be in the Faraday Cage, but it seemed smart to have them stored in the same place. He'd also found an inexpensive video drone—the most recent piece of equipment added—along with a second set of four handheld two-way radios.

Gazing at his stock of essential supplies, he took a deep breath and sighed at the thought that his foresight was now going to come in handy. He steeled himself as he pondered the most efficient way to load the gear for their journey—a journey they'd have to take all too soon.

Clearing his throat, Abram marched to the bottom of the basement stairs and craned his neck back, looking up the stairs to the cracked-open door above.

"Shelly?" he yelled up into the main house.

"Yeah, dear?"

"Make sure Emma's bug-out bag is stocked."

"What are you talking—"

His booming voice cut through his wife's question: "We're leaving, and this is not a drill."

Nick Caulfield placed the paper on the dining room table as silverware clinked against plates intermittently, the only sound that could be heard in the room. His teenaged son and six-year-old daughter munched on their meals in silence as Nick waited, pensively. He didn't like the idea of the grilling that would ensue, but as a single parent, it was the best he could do.

He glanced at his offspring in turn. They both bore a striking resemblance to his own appearance—light brown hair and eyes contrasting their pale skin, a testament to favoring the indoors, especially during the frigid New Hampshire winters. His daughter's hair was done up in pigtails; they bounced as she tinkered with her food. His son's, on the other hand, was unruly.

His daughter peered over at the paper, a quizzical look on her face. "What's that, Daddy?"

"Rae Ann, this is Corey's report card. Finish your veggies, now."

Corey kept his eyes on his plate, neither looking at his father nor at the report card that sat between them like an exposed dirty secret.

"I don't like broccoli," Rae Ann continued, breaking the

silence. She lifted her stuffed bear from her lap and set it next to her plate. "But Louisa does."

"No toys at the table, honey," Nick said, still focusing on Corey, who hadn't raised his eyes.

Rae Ann sighed and placed Louisa in her lap. She looked at her broccoli and then at her father, who tore his gaze from Corey and raised an eyebrow at her. She squirted ranch dressing on her plate and dipped the tiny green trees in it. Rae Ann was much easier to keep in line than her older brother.

"Corey," Nick said, "look at me when I'm talking to you."

Corey shot a look at his father and huffed. "If Mom were here, she wouldn't make a big deal about me failing that class. Nobody even speaks French around here, so what does it matter?"

Nick took a deep breath and exhaled slowly. It had been five years since the passing of his wife, and the pain hadn't gone away. He doubted it ever would.

A knife screeched against a plate, the sound halting abruptly, but Nick's teeth were still on edge. "You know the rules, Corey."

"I know," Corey said, looking back at his uneaten mashed potatoes and veggies. "Get at least Cs—"

Nick finished his sentence, "—or I get the game console. And no social media."

Corey suddenly looked back up. "But I got an A in math, Dad."

"Let me make this very clear: a failing grade in any class is unacceptable."

"I forgot to turn in a paper—"

"Not good enough. I'm taking the game box—or cube,

whatever it is—until I get a call from your French teacher saying you're caught up again. I don't want you failing the eleventh grade. Do you understand?" Nick narrowed his eyes at the boy.

"It's not fair," Corey said. He stood up and shoved his chair under the table. He began to stomp away, but Nick called him back.

"Clear your dishes, Corey," he said.

Corey worked his jaw as he picked up his dishes and delivered them to the kitchen sink. Nick watched his retreating back and sighed inwardly. Had Corey just forgotten a paper, or was it more than that? If he wanted the truth, Nick was going to have to call the school on Monday. Corey wasn't an unreasonable kid but wasn't beyond manipulating the truth to his own advantage. He had the feeling that these last two years of high school and getting Corey into college was going to be hell on wheels.

"Finish up, honey," Nick said to Rae Ann. "I need to get back to work."

"Can I have ice cream?" Rae Ann asked, chewing the top of a broccoli floret.

"You know we only have dessert on Friday nights," Nick said. "Finish up and clear the table, please."

Satisfied that most of the vegetables had been eaten, Nick stood up and cleared his own plate. He rinsed the dinner dishes and placed them in the dishwasher—it was Corey's job, but he just didn't feel like another argument this evening.

"Is your homework done, honey?" he asked.

His daughter was sitting at the kitchen table again, talking with her stuffed teddy bear. That toy was her constant companion.

"I'm only supposed to read out loud to you, Daddy."

"That's right. It's Saturday." Nick shook his head—was work consuming him so much that he'd forgotten what day it was? Looking back at Rae Ann, he continued, "Get your book, honey, I'm almost done here."

Nick grabbed a soap pod from under the sink and started the dishwasher. By the time he'd dried his hands on the dishtowel, Rae Ann was back with her book.

He bit his lip and listened patiently about a porcupine named Fluffy, while Rae Ann read. His instincts said to correct her, or to make her reread passages until she was fluent, but her teacher had told him in no uncertain terms that he was to keep his mouth shut and only praise at the very end. She would do the teaching, all he had to do was listen. But it was excruciating.

Once she finished reading to him, Nick praised her and sent her upstairs to get ready for bed. He made his way through the front room to his office and heard the faint noise of a TV that had been left on in the living room. On the TV, a man was droning on about some phenomenon happening on the sun. Flares, it looked like from the images.

Nick turned it off as he strode by and tried to mentally prepare for the long night of work ahead of him. It didn't take long—work-mode was his default mode.

Standing in his garage, Abram felt his cell phone buzzing in his pocket. Outside, the faint sound of a basketball bouncing against the blacktop of a neighbor's driveway started up—whoever was playing was oblivious to the dangers that would soon engulf the region. Now was not the time to be playing—it was the time for action, plain and simple.

He pulled it out and answered the call. "What's up, Gary?"

He heard his best friend's voice on the other end: "You all packed up?"

Abram stepped toward his 1976 Land Cruiser and peered into the cargo area. He was sure that everything was there—the bug-out bags, the Faraday cage, and several pieces of equipment that were too expensive to keep an extra at the compound, like his night vision goggles.

"Everything I planned on taking, yes," Abram said. In truth, he had been planning on stowing an extra can of fuel in the back but knew Shelly and Emma would complain about the lack of leg room during the entire journey. Besides, the five hundred gallons he stored at the compound would probably suffice.

"Good," Gary said. "I'm leaving now. I want to get out of here before the general public gets wind of what's going on and starts clogging the roads. It's bound to get out soon, if it hasn't already."

"You'll probably make it to the compound before I do."

"When are you leaving?"

A fly buzzed by Abram's ear, and he swatted at it, missing narrowly. "I have to wait until my sister-in-law gets here."

"And when's that?"

"Near dawn."

"You need to leave as soon as possible, man. Middle of the night is ideal—less suspicion from the neighbors and all."

"Maggie's insisting on working her last shift at the hospital, and Shelly refuses to leave without her."

"I'm so glad I don't have a wife to kowtow to," Gary said.

"You should just tell them what's what. Order them into the car."

"A little hard to do when there isn't any hard evidence, and no, some pictures from the internet don't count when the news all says it's nothing to be worried about. The ladies trust the authorities not to mislead us." Abram sighed. "I'm glad I'm not that gullible."

"And irrational."

"They aren't irrational, Gary. They are just not as informed as you or I. They might point out that our sources could be called unreliable."

"Whatever you say—I'm not getting into that again. Listen, I'll meet you up there. Just get up there as soon as you can, man."

"Will do. Open the cabins when you get there, will you?"

"Yeah. And I'll gather all the fresh produce I can. What we can't consume, we can preserve."

"Sounds like a plan."

"See you tomorrow, Abram."

Gary hung up, and Abram pocketed his phone. He stared into his vehicle's cargo area again and furrowed his brow, thinking of any last-minute supplies he could cram into any available space.

The door to the house opened, and Abram turned to see Emma walking out into the garage. At sixteen, she was looking more and more like a woman every day.

"Are you ready to go, Em?" he asked.

"I'm ready, Dad."

"I've got your bug-out bag, but if you have any personal items you want to bring, you should get them ready to go."

Abram looked at his daughter and noticed the unease painted on her face.

"What's the matter, Em?"

"I'm worried about Corey. We have room, and—"

"No, we don't," Abram said. "We've got your Aunt Maggie coming with us, and I think that's enough."

"But Corey could help."

"There isn't enough food to go around, Em. Simple as that."

She took a deep breath and let it out slowly. "Corey could be an asset," she said. "He's strong, and he knows how to fix things."

"I'm sorry, Em," Abram said. "I don't know how long we're going to be in Vermont. If we took the boy, we'd have to take his dad and sister too. There's no way we can do that."

"But he's my best friend, Dad. He's part of my family. If we don't take him, I might not see him again."

Emma looked away from her father, not meeting his steely gaze. He hated doing this to her, but he was focused on her safety, and asset allocation was an important part of the equation.

"Emma, we can't take them, and that's that. Now go pack your things." Abram pursed his lips.

Abram turned to head back toward the Land Cruiser, and heard his daughter's pleas behind him.

"There's plenty of room," Emma said, "and we've brought up tons and tons of food. Cans and military rations and barrels full of flour and rice. There are the lake and the river near the camp. We could help the Caulfields survive."

Standing at the back of the vehicle, Abram glanced over

at his daughter. He could see the flush in her cheeks despite being dozens of feet away.

"I know it seems like a lot of food, but really, it's not," Abram said. "If this solar flare takes out a large area, it could be a year before everything is back to normal. We just don't know how prepared the government is, or the power industry. I can't take the chance that you won't have enough to eat because we tried to save too many people."

"You are going to let my best friend die!" The pain in her voice was palpable.

Abram knew he was going to be paying for this for weeks to come. He thought of the pain of living with an emotionally injured daughter versus the pain of watching that same child die of hunger, and he knew which one he was willing to endure.

"I'm sorry, Emma, but my responsibility is to my own family, no more, no less. Now go gather anything else you might need. I need to talk to your mother."

Emma ran back into the house, slamming the door behind her.

Abram let out a sigh at the thought of taking a sulky, angry, and self-justifying teenager to their compound, but that was just another part of having children. She would see the wisdom of his ways one day...or not. Either way, she'd be alive, and that's what mattered most to him.

He closed the back of the vehicle and padded toward the door leading into the house. Once inside, he closed the door gently behind him, hearing Emma's distant cries. It was going to be a long night.

2

Emma Patterson's phone vibrated, and she opened her eyes into the gray light of the pre-dawn. She hadn't given her phone to her father when he'd asked for it, telling him she'd give it to him in the morning. Instead, Emma had checked online for instructions on how to make her own Faraday cage out of a small cardboard box, padded on the inside with a headscarf and wrapped in multiple layers of aluminum foil. When they reached the compound, she would put her phone in her own personal Faraday cage after she'd shared her location with Corey. The bug out place was hard to find, and she was proud of herself for thinking of it.

She eased herself out of her narrow bed and took a few steps to reach a nearby second-hand chest of drawers, getting dressed as quietly as she could in jeans, a t-shirt, and Doc Martins. Goosebumps sprung up on her arms, so she pulled on a gray hoody too. Glancing in the mirror that backed the dresser, she pulled her dirty-blonde hair up into a ponytail and wiped the sweat residue from her tanned forehead. It was going to be a long day, but she was ready for it.

Grabbing her phone from her nightstand, she tried once again to call Corey.

No answer.

She figured he must have gotten into another fight with his dad over grades. His dad sometimes took his phone as well as his game consoles when they weren't getting along—that must be why he hadn't responded since dinner time last night.

She texted him that she needed to talk to him, and was going to leave a letter through his mail slot in case he wouldn't be able to reach her in time.

Sitting down at her desk, Emma pulled a piece of blank paper from her sketch pad and started on the note:

Corey,

Dad says there is going to be some kind of solar event that's going to take out the power grid, and we are leaving for the compound in Vermont. This map is how to get there. Dad says there might not be power or communications for a year! The safe house has lots of space and food and is set up off the grid. You have to come. I can't live without my best friend for a whole year.

Emma

Below her note, she drew a map from their neighborhood in Manchester, New Hampshire to the compound in the mountains of central Vermont. She knew the last ten miles could be problematic, as it was little more than a track. There were a lot of dirt roads, and the two-mile drive to the cabins wasn't marked. Not even a mailbox to show where to turn. She wrote a note at the bottom of the page that she'd turn on location sharing on her cell phone, but that might only work until the event reached Earth. Then her phone would be fried, or the cell phone towers would be out of commission, or...

She shook her head to dispel the thoughts—thinking about a world without power and modern communications made her sick to her stomach.

But those feelings were nothing compared to the void she'd feel without Corey by her side during the end of the world.

Emma slipped the letter and map into an envelope and wrote Corey's name on the outside. Sealing it, she stepped into the hall and passed the partially open door to her parents' bedroom. Beneath her feet, the floorboards creaked softly, disturbing the early morning silence that lingered between her father's light snores.

She froze when her father's snoring abruptly stopped, cursing the fact that he was such a light sleeper. Men in his line of work typically were.

Dammit, she thought. *If he catches me with this note...*

She eased off her right foot, expecting the floor to creak again, but there was no sound. She heard her father turn, probably rolling onto his back.

Was he awake?

Her question was answered when his light snoring started up again. How her mother dealt with that racket was beyond her, though over two decades of practice likely had something to do with it.

Emma continued down the hallway and descended the steps.

Just then, her father's alarm blared.

Crap!

Hearing him lumber out of bed, she hurried across the linoleum kitchen floor and out through the garage door that led to the side of the house.

From the side of the garage, she could slip out the gate and out onto the street. She took a quick look to make sure that her dad wasn't looking out her parents' bedroom window, but there was no one there, thank goodness. The sun was on the verge of rising, and her parents were prepared to leave as soon as Maggie arrived. She had to make this quick—and not get caught.

She jogged next door to Corey's house, feeling the crisp morning air against her face. A few sparrows chirped nearby as she reached Corey's front door. Without a moment's hesitation, she shoved the letter through the mailbox and ran back home before the sun came up over the horizon.

Back in the kitchen, she let out a sigh of relief when footsteps creaked upstairs. She grabbed a box of cereal and a bowl, not worrying about making noise as she poured the sugary goodness into the bowl. Sitting down, she could feel her heart still racing in her chest, though she was in the clear—she'd be finishing her breakfast by the time her parents came downstairs, and they'd never know the difference.

Nick was up and working at his desk in his office before dawn. Neat stacks of paper flanked him as he worked out the kinks in a new product, the "ISO-mug," that would keep beverages at a constant temperature for more than twenty-four hours. The initial design paper had asked for a stable temperature container, but he'd awoken in the middle of the night with an idea for a product the consumer could adjust, so the temperature would be perfect for each individual. He figured both mugs would be marketable. The entry-level model that just featured one constant setting and the up-market model that could be adjusted.

Now, he just needed to figure out how to implement the new feature.

A sound at the front door broke his concentration. He lifted his head to listen, but it was all quiet. Must have been a breeze or his imagination or something.

He got up and brewed himself a cup of coffee, tasted it, decided it was too hot, and carried it back into his office where he kept a thermometer. When the coffee was his perfect level of "hot," he measured it. It was one hundred and fifty degrees, but he liked his coffee hotter than many people. He really should have someone take a poll. Except most people didn't know what temperature their coffee was; taking a poll would be useless. He'd need to go to a coffee shop with a thermometer and test people's coffee. For now, he'd say one hundred and forty degrees.

A short time later, he was beginning the math that would tell him how much of the iso-thermic substance his company had designed would be needed when the sound of an engine starting pulled him from his concentration. It wasn't just any engine—it was his neighbor's Land Cruiser.

Nick stood up to look out the window, in time to see Abram driving away, the vehicle full, with the passenger seat and both jump seats in the back occupied. It looked like there was a lot of stuff packed around the people in the cargo area, as well.

"What the hell," he muttered. This was unusual, to say the least. Sunday mornings were an odd time to head off on some trip, with the beginning of the school week quickly approaching. Regardless, he hoped they weren't going far—those people in the rear were in for an uncomfortable ride if they were.

Sitting back down, Nick refocused on the task at hand, even more convinced that there was a need to offer more than one temperature. If not a mug with a temperature setting, then perhaps mugs set to different temperatures. Then, the customer would buy the container that corresponded to the hotness that suited their taste, and mugs would be easy enough to produce—each mug would simply have a different amount of the isothermal material in the sleeve of the cup. Still, he would rather create a mug that was adjustable. He was going to continue to work on that as well—beyond "ISO-mugs," the applications could be endless.

Corey peeled his eyes open and rolled onto his side. The early morning sun shone through his partially open blinds, glinting off the band posters that consumed most of the wall space in his room. Every band represented had reached its prime well before he was born, but he loved them nonetheless.

He let out a long breath. For a Sunday morning, he was up early and was confused about why. Had he heard something? His dad had returned his phone in the night—it was on the bedside table. Corey checked it to see that Emma had been calling him, but there were no voice messages, and the texts only said, "Call me." He hit the call button, but Emma didn't pick up.

"I'm calling you back, Em," he muttered after the beep. "What's going on? Call me."

Taking the phone off its silent setting, he placed it back on the table and lumbered out of bed. He dodged several piles of dirty clothing on the floor and moseyed over to his dresser, which had a few articles of clothing strewn about. He rummaged to find a pair of jeans and a wrinkled black t-shirt that both passed the "smell test." Bingo.

Dressing slowly, he thought about Emma and what in the world she could have been calling about so early in the morning. The one thing he thought he could guarantee was that she would be fast asleep at that hour. So, what would get her up? Or maybe she hadn't gone to sleep? Was something wrong? He worried and wished he'd had his phone overnight, and that the ringer was on when his dad had returned it. He would have been awoken by the ringtone and could have helped her. Would have been there for her.

Once fully dressed, he picked up his phone and slid it into his pocket, then headed downstairs to get a bite to eat.

Another day in paradise...

As Corey passed the living room, he saw that his father was in his office. Working early again. Well, it was understandable—once Rae Ann was up, she wouldn't give him any peace. She didn't believe in parents working on the weekend.

Corey was about to turn into the kitchen when he spotted an envelope on the floor just inside the front door. Mail didn't come this early in the day, and never on Sunday. He went to retrieve the letter from the entryway and was surprised when he saw his name written on it in Emma's curvy handwriting.

"Huh?"

He carried the envelope into the kitchen and set it on the table while he poured himself cereal and put bread in the toaster. There was already coffee in the pot, so he poured himself some, but when he tasted it, the coffee was tepid, and he had to microwave it to make it drinkable. His dad had said something about a mug that kept coffee at the correct temperature. He should make a coffee carafe that did the same thing.

Finally, he sat at the table with his cereal, toast, and coffee and took a bite. Then he opened the letter and pulled out a single piece of paper—on it was a note and a map. He took another spoonful and considered what she'd written.

"A solar event?" he muttered between bites. "What's she talking about?"

He pulled out his phone and searched the web. There were hundreds of articles on the upcoming flare, but none of them indicated that the public should be worried. Well, almost none. Some prepper—like Emma's dad—had written a blog post saying the government was concealing the severity of the storm and that the images he'd seen indicated a coronal mass ejection strong enough to take out the power stations and communications in the path of its field.

Corey figured her dad must agree with this guy. But why would it matter where you were when the flare hit? If the entire east coast was going to be without power, why not just stay put? Well, he reasoned, maybe you could drive far enough that you'd be out of the range of the pulse wave, or whatever. You could move to a place where life would go on as usual until New England was up and running again. Unless the entire continent was affected. Then, where would you go?

Emma's dad obviously had a place in mind—a compound in Vermont, by the looks of the note. Maybe it was a bug out location. Corey had heard of those. Places to retreat to where you could be safe while civilization was falling apart. He studied the map again. It showed how to get to the compound. So maybe the place was a safe place for shelter until the world was back to normal.

He checked his phone; she hadn't shared her location yet, so it must take a while to get there. Well, yeah. Vermont was two hours away, and he'd bet that the hideout was up in the mountains, someplace remote. A spot where it would be hard to find them. He'd check again in an hour. It was possible she'd be there by then. Or maybe they hadn't left yet. That was possible.

Corey carried his dishes to the sink and let himself out through the patio door. He hurried through the gate that Dad had built for him and Emma when they were younger so they could go to and from each other's houses without going onto the street. Dad had always feared child abduction, and Corey could never figure out why. No one he'd ever known had been taken.

Still, the gate was handy, and he climbed the back steps to the Pattersons' kitchen door. He knocked, but there was no answer. He peered in the windows but didn't see anything, so he walked around the house and went in through the door to the garage. Mr. Patterson's Land Cruiser was gone. Would he take the Jeep-like vehicle all the way to Vermont with Emma riding on a jump seat in the back? That seemed like cruel and unusual punishment to him. Maybe they could switch off so that no one had to ride the entire trip in the rear.

Mrs. Patterson's car was in the garage, as well as a car that Corey didn't recognize. Had they gotten another vehicle? It had Rhode Island plates. Emma's Aunt Maggie was from Rhode Island—maybe this was her car. That meant two people in the jump seats in the back of the Land Cruiser. Pure torture. Four people headed for Vermont in a four-wheel-drive vehicle. If Aunt Maggie had come, this must really be serious. He was pretty sure Emma once told him she had some kind of high-powered job. No one would leave that kind of responsibility on a whim.

He leaned against the door and thought. If he was going to convince his father to drop everything and drive to Vermont, he was going to need more facts. A note from Emma wasn't going to be enough to convince his scientifically minded dad. He was going to need evidence, hard evidence. Right, then he'd have to find it.

Corey exited the garage, ducked back through the fence, and entered the house the same way he'd gone out. He took a quick minute to rinse his dishes and put them in the dishwasher. No point in attracting his dad's ire when he needed to be able to influence him. Especially after what happened at last night's dinner.

Upstairs in his room, Corey fired up his laptop and printer. He was going to need a stack of papers with hard evidence if his dad was even going to listen. He would start with the images the national weather service had put up, and then contrast them with the pictures the prepper bloggers posted and those from other governments and scientists that weren't governed by the NWS or NASA or any other part of the United States Government. Then he would pull information about the effects of CMEs, including the shutdown of a power plant in Quebec in the late 1980s.

His fingers flew across the keyboard as he pulled up the facts that he needed. He was going to need a new print cartridge after printing all these color images. He found the documentation he needed on CMEs and their effects, and then he hit the jackpot: an article by a government insider warning about what would happen if the threat of a CME was broadcast to the general public. Basically, murder and mayhem, as well as people stranded on freeways full of cars that would no longer run, either because their electronics had been knocked out or because they'd run out of gas. He printed that too.

He finished gathering his papers, placing Emma's note on the top, when Rae Ann stuck her head in the door. "Do you want to have breakfast with me?" she asked.

"I already ate, Rae," he said, "but how would you like to go on a road trip?"

3

NICK SLAMMED his hand on his desk, then ran both hands through his hair.

"This isn't right," he muttered.

He was frustrated with what the numbers were telling him about the insulating material in the ISO-mug. If his calculations were correct, they would need so much of the product that it would be like drinking from a container the size of a flowerpot just to get a cup of your favorite hot beverage.

"I have to be doing something wrong," he said.

That might've been true, but when they had researched this material, he was sure they'd done tests that gave better yields with less content. Had he studied the wrong stuff? He knew his boss had worked on this before sending it his way for design work. Something was way out of whack. He felt his frustration rising and decided to take a step back.

He analyzed the specs that came with the file when he took on this project, and he was surprised when he found two materials sheets. He would have sworn there was only one when he'd checked before. He was confused for about thirty seconds, and then decided he'd be thankful instead. If there was a second compound, then maybe he wasn't designing mugs the size of coffee cans after all.

Nick started punching in numbers for the second material, hopeful that he'd still be able to design an elegant hot liquids container.

The calculations were looking better, but he double-checked both, just to make sure he wasn't in error. He didn't usually make rookie mistakes like that.

He was deep into the specs when a knock on the door disturbed his concentration, and he swiveled to see Corey entering the room.

"I'm busy, Corey," Nick said. "Can this wait?"

"No," Corey said. "There's a solar flare that's sending a solar storm toward Earth."

"Corey, your science project can wait, can't it? I'm swamped here," Nick said, turning back to his computer.

"This isn't a science project, Dad. You've got to listen to me."

Corey stepped over to his desk and put some papers on it.

"Corey," Nick said, picking up the papers and handing them back to his son. "You know not to disturb me when I'm working. Take this away, and I'll talk to you later."

Nick fixed his eyes back on his computer screen, but out of his peripherals, he saw his son still standing there.

"It can't wait, Dad. I know you think Emma's dad is a doomsday nut job, but I think he's right this time. It's on the news."

"What?" Nick turned back to his boy.

"Pull up the news, Dad. It's crazy what's going on." Corey motioned to the computer screen.

Nick opened his browser and pulled up his favorite news website. On an embedded video, a group of talking heads were debating the problem. Corey crowded in behind to look over Nick's shoulder as a couple of men argued over the impact of the solar storm.

The speakers' names weren't listed, but Nick saw a bald man in glasses who was explaining that most people wouldn't even notice the interruption in service. The guy across the table from him shoved his chair away from the table and called the bald guy an idiot. Then he picked up a chart that showed the severity of this event, that it was way beyond what humanity had seen before.

But then a banner flashed across the bottom of the screen, saying that people were best sheltering in place, not to panic and clog the roads. FEMA and the Red Cross would be setting up centers to help people get through the crisis.

"See that," Nick said, pointing to the banner. "The authorities are advising that we don't travel. We should do what they say and stay put."

"Emma's dad didn't believe that," Corey said. "They've gone to the hills in Vermont, so they'll be safe. I think we should go too. They left us the directions."

"If Abram wanted us along, he would have come and told me about this, Corey. A note from Emma does not constitute an invitation."

"He didn't have time. That's why Emma drew us a map. And she's going to share her location with us so we can find our way there."

"Share her location?"

"With her cellphone, Dad. Listen, we can't stay here. We won't have power or water and then it'll be chaos with all the people around here."

"Corey, the corps of engineers will sort it out," Nick said. "We should stay here in our own beds. We've got plenty of food for a few days. The 'crisis' should be over by then."

"No, Dad, it won't. Mr. Patterson thinks it could be a year or more before things are back to normal. We could be herded into the Verizon Arena, or someplace like that. You don't want to be stuck on a cot, fighting for food with a bunch of strangers, do you? Especially when we could be safe with people we know."

"Corey, if there's no electricity, how are we going to gas up our car for a trip to Vermont? We need a full tank to get up into the mountains." Nick frowned at his son. Why was he pushing so hard on this? Of course—Emma. The two couldn't bear to be separated.

"If we go now, you'll still be able to get gas. The solar storm hasn't hit yet. But if we wait, then the roads will be full of cars that can't move, either out of gas or their computers fried. We need to go now, Dad."

The computer monitor was displaying pictures of a flare jumping off the surface of the sun. Nick was fascinated. How could something so far away possibly affect them? It seemed like nonsense. A solar flare taking out the power infrastructure of the eastern coast of the continent? It was ludicrous. And he had work to do—he couldn't be heading off to Vermont just in case there was an emergency. Especially when he had his doubts about his welcome when he got there.

"All the official government announcements say to stay

put, Corey," Nick said, pointing again to the rolling banner at the bottom of the computer screen. "Look here. 'Shelter in place. Don't clog the highways. Assistance will be available in your location.' Why leave when everything will be fine here?"

"Because it won't. Why can't we just go where we know it will be safe?"

"Corey, if we are going to lose power, I really need to get this work done. I'll think about leaving when these calculations are done, okay? I can't really focus on anything else until this is done. Go spend some time with your sister, and I'll talk to you when I'm done here." Nick made a sweeping gesture with his hand, indicating the papers and file folders on his desk.

Corey let out a small sigh of defeat. "Don't blame me if we end up stuck here with no food or running water. No heat when the cold weather sets in, and no lights when it gets dark at four in the afternoon."

"Don't you think you're being a little over-the-top, Corey?" Nick asked. "There is zero chance the world is coming to an end. I'm sure the power will go out for a day or two, but we've dealt with that before. Now please let me finish my work."

"You never listen to me," Corey said between clenched teeth, then he slammed out of the room.

Nick looked at the door for a moment, hearing Corey's footfalls fade as he stormed away. Then Nick closed his internet browser and shook the thoughts of the "event" out of his head. He had work to do.

Corey lay on his bed and ran the conversation with his father through his mind. It was just like his dad to ignore what Corey had to say. And it wasn't only Corey, but Mr. Patterson too. His dad wasn't stupid; he was arrogant. He thought he knew everything about everything. Corey slammed his fist into the bed. He just had to get to Vermont, and he couldn't leave his dad or his sister. And anyway, he couldn't drive himself; he only had a permit.

Rae Ann poked her head around his door. "What's wrong, Corey?" she asked.

"What makes you think something is wrong?"

"I heard you stomp into your room," she said.

"Yeah, Dad won't listen to me, and it's really important this time."

"Why?"

"Because there's a solar storm and we might lose all our power," he said. "We should go somewhere safer."

"What's a solar storm?" she asked. "Is it like when it's too sunny?"

"No, Rae, it's when the sun shoots a solar flare from its surface, and the electromagnetic waves reach the Earth. It causes the power to go off. Here, let me show you." He opened his laptop, and Rae Ann sat cross-legged on the bed next to him. He pointed to an image of the sun with a flare erupting from its surface. "See that? That's a solar flare."

"That's not big enough to reach the Earth," Rae Ann said, pointing to another picture that showed the Earth in relation to the sun. You could hardly see the flare in that picture.

"It shoots out invisible waves," Corey said, "and they hit the Earth."

"Will the school be okay? It won't explode the school, will it?"

"No, it doesn't explode buildings, just electronics." He noticed she was looking at the computer with wide eyes. "The computer wouldn't explode, silly, just stop working. I don't think anything actually explodes. Everything just stops working, and the world goes dark."

"Even in the day?" Rae Ann was looking fearful again.

"No, not during the day. It's an expression—when electricity stops working, they say the world goes dark. But obviously, if the sun's out, there's still light. It's just that there are no radio signals or light coming from Earth anymore. Or at least the part of the Earth affected by the pulse." Corey realized it was probably more complicated than that, but it was above his pay grade.

"How do you know the sun's going to spit rays at us?" Rae Ann asked.

"Because the news says so. Scientists know all about the sun, and they take pictures every day to see what it is doing," Corey said. "And Mr. Patterson said so too."

"Dad says Mr. Patterson is a nut job and I shouldn't believe a word he says."

"I think Mr. Patterson's right this time, Rae. The science backs him up."

"But the news people are telling us not to leave. They say nothing bad is going to happen and that we should stay home."

"Since when do you watch the news?"

"You left the TV on last night, and I heard what they were saying. I think you are making it up because you want to hang out with Emma." She turned to leave. "Corey and Emma, sitting in a tree," she chanted as she left.

He threw a pillow after her retreating form, but it hit the door as she closed it after herself.

"She thinks she's so funny," he muttered.

Corey studied the map on Emma's note and checked his phone for her location. She hadn't arrived there yet. He wished his dad hadn't had his phone when Emma called—maybe he could have gone with her. Except family was on the top of Mr. Patterson's list of essential things. He would say that Corey needed to stay with his own family, even though Corey felt like Emma was his family.

What did he have to do to get his dad to pay attention?

Soon, when the power went out, it would be too late.

He pounded his mattress again.

4

Emma sat cramped in the back of the Land Cruiser, a plastic crate containing supplies jammed into her knees. The jump seat wasn't the most comfortable at the best of times, but now there was no place for her feet—they were stuck under a duffle on one side of the crate and a grocery bag on the other.

She supposed it could be worse. Most of the luggage was on top of the truck—if the weather were wet, that would be in here too. She didn't know why it was such a noisy vehicle, but it was a good thing they weren't trying to have a conversation, since no one would be able to hear.

She didn't want to talk anyway. She was upset with herself for not ringing Corey's doorbell that morning. Who cared if Corey's dad would be upset with her? This was too important to just leave a stupid note with a map. What if she left something out? How would he ever find her?

Why hadn't she rung the doorbell?

Or she could have thrown rocks at Corey's window.

Anything but nothing.

She felt so stupid.

Her Aunt Maggie leaned forward, and Emma glanced at her for a moment. A few years younger than Emma's mother, Maggie bore a striking resemblance to her only sibling. She had long, brown hair, and her face was somewhat tanned, though Emma knew she had spent most of her days indoors. Noticing the bags under her aunt's hazel eyes, she remembered that the woman had just worked a long shift at the hospital.

"Are you all right?" Maggie asked loudly, looking concerned.

"The world is coming to an end, and you're asking me if I'm all right?" Emma asked.

"Don't talk to your Aunt Maggie that way," her mother shouted from the front of the car. "Show some respect."

"But, Mom, it's true. Everything is not okay. I abandoned Corey." Tears sprang to Emma's eyes, and she wiped them away with quick flicks of her fingers.

Abram's voice carried from the driver's seat: "Enough about Corey. We can't support everyone."

"It's all about facts and figures with you, Dad," Emma said, "but real life is more than that. It's about helping those you love."

"So, you love this boy?" her father asked. "You're only sixteen. What do you know about love?"

"I know what love is," Emma said. "I know you don't abandon people you care for. A loving heart doesn't sneak away when no one is watching, without even warning your neighbor what's coming."

"Nick Caulfield would laugh in my face if I told him what I believe. I'm not wasting my time on that family." Her father practically spat the words.

"You could have convinced him," Emma said. "You could have shown him the facts that convinced you. But you didn't even try."

Abram's jaw tightened, but he didn't speak. Emma felt her mother's eyes on her in the rearview mirror and noticed the brief shake of her head.

Aunt Maggie reached across the gap between them and took Emma's hand, squeezing it in support, but Emma's mouth tightened into a thin line as she gazed out the window. There was nothing new to catch her attention out there. Nothing but trees from Concord to Lebanon, New Hampshire, then there was maybe five minutes of country homes, commercial buildings, and shops before they crossed the bridge into Vermont. She caught a glance of the VA hospital there, and then it was almost nothing but trees and rock face next to the road until they took the off-ramp from the interstate.

To Emma, this was the most boring drive in the world. There was nothing to take her mind off Corey, and the ache in her chest increased the further they traveled away from home.

Nick was having trouble focusing on his work. The idea that Corey and Abram might be right kept creeping into his consciousness and breaking his concentration.

Finally, he reopened his internet browser and searched for solar storms and CMEs. He stayed away from the mainstream news and instead focused on scientific websites like NASA—the National Aeronautics and Space Administration

—and NOAA—the National Oceanic and Atmospheric Administration. He also pulled up scientific pages from independent scientists that weren't required to follow the government line and downplay the seriousness of an active flare.

What he learned chilled him. The power outage resulting from a solar storm could cause power to be out for months, if not years, if it was strong enough. Already, there were alerts stating airports were shutting down in preparation for the next big flare. Part of the problem, he read, was that the electromagnetic energy released during a solar flare traveled at the speed of light, so their effect on the Earth happened concurrently with their appearance. The science of prediction was not exact, so the blackout on Earth could not be predicted in time or duration or amount of damage done to the infrastructure.

Nick switched back to the local news channel to find that grocery stores and pharmacies were overrun with shoppers, and some people had resorted to looting. There was talk of shutting down the central power generation plants to reduce damage to the large power transformers. Why it mattered if power was flowing through them when the pulse hit, Nick didn't know.

What he did know was that he was totally unprepared for this kind of emergency. The house held what water would come through the pipes and into the hot water heater, and a day or two worth of food, and that was all.

But he was pretty sure that Abram would have invited him to the mountains if he'd wanted Nick's family there, and wouldn't have left it to a teenaged girl to issue the invitation. It went against the grain to go there and ask to be let in. Nick didn't need help. He was perfectly capable of taking care of his family on his own. Hadn't he taken on the role of both father and mother when Rochelle died? Yes. Had he asked for help from anyone? No. He'd turned away the traveling nurses and the social workers and the volunteers who offered to babysit the children. He'd taken meals brought by neighbors only because he did not want to hurt their feelings, careful to discourage any repeat offerings by telling people that his children were picky eaters.

They were not.

He just didn't believe in taking assistance of any kind. If you couldn't support your own family, then you were a failure. But, on the other hand, he hadn't anticipated this emergency, and he didn't have the skills to ride it out here at home. He would eventually have to take his children to a shelter with thousands of strangers, and he assumed Abram's camp would be preferable to that. Even if he were unwanted, at least they would be with people they knew. And he'd be able to help there, not just lay around on a cot all day.

But what if he decided to stick it out here in his home?

What would he have to do?

He knew he'd have to find food and water, not to mention sterilize water for drinking.

He'd have to somehow warm the house and find a way to heat water for baths.

And he'd also have to continue his children's education...

He could do these things, couldn't he?

But what if Rae Ann or Corey got sick? What would he do then? He'd have to find his way to the shelter to get medical help. Wasn't Abram's sister-in-law a nurse? The head honcho at a hospital in Rhode Island, if he remembered correctly. If he journeyed to Abram's, then she would be a resource. Their own private health practitioner.

Unless Abram refused to let them in...

Nick held his head in his hands, not knowing what to do. Or rather, knowing what to do, but not wanting to do it.

If staying here were not an option, then the choice between Abram and the Red Cross shelter in the company of tens of thousands of people was easy. He would take the kids to Vermont.

He heard a sound behind him and found Corey standing there.

"Dad, we really need to—" Corey started, but Nick cut him off.

"I know," Nick said.

Corey's face betrayed the shock he felt. He had clearly been expecting a fight. "We're going to Emma's dad's place in Vermont?"

"Against my better judgment," Nick paused and took a breath, "yes. Abram may not welcome us there, but it's our best chance of survival with a little dignity."

"Emma said he invited us, Dad," Corey said. "Look at the note."

"Either way, we're going."

Corey nodded, but remained silent.

Nick continued, "Find Rae Ann, and the two of you get packed. We're leaving as soon as possible."

5

"WHAT TO BRING..." Nick said, standing in the closet that served as the home's pantry.

Obviously, anything perishable needed to be eaten now or thrown away. He would pack the contents of his freezer into his cooler, minus the ice cream which wouldn't last as far as Vermont.

He started packing anything that wouldn't go bad, then loaded the boxes in the back of his SUV. He filled all the sports bottles they'd accumulated from soccer camps and other sporting events over the years with water and packed those too. He emptied the fridge and some of the freezer into the garbage can and rolled that to the curb. The meat went into the cooler as planned, along with all the ice and frozen vegetables. He loaded the cooler into the car and rushed upstairs to pack his bag.

He stuck his head in Rae Ann's room. "Are you packed, sweetheart?"

"Yes, Daddy. Will we be back in time for school tomorrow? I don't want to miss reading time with Miss Stewart. Fluffy the porcupine is going to France."

"I don't think they'll be having school tomorrow, Rae Ann," he said. "Open your bag and show me what's in it."

She unzipped her suitcase and flipped back the lid. It held nothing but toys.

He sighed. "Rae Ann, you need clothes to wear. Take the toys out and put in pants and t-shirts, underwear and socks. Then get your coat and at least two sweaters or hoodies. Then, if you still have any room, you may put toys in."

"But, Daddy..."

"Do it, Rae Ann."

She looked mutinous but started pulling the toys from her bag. He left her to it and went to follow suit, packing casual and outdoor work clothes and leaving his nicer attire in the closet. On his way back downstairs, he checked in with Rae Ann again.

"Did you get your clothes packed?" he asked.

"Yes, Daddy," she said, holding Louise the stuffed brown bear tight to her chest.

"Where is your suitcase?" he asked, looking. It wasn't anywhere in her room.

"In the car," she said. "Corey took it down for me."

"Did he check it?" he asked.

"I think so," she said, a worry line appearing between her brows.

"Okay. Let's go." He turned to leave, and she followed him, still clutching Louise.

When they reached the garage, he found Corey had already pulled the car out and had the rear hatch open, rearranging the suitcases and boxes in the back. He grabbed

Nick's case, slotted it into the back, and turned to his dad as he closed the hatch.

"We're all set, Dad," he said.

"Did you check Rae Ann's suitcase?" Nick asked.

"Yep. Full of clothes. And I made sure she brought practical stuff and not just her tutu." Corey grinned.

"Okay, everyone, get in. Time to go."

Nick closed and locked the garage door, circling the house to check that it was locked up tight, and then got in the car.

"I guess we're in for an adventure," he said and started out of the drive.

The first problem was the need for fuel. Nick could tell from his gas gauge that they didn't have enough to reach Vermont, but every gas station he drove past was blocked up with lines of cars. His usual station had a line blocking travel right around the block, so he gave up and got on the I-93 freeway, where there were still more cars.

It took them twice as long as usual to reach the rest stop before the off-ramp to I-89 that boasted a gas station, restaurant, convenience store, and bathrooms, but there was a line for fuel a quarter mile down the shoulder of the freeway.

He kept on going, hoping that he would reach exit nine on I-89. That was a decent place to stop, and it wasn't near a major town. Perhaps the lines there wouldn't be as long.

Rae Ann was singing in the back seat, and usually, Nick would put an end to that. But if it kept her happy, he'd let her sing today, and his nerves could just take the beating. It was better than listening to her ask, "Are we there yet?" endlessly. His wife, Rochelle, had loved it and would join in, singing at the top of her lungs, not caring if she got the tune or the words right, but just enjoying the joy of it. He regretted the times he'd asked her to stop. If he'd known she would die so young, he would have put up with all her quirks. Now it just hurts to think of it.

They crept along I-93 to the I-89 exit, and once they'd taken the clover leaf, the traffic lessened some. It seemed like most people were heading toward the cities, rather than away. Was he doing the right thing, taking his kids to Vermont? Or was he putting them in even more danger with fewer resources? No. He'd decided to follow Abram to Vermont, and that was what he was doing.

He gripped the steering wheel tighter and tried to push his doubts out of his mind. He needed to be decisive and not waffle around in self-doubt.

He was confident in his work, and he knew he should've been so in all parts of his life. But, instead, he tended to ignore those other pieces of himself and focus most of his energy on the things he did best. He knew he should be more hands-on with his kids, the way Rochelle was, but he didn't have the confidence. And anyway, they were learning independence. He didn't do their homework with them or for them, so they had to be self-reliant. That was a good thing. They should be self-sufficient. He just wished he felt better about it. He had the feeling that Rochelle would be disappointed in him.

They made it to exit nine before they reached the bottom of their gas tank, and Nick was rewarded with the sight of two gas stations with a line of only two or three cars. He pulled in behind what appeared to be the shortest line and killed the engine. He'd hate to run out of gas before they reached the pumps.

He noticed the signs about limiting the amount of gas

each customer could purchase to ten gallons. That worried him a little. He figured he could reach central Vermont on ten gallons, but if they had to drive a long way into the mountains, it could be tight.

The minutes ticked by as he waited. At the front of the gas station, he spotted the logo of a popular cigarette brand, the latest carton price scrawled out below. If society collapsed, a pack of cigarettes would probably be perfect for barter. He'd read that somewhere, and figured if that were true for cigarettes, it would be doubly true for canned food, potable water, and ammunition. The gold-bugs he'd talked to had thought hoarding gold was the answer, but you couldn't eat gold.

Nick drummed his fingers on the steering wheel, hoping things wouldn't get so bad that people would need to barter in order to survive. He lowered his window a crack. Music from overhead speakers calmed him, but as he took a deep breath, he gagged from the potent stench of gasoline—someone must've spilled some nearby. Coughing, he raised the window, sealing off himself and his family from the outside world.

After another ten minutes of waiting, Nick turned his key in the ignition, pulled the SUV up to the available pump, and killed the engine again. Outside the car, he dispensed his ten gallons of gas. Before he hurried into the station to pay, he stuck his head in the car.

"Lock the doors," he said, and as Corey opened his mouth, he cut him off. "Listen, I know it's a small town in the middle of nowhere, but just do as I say and lock the doors. Okay?"

"Okay, Dad," Corey said, rolling his eyes.

Nick gave him a look, and Corey placed his hand on the door handle, his finger poised to do the deed.

"Thanks," Nick said, and disappeared inside the station.

Corey watched his dad walk into the gas station and slumped back in his seat. It was taking forever for them to get anywhere, and Emma hadn't shared her location with him yet. It was a good thing they had the map.

He tried texting her, but she didn't respond. Maybe her battery had run out, or maybe her dad had made her leave her cell phone behind. There was no way to know, but it bugged him that they were out of touch.

A man was walking toward their car from the direction of the station, but Corey hadn't seen him come out of the building. There was something about him that Corey didn't like, even though the man was smiling and appeared friendly enough.

"Lie down, Rae Ann," Corey said. "And be quiet."

For once, Rae Ann did as she was told and curled up on the seat.

The man tapped on Corey's window. "Open the door," he said. "I want to talk to you."

Corey shook his head, thankful now that his dad had made him lock the car.

The man frowned and tried the door. "Come on, kid, open up."

Corey's heart was beating hard, and he was having trouble drawing breath. A panic attack. He'd had them before when he was scared. He tried to slow his breathing and think.

What should he do? He reached over and pressed the horn, hard.

The man jumped back and swore, but he didn't go away. Instead, he reached behind his back and pulled out a gun.

Nick was paying for his purchase when a horn blared outside. He jerked his head around to see what was going on—his kids were out there. There was a man with his hand on Corey's door, tugging at the handle with one hand and holding something in the other. Could it be a gun?

He rushed from the store, yelling, "Hey, get away from my kids!"

The gun was gone now—did he imagine it?

But when the stranger swung around, the gun was back in his hand, and he was aiming it at Nick.

"I need your car," he said, his voice low and steady.

"I have kids," Nick said. "Please, don't do this." He managed to keep the desperation out of his voice.

"Yeah, so do I, that's why I need your car," the man said, flicking his gaze toward Corey. "Tell the boy to open up."

"What if I don't?" Nick asked. "Are you going to kill me in front of my kids?"

"I'll shoot you if I have to—a bullet hole in the leg would probably do it."

Nick noticed that people were rushing to their cars to get away. Even vehicles in line behind him were pulling out, escaping the danger. No one was going to help. He heard the door to the station lock behind him. He was on his own here.

"I don't want any trouble, but I need my car," Nick said.

"The kids and I have got a long way to go." He opened his palms toward the man.

"Too bad," the man said. "The only way I can get to my kids in time is with your car. Be thankful that you have them with you. Now tell your son to open the car, or I'll start shooting."

"Maybe we could give you a ride to where your kids are."

"I'll still need the car...sorry. Now get the boy to open up." He cocked the gun and aimed it at Nick's leg. "You're going to have a tough time getting where you're going if you can't walk."

Nick saw a hardness in the man's face that told him he wasn't kidding. If he had to shoot Nick, he would. He was still trying to figure a way out when Corey got out of the car.

"You can have the car, man, but let me get my little sister out of the back seat." Corey opened the door and unbuckled Rae Ann. "Come on, Rae Ann," he said, "we're giving the bad man our car."

Rae Ann got out, clutching Louise. "My suitcase," she whimpered and gave the man a frightened glance.

"You can take your stuff," the man said. "Just hurry up about it."

Corey looked at Nick. "I couldn't let him shoot you in front of Rae, Dad," he said, his voice merely a whisper. "I'm sorry."

"It's okay, son. I understand," Nick said. He squeezed Corey's shoulder, and they joined Rae Ann at the back of the car. Rae Ann had one suitcase out and was reaching for another. "Just one suitcase, honey," he said. "You can only take what you can carry."

"They are on wheels, Daddy," she said. "I can pull them."

"It's a long way home, honey. One is going to be more than enough."

She threw the suitcase that she had by her side back into the car. "Then I want that one," she said, pointing to the second suitcase.

"Hurry up," the man called, waving his pistol.

Corey grabbed it and quickly set it on the ground next to her. Then he grabbed the duffle he'd packed his belongings in. Nick grabbed his rolling suitcase, a Bungie, and the bag with the snack foods.

"Okay, that's it," the man said. "Give me the keys."

"Wait," Nick said. "We'll need water." He reached in and grabbed another fabric grocery bag. "Okay, now you can have it. The keys are in the ignition." He slammed the rear hatch and dragged his belongings to the sidewalk that surrounded the minimart. "Come on, kids, get out of the way of the cars."

6

Nick pulled out his cell phone and dialed 911 as his car drove out of the parking lot. He was furious with the loss of his vehicle and shaking with the after-effects of the adrenaline rush.

"What's your emergency?" a female voice answered, efficient but also warm, the kind you wanted to hear when you were in the middle of an emergency.

"My car has been stolen," Nick said into his phone.

"What's your location?"

"I'm at a service station just off the I-89, exit nine."

"What is your name, sir?" She was calm and unruffled.

"Nick Caulfield."

"Can you be reached at this number if the call is dropped?"

"Yes, this is my cell phone," he said, furrowing his brow.

"Are you safe and uninjured?"

"Yes, we are safe and uninjured," he said, "but while you are asking me all these questions, the guy who stole my car is getting away."

"Sir, I hate to tell you this, but the world has collectively lost its mind. There are so many emergency calls right now—I can't even tell you how long it's going to be before an officer can reach you. Was there a weapon involved in the incident?"

"Yes, he had a gun and threatened to shoot me," Nick said, keeping an eye on Rae Ann to make sure she wasn't listening.

"Can you tell me exactly what happened?" she asked.

He detailed the carjacking, giving as much detail as he could remember about the thief. Told her he was with two children, and that if an officer wouldn't be showing up for a while, he was going to start walking home.

"Where do you live, sir?" she asked.

"The south side of Manchester, New Hampshire," he said through gritted teeth. He should have never left home.

"I'd say that is a multi-day walk with children, sir," she said. "The Warner Police Department is only a quarter mile north of your present location. I'm sure they can take your statement if you go to them."

"I'll think about it," Nick said. "Meanwhile, I need to get off the phone. I don't have any way to charge it if the battery dies."

He punched the call off with his finger and gestured to Corey to come here.

"We are going to walk to the police station," he said, "then I think we should start home."

"Dad, we are almost halfway to Vermont. We should keep going."

"I don't want to argue about it right now, Corey. Let's go report our car stolen and see if there are any car rental agencies around here. If not, I'll call Mike or someone to come get us. I want you to hold Rae Ann's hand—it doesn't look like this road is meant for pedestrians."

They started north, walking on the bike path separated from the traffic by a strip of grass. Cars were whizzing by and Rae Ann kept flinching and trying to pull away from Corey.

"Stop pulling, Rae Ann," Corey said. "I won't let a car hit you."

"I don't know how you could stop it, Corey Caulfield," Rae Ann said. "They are big and fast."

"I'd throw you out of the way before they hit us."

She sulked and made Corey walk as far away from the traffic as possible, dragging him into the bushes that bordered the path. But it was only a couple of minutes later that they were crossing "N" Road, then the grass patch that separated the parking lot of the police station from the road.

Inside the station, a clerk behind a glass partition glanced at them as they came in. Her hair was gray for three or four inches from her roots to the bright red that she'd presumably been dying before she'd changed her mind about the color. Her eyes were just as red as the ends of her hair, perhaps from a lack of sleep, and Nick wrinkled his nose at the old-coffee smell that lingered in the stale air.

"You're lucky," she said as they approached. "We aren't usually open on a Sunday, but it's so crazy out there that my boss asked me to come in. Are you the gentleman whose car was stolen at the gas station?"

"Yes." Nick set down his suitcase and leaned on the counter. "Do you have paperwork for me to fill out?"

"Usually an officer fills out the paperwork," she said, bouncing her head back and forth, "but I guess, as things are so busy, I can give it to you. What are you going to do with these children and no car? It's just awful how people have gone wild in anticipation of this solar storm that's coming."

She didn't appear to need an answer from him, so he took the paperwork and began to fill it out. Corey and Rae Ann rested in two of the three orange chairs that were set against the wall. Rae Ann clutched Louise, kicked her feet, and hummed. Corey had his earbuds in, probably listening to music. Just as well, as it was going to take a few minutes to finish these forms.

He'd been working on them for five minutes or so when he realized the woman was trying to get his attention.

"Yes?" he asked.

She put a finger to her lips and pointed to a jar of candy on her desk, and then to Corey and Rae Ann.

He frowned at her.

She made the motion again.

"I'm sorry," he said, "I've just had my vehicle stolen after spending four hours on what should have been a one-hour drive. I don't understand what you are trying to tell me."

"I was trying to ask if it's okay for your kids to have a piece of candy," she whispered, but the sound carried through the room. "But I didn't want to say it out loud in case the answer was no."

Corey's gaze was fixed to the floor, head bobbing to the music piping through his earbuds, but Rae Ann perked up immediately.

"That would be fine," Nick said.

The woman gestured to Rae Ann to come to the window, and she slid the jar of candy out in front of the girl.

"One for you, and one for your brother," she said.

"Thank you," Rae Ann said, and reached into the jar for two pieces.

Just then, the door slammed open, a woman rushed in, and Rae Ann jumped, knocking the jar to the floor and spilling candy everywhere. Rae Ann hid behind her father as the woman from outside rushed forward to the desk, stepping on the candy and rolling her ankle. She gasped with pain and grabbed the counter to keep from falling. Nick moved over to steady her, kicking the jar, which impacted the ankle she'd just injured.

She shook off Nick's helping hand. "Never mind about me, there's a robbery at the McDonald's. They're armed with guns."

The clerk turned and began to speak into the radio on her desk, then glanced back to the woman. "Any shots fired?"

"Yeah. They shot up the interior of the restaurant before they demanded money and all the food that was ready to eat."

Nick figured if he were going to rob a restaurant, it wouldn't be a McD's, but then they were probably mostly after the money, and the food was just an afterthought.

The clerk turned to the radio and requested all cars respond to the robbery.

Nick returned to his paperwork, and when the woman who reported the robbery left, he handed his paperwork in.

"I've filled it out to the best of my ability," he said. "An officer can call me if they need more information."

"If we have any communications after the power goes out," the clerk said. "Feel free to check back in."

He nodded and took a seat next to his kids. "I think we should try to get home," he said to Corey.

"We can't," Corey started.

Nick raised his hand to stop him. "Corey, I'm sorry, but we're expecting a major disaster to hit any time. We have no way to get anywhere, but at least we know where home is. We aren't even halfway to Vermont yet. I'm taking us home.

"But—"

"Please don't argue with me. I tried to get to Vermont, I did. I just don't see how we can get there without a car. But with all the traffic going toward the city, maybe we can find a ride home. Come on." He stood up. "Let's get moving."

They went outside and crossed the grass to the road. The cars that had been rushing by them earlier were now at a standstill, as a roadblock had been erected around the McDonald's. They walked to where an officer stood on the bike lane.

"Will we be allowed to go by?" Nick asked.

"We wouldn't want to put your children at risk, would we, sir?" the officer asked. "We have a hostage situation, so I suggest you find a different route."

Nick turned away. He didn't know the area well enough to find a different route. As far as he knew, it was ten miles to the nearest freeway exit and he had no idea how to get there.

"Let's go back and ask the clerk if there's another way to go," he said to the kids.

But back in the police station the clerk just shook her head. "If you are walking," she said, "you might as well just stay put until they open the road. You'd have to go ten miles or more in the wrong direction before you could get straight again."

Nick thanked her, and they went out to stand on the grassy spot again.

"Dad," Corey said, "this street, what's it called?" He scanned for a sign. "N Road."

"N Road? Who names these roads around here?"

"I don't know, but look, Dad, it runs alongside the interstate going north."

"We need to wait, Corey."

"But we could get to Vermont this way, and maybe catch a ride at the next freeway entrance. It would be better than just waiting here for hours."

Nick took a deep breath and let it out slowly, feeling a slight breeze pick up. He pondered the situation for a moment, then focused his gaze on his son. Sure, they could return back home and hole up for a while, like he wanted to do, but if society fell apart, he realized they wouldn't last long. With no way to defend themselves, they would be at the mercy of those with looser morals. Making the journey to Abram's was vital, and he knew Corey was right to make a push for it.

Nick pursed his lips, not wanting to speak the words on his mind, but then gave in. "Okay, Corey, we'll do it your way. It doesn't look like we'd be any worse off. It could be hours before they let us through." Nick grabbed the handle of his suitcase. "This way, kids. We're walking to Vermont."

7

Abram was happy with the time they were making. In another fifteen minutes, they'd be in Vermont and only an hour or so from their destination. Emma hadn't made any comments from the back in quite a while, and he was hoping she'd given up on her vendetta against him. He knew she would miss Corey, but it was time for her to branch out and make other friends. After the emergency, the two of them would have had a clean break, and maybe it would be easier for her. After all, he figured it would be at least several years before civilization was up and running again.

Not that he disliked the boy, but Abram was afraid of what the friendship might develop into if it was left unchecked. It would be a mistake for Emma to get involved with the boy. She'd spent her entire childhood with him, and she needed to spread her wings and experience the world.

They were still on the interstate, almost at the bridge across the Connecticut River, when the car in front of them screeched to a halt as a transformer on a powerline next to the freeway exploded and set the pole on fire. Abram and his family came to a stop right at the West Lebanon exit, and the stop light at the end of the off-ramp went dark. There was a collision in the intersection. Newer cars, like the one in front of them, stopped running. Some restarted, but others did not, and people began abandoning their vehicles where they stood, causing the cars that would still run to have to wind around them.

Shelly gasped as two cars collided.

"What's happening?" Maggie asked.

"I think the first waves from the coronal mass ejection just hit," Abram said.

"They need help," Emma cried from the back seat. "Dad, those people need help!" She pointed to a family with children who were trapped between two dead vehicles, with two more trying to pass between the cars in the space the people occupied. Luckily, the two moving vehicles stopped before they crushed the family.

"We can't help them," Abram said.

"Why not?"

"If we go down there, we become part of the problem. It's not our fault that they are unprepared."

Abram swung his Land Cruiser out and around the car stalled in front of them. The Toyota was old enough that it didn't have electronic ignition or any computerized components. The electromagnetic pulse couldn't affect it.

There were people and cars on the roads below, chaos without the aid of stoplights.

They crossed the river into Vermont and left the mess behind. There wasn't a stop light to be found between their current location and their destination. The backwoods of Vermont didn't have traffic lights; it was one of the things that made it perfect as a bug out location.

"I can't believe we didn't try to help those people," Emma said.

Abram glanced at her in the rearview mirror. Her face was mutinous. Well, that was just too bad. They couldn't let anyone slow them down now.

"The problem is too big for the four of us to solve," he said. "We'd just compound the problem if we tried."

Emma crossed her arms, shifting her steely gaze toward the passing trees out the window.

Abram glanced in the rearview. He felt like her behavior was a failure of their parenting, this affinity for the sulks and speaking her mind. His sister would never have dared talk back to their father, nor would he. His siblings knew who was in charge of their household, and it wasn't the children.

He pursed his lips.

There was still more traffic headed south than north, but after they passed the junction with I-91 at White River Junction, traffic picked up.

Abram wondered where people were going. Could it be that they assumed there'd be power if they crossed the border into Canada? Surely, they weren't headed to Burlington…

Burlington was the largest city in Vermont, but at just over forty-two thousand people, it wasn't huge. The city of Boston's population was higher than that of the entire state of Vermont. If you were looking for help, Vermont wouldn't be the first place he'd think of. Unless, of course, they were bugging out to Vermont, the way he was. If you were looking to get away from the hordes, then Vermont was the perfect place to be.

Abram pulled off the interstate at exit two, nearly twenty miles from the border. Freeway off-ramps in Vermont tended to be ten miles or more apart, unlike other places where they seemed to come one after the other. He figured this was because so many states were built up and contained countless miles of urban areas. The two Vermont interstate freeways were instead surrounded by miles and miles of trees. If you wanted to find the towns, you had to get off the interstate and drive the state routes.

And there, at the junction of Routes 110 and 14, was the quaint town of Sharon. There was a huddle of maybe twenty-five people on the green, and Abram pulled over and let Emma and Maggie from the back so they could stretch their legs.

They stood next to the car and Abram excused himself and walked across the green to a smaller knot of people standing in front of an old church.

"Power's out?" Abram asked as he approached.

"Yep, I guess what they've been saying on the radio is true." This, from a tall man in Bean boots, jeans, and a flannel shirt. "Half our vehicles won't start anymore."

"What you need is a seventies vehicle like mine," Abram said. "No electronic parts."

"A little late for that now," the man said. "But, luckily, some of our cars restarted when we disconnected then reconnected the batteries. And Norm here has an old pickup that'll run, but it's well past its prime." He indicated the man standing next to him.

Norm stuck out his hand, and Abram shook it, saying, "Abram."

There were introductions all around at that point, the man Abram had spoken to first being Tom, then there was Jim, Geo, and of course, Norm.

"What are you all doing out here on the green?" Abram asked.

"If we thought this was just a normal power outage," Tom said, "we wouldn't be out here. It would be life in Vermont. Power outages are business as usual. But the word is that this could last a very long time. We're trying to formulate a plan. Food is going to be an issue, even for those of us who farm. We need fuel to bring in the crops and take them to market. And who knows if money will be any good after today."

Jim spoke up: "I've got a cousin up near Randolph who uses horses to bring in his crops, but there's only him and the one set of nags—what are the majority of us going to do? Bring them in by hand?"

"And how do the dairy farmers run their milking machines or refrigerate their milk?" Geo asked. "Some of us have backup generators, but the fuel won't hold out forever."

"A return to community harvesting?" Abram asked.

"Possibly," Geo said. "Or perhaps a different way of buying into a farm share using labor instead of money. The problem is, even though we're used to living without electricity—we get power outages at least a couple times a year—our vehicles have never stopped running before. And we've always had access to engine fuel. It's going to take some doing to work these problems through." Geo shrugged.

"Yeah, I'll say," Abram said, pursing his lips. "Well, it's

time for me to move along. Good luck. I'm sure you'll work it out."

Abram said his goodbyes to the men and stepped back toward his vehicle. Once they were all inside, he pulled out of the town and continued on, heading closer and closer to the safety of his compound.

Corey shouldered his backpack and followed his dad and sister down N Road, going northeast. The tree-lined road was filled with meandering cracks—as a road that ran parallel to the interstate, it was sure in disrepair. Power lines crisscrossed over the neglected road, delivering electricity to the few homes they walked past. Soon, the power would cease to flow, and the occupants of those homes would be in trouble.

A few minutes later, they reached a section of road that featured no buildings at all. A few distant horns honked off to their left, and Corey swung his head to see, but the highway was still cloaked by the dense forest. Corey figured there was probably a traffic jam on the highway—more people were growing wise to the looming threat.

As they walked, anger stewed in Corey's belly at the thought of the man who stole their car. He'd needed the car for his kids, he'd said. But what about Corey and Rae? They were kids, and the man's actions had endangered them. He hoped the man who stole their car was stuck in traffic, where the cops would find him. That would serve him right.

For a moment, he wished his father owned a gun. In truth, what he really wanted was his own gun. He'd have been able to keep the car from being stolen. He could have opened the window and blown a hole in the guy's leg. That would have stopped him from taking their car. They would have been on the interstate and almost to Vermont by now. If he ever got the opportunity to learn how to shoot, he'd take it.

Anger burned within him at the man who stole their car, but not just at him...at his father, too, who let it happen. And then at himself. He should have shoved the car door into the car thief. If he'd been thinking clearly, that's just what he would have done.

The thought he could have prevented this disaster shamed him, which just angered him more. All he would have had to do was to slam that door into the man's legs, and he hadn't thought of it. What was the point of being angry at his father when he hadn't done any better himself?

He groaned inwardly. This was his fault as much as it was his father's. And now it would take them days to reach Emma.

Somehow, thinking of Emma also made him think of high school. He wondered if they'd ever finish the year, or if they'd have to do the second semester over again. He hoped not. It would be better if they never had to go back to school at all, except that he wanted to do things with his life, and he'd have to go to college or get some kind of specialist education. Would they waive the need for high school since the power had gone out and made school impossible?

"My feet hurt," Rae Ann said, breaking his thoughts. She was hugging Louise to her chest with one arm as she pulled her rolling bag with the other.

Corey dropped his gaze to her feet. She was wearing a pair of princess shoes.

"Of course, your feet hurt," he said, "you're wearing dress up shoes."

Their father stopped and looked at her feet. "Rae Ann, you can't walk in those shoes." He glanced at the suitcase she was pulling. "Do you have a better pair in your suitcase?"

She stepped in front of her bag. "No. They are in the car," she said. "I changed my shoes in the car."

"Let me see," their dad said and grabbed the suitcase from behind Rae Ann.

"No," she cried and reached out to try and grab the bag from her father.

But he was already crouched down, unzipping the case. She grabbed Corey's arm and hid behind him.

"What are you doing, Rae?" Corey asked, trying to turn and look at her.

But she kept avoiding him by stepping behind him as he moved. His father gasped, and he looked to see what was up. His dad was staring into Rae Ann's case, which a doll and a stuffed elephant had fallen out of, and not a pair of shoes to be seen. Or any other items of clothing, for that matter.

"Rae!" Corey exclaimed.

Their dad stood up. "The bag you left in the car was the one with your clothes?" he asked.

Rae Ann nodded, her eyes wide and fixed on her father's face.

"There's no point in looking at me like that," their dad said. "This is your doing, not mine." He stuffed the doll and elephant back in and zipped the bag closed. He stood up and handed the bag back to her. "Let's keep moving. But I'm not carrying that bag when you get too tired or sore to walk."

Rae Ann took the handle and dragged the bag behind her, tears welling in her eyes.

"It's okay, Rae," Corey said. "I'll help you with your bag."

She wiped her nose with her sleeve and stopped crying, giving him a half smile.

They were coming to an intersection ahead, a traffic light blinking yellow. There were more buildings visible now, more signs of life. A car from the right came to a stop before making its way forward again, in the direction of the interstate. Then, as Corey watched, a transformer on the corner fizzed and popped, and the light went dark. The car, which hadn't passed out of sight yet, stopped dead in the road. Then, a moment later, the car started and moved forward again, but the traffic light remained dark.

When Corey, Rae Ann, and their dad reached the intersection, they looked down the road to see a traffic jam. Several cars were stuck in the way, and their owners were out of the vehicles gesturing at the autos that were still running but stuck behind them. Other people were trying to snake their way through the cars that were stopped on the road.

"Should we go help them push the cars out of the way, Dad?" Corey asked.

"No, son," his dad said. "I don't think we should get involved. We've got a long way to go, and frustrated people can be difficult to work with. We've got Rae to think of. Let's keep moving."

They crossed the road and kept moving on, but Corey couldn't help thinking that it was wrong not to help. It wouldn't have taken them long to push the cars to the side of the road. He noticed that there were more people on the street now. Lots of people whose cars wouldn't run anymore, and the people whose cars were working had to weave around the people on the road.

As he watched, a group of walkers surrounded a car and tried to get the driver to stop. They wanted a ride. But the driver was afraid—Corey could see it in his face, still visible through the crowd of people. The man revved the engine, and when the group didn't move, he pressed the accelerator to the floor, scattering the people in front of him.

No one looked severely hurt. Corey watched them get to their feet and start forward again, but he was worried now. A hard pit grew in his stomach as he began to see what fear did to people, how dangerous the world was at this moment.

The grid had just collapsed, and people were already panicking, causing even more chaos. Perhaps they knew of the struggles to come, and how terrible things would truly get...

Corey wondered how these people would get to where they felt safe. How would they survive? And, come to think of it, how would he, Rae Ann, and his dad do these things? Would they make it as far as Vermont? Or would something awful happen to them out here on the road?

He walked close to Rae Ann, keeping an eye on the people that they passed. Walking between Rae Ann and the strangers made him feel better. More in control. But he encouraged her to get closer to their father, so that she was protected on two sides and he could be sure that no one came up behind them and snatched her. Not that he had any idea why anyone would take his sister, but he'd heard of such things, and he wasn't taking any chances.

He kept an eye on the people around them, watching as people passed by.

As long as no one came too close, they'd be fine.

He noticed that his father was doing something similar, leading them away from the people around them. Staying well away from the tight packs of men that seemed to gravitate to one another. Friends on the same road, finding each other. There were no friends here for the Caulfields. And Corey thought they'd better remember that.

8

WHEN THE ROAD turned from pavement to dirt, Nick felt uneasy, but it was maybe ten miles down the road that Nick's stomach really began to churn.

They'd been walking through Mount Kearsarge State Forest for a while now, Rae Ann on his back and Corey carrying her suitcase, since one of the wheels had developed a flat spot. And while there had been some traffic—cars that still ran, bicycles, motorcycles, and even a pedal-powered auto—it had remained relatively light. There hadn't been crowds since they'd left the more populated areas around exit nine behind.

Now, as they reached Kearsarge Regional High School, and the road turned to pavement again, there was a sudden influx of people. People were sitting in their cars in the high school parking lot, and Nick wondered why. Had they been sitting there for the last five hours? Then it occurred to him—this was a high school. People were probably here when the power went out, for sports events and other community gatherings. And more people appeared to be coming.

"What's happening, Daddy?" Rae Ann asked from his shoulders. "Why are there so many people here?"

"I already told you, Rae," Corey jumped in. "This is it. No more power. Everyone is in big trouble, and they know it. They're all scared. That's why we have to get to the Pattersons' ref—"

"Corey!" Nick snapped. "Let's not broadcast it, son." He glanced around. Plenty of people would happily follow them to a safe haven. There were a lot of panicked people around here.

"Hey," a guy across the street called, apparently having spotted someone he knew. "FEMA is setting up a station at the New Hampshire Country Club. I'm going up there."

"Where?" "What did he say?" A chorus of questions sounded around them. People started moving past the high school, moving north.

At the same time, there was a shout from the school, and a dozen people were running out the main doors, their arms full of supplies. Food from the cafeteria, toilet paper and paper towels from the janitor's closets. They were looting the high school.

Nick shook his head. Didn't they know that they were going to end up back here when there was no water and no food anywhere else? They were robbing themselves of future supplies.

The crowd carried them along, pushing them toward the FEMA station. But Nick did not want to end up there. Just another small family in a sea of families, so when the crowd veered right, up Kearsarge Valley Road, Nick guided his family further up N Road, away from the crowds.

"Why aren't we going to the FEMA station, Daddy?" Rae Ann asked.

"Yeah, Dad, are we going the right way?" Corey added.

"We need to stay away from the crowds," Nick told them. "Crowds are dangerous, and I don't want us to get stuck in the middle of a riot, or have our supplies stolen. We have a goal, and this road is taking us toward our goal. I know it seems strange to be going away from all the people, but believe me, we don't want to be stuck there."

"We're still headed toward the Pattersons'?" Corey asked.

"We are still headed northeast, son," Nick said. "We can't do more than that for the time being."

"But you are sure, right?" Corey insisted. "This is the right way?"

"Yes, Corey," Nick said calmly, smiling at the boy. "This road follows the freeway almost all the way to Vermont. It's going to be a long walk, but maybe tomorrow we'll get lucky, and someone will give us a ride."

"How many of the cars do you think have stopped running, fifty percent?" Corey asked.

"Truthfully, it doesn't matter. Without electricity, there will be no pumping the gas from the service stations, so if they didn't stop running today, it's just a matter of time. I'd admire those people who still have bicycles—they can get around their communities, at the very least."

"I liked that car where all the people were pedaling," Rae Ann said. "It looked like fun, and you wouldn't have to worry about falling off." Rae Ann fell off her bike a lot, in Nick's estimation. He still hadn't got her steady on it. A pedal car was probably really attractive to her.

"You'll get better on your bike," he said to her. "Don't worry."

"But my bike is back in our garage. I'm not going to see it for a while, am I?"

"There will be other bikes, Rae Ann," Nick said.

She sighed. "Okay," she said, as if he were sending her to bed half an hour early.

"Bikes are fun," Corey said. "You can get places fast."

"They may be fun for you," Rae Ann said. "You didn't scrape all the skin off your leg falling off yours."

"Dad told you to ride in pants and shoes—I heard him," Corey said. "You wouldn't have hurt yourself so badly if you'd listened."

"Okay, Corey," Nick said. "That's enough. Rae Ann knows what happened and why. Did Emma send her location before the internet died?"

Corey checked his phone. "No. Maybe they hadn't gotten there yet," he said. "But she sent the address, and I got the directions. If my phone doesn't die—"

"Turn it off for now, son," Nick said. "It's not like you'll be getting any texts. We'll look at it again when we get to the little town that's close to the Pattersons' place—Fenton, I think it is. For now, let's save your batteries, okay?"

"Okay," Corey said and powered off his phone.

Nick could tell it bothered his son to be out of contact with his friends, but he was just going to have to adapt. They'd been thrown back in time and would have to learn to live with simpler amusements and make friends with the people at hand. There was just no other choice.

"Daddy, can I have a snack?" Rae Ann asked. "Louise is hungry."

"In a little while, sweetheart," Nick said, "when we stop to rest."

Rae Ann sighed again and rested her head on top of his, her legs sliding so her knees were bent over his shoulders. He kept a hold on her ankles and glanced at the silly princess shoes. She was going to have to grow up faster now. Too soon, and it made him sad. It was his job to protect her, but how could he protect her from this? Bad choices in a world like this could be deadly. A blister could get infected, and there would be no medicine to give her except what was in the first aid box. Then he remembered the medical kit was still in the car. How could he have missed something so basic?

"Where do you think we'll sleep tonight, Dad?" Corey asked. "In somebody's barn, maybe?"

"We'll have to see what the end of the day brings, Corey. But be happy it's not raining, because we might be stuck sleeping outside." Nick shook his head. If only they hadn't lost the car.

"Would our car still be running?" Corey asked, as if reading his mind.

"I don't know, Corey. It had electronic ignition and other computers in it. But some cars seem to be able to run, while others don't. And I don't know enough about the science to know why. Maybe if I was an electrical engineer, but my area of expertise is materials. I just don't know if the guy who stole our car is now just as stuck as we are."

"I hope he is," Corey said. "It would serve him right."

His son was quiet a minute.

Finally, Corey added, "I wish I'd slammed the car door into him, Dad. We might have been able to get away."

"I wish I'd done things differently too, son," Nick said,

"but I didn't. There's no point in worrying about it or blaming yourself. We're all still alive and in one piece—if you don't count Rae Ann's suitcase—and that's something to be thankful for."

"But how are we going to make it all the way to Central Vermont? It's a really long walk." Corey sounded depressed. "It could take us weeks."

"If we get stuck, tired, and hungry," Nick said, "then we'll stop at a FEMA site and rest up. I don't like the idea of being in those crowds, but if we have to, we will. We'll rest as many times as we have to, and eventually, we'll make it."

"But couldn't we ask for a ride? Flag down one of the cars that are still moving?" Corey asked.

"I'm not sure that's safe, Corey. What if they didn't take us to where we wanted to go? What if they stole our stuff or tried to hurt Rae Ann? No. I don't think we'll be catching a ride. But when we get into a more populated area, we'll start trying the cars that have been abandoned. Someone might have left a car that still runs. We could catch a break that way."

Corey nodded. That seemed like it was acceptable to him. *Thank goodness*, Nick thought. He needed the boy on his side to get through this.

Abram started to relax when they finally turned onto the dirt road that led to his property, skirting the nearby town of Fenton. Three miles down this road, then half a mile up the drive, and they'd be home free. You just never knew what was going to happen when you traveled during an emergency. But all the people they'd run into had been ordinary. Vermonters were accustomed to working together as a community, taking care of their neighbors and doing what it took to keep everyone alive and well. Most of them lived in small enclaves, towns, and villages where, if they didn't know everyone, they knew *almost* everyone. They certainly knew their neighbors, and that's what counted most.

The dirt road was relatively smooth, as they weren't uncommon in Vermont and were very well taken care of, but when he pulled into the drive, he had to slow way down. The winter had left it pockmarked with potholes, and the spring rains and the melting snow had washed portions of it away. More than once, the women in the back gasped, complained, or cried out in pain as he hit a pothole and their heads hit the roof. Perhaps he should have gotten a different model, but this Land Cruiser was really the best for what they needed—once they were here.

He hadn't offered for anyone else to drive, and maybe that was selfish of him. He hadn't had to spend any time in the back, as his wife, daughter, and sister-in-law had. But, as he knew the way, and wasn't afraid of driving through the cars stopped dead on the highway, it was probably for the best. He wouldn't put it up for a vote, though. He knew better than to ask his wife and daughter if his decisions were the correct ones. Better to ask forgiveness than permission.

They navigated a bend in the drive, and there was the compound laid out before them. He had to stop and open the gate—Gary was here somewhere, but Abram didn't really expect him to come running just because they had arrived.

"Should I get the gate?" Shelly asked.

He shook his head. It had a lock on it, and only he and Gary had a key. But he didn't say that out loud, since then the women would all want a key as well. They would feel trapped if they knew they couldn't walk out the drive to the road. The compound wasn't fully fenced yet, and if they walked through the woods, they could eventually get around the fence, but that was rough going. And he wasn't about to tell them about it. The less anyone knew about the details of this place, the better off they would all be.

Beyond the gate was a pole barn where chickens and Guinea fowl were housed. They also kept some supplies there, the decoy supplies used to fool thieves into thinking they'd gotten all that was here. One hoped that it wouldn't come to that—they didn't want to lose those supplies—but it was a loss they could afford to take, especially if it fooled the interlopers into thinking that's all there was.

Past the pole barn another quarter of a mile, they came to the garage, and Abram parked the Land Cruiser in one of the large bays. The old farmhouse lay down the hill from the garage and Abram could see that Gary had been installing the functional shutters on the windows. They resembled the decorative shutters that could be seen on houses all over Vermont, but these were steel and nearly impossible for an intruder to get through. The doors were steel, too, making the home almost impenetrable when locked down. That was one of those places they had not skimped on funds.

A noise was coming from the outbuildings—barns and sheds that lay lower down the hill than the house and off to the east—so Abram figured Gary must've been down there working. He'd go find him in a while after he'd settled Shelly, Maggie, and Emma in the house.

He led the women down the path to the front door of the house that Gary had kindly left unlocked for them. They piled their luggage in the entryway and went back up the hill for the other supplies they'd brought with them.

"Emma," Abram said, "come upstairs. I'll show you your room. You too, Maggie, if you don't mind." He led them up the stairs, catching a whiff of the stale air, and showed Emma to a room on the right at the end of the hall. Her room spanned the side of the house, with views on three walls. It was a light room with a high ceiling, and he thought Emma would like it.

Maggie's room was at the other side of the house, similar to Emma's except it faced the north and the views were of the hill and the garage, and the light wasn't as bright. Still, it was a large room, and he thought Maggie would be satisfied.

The four rooms in between Maggie and Emma were smaller by more than half, and although they did have views, there was only one window per room. There was also a full bathroom, fed from a water cistern mounted on the roof and fed from a spring further up the hill. The gravity-fed water system didn't need a pump. It was one of the things Abram had appreciated about the place when he'd been shopping for a compound. There was a least one system that they didn't need to find a way to power.

He left the women upstairs and went down to show Shelly their bedroom. It was a smallish room but had two large windows overlooking a line of apple trees that separated the house from a large pasture that used to be a hayfield. Past the grassland was the edge of the forest that surrounded the property for miles around. They were an oasis of sun in an ocean of green. Plenty of space for growing food, existing fruit trees, and outbuildings for farm animals and working.

He left the house and strode to the garage to get the cans of gasoline he had strapped to the back of the Land Cruiser and haul them down to the shed, where they were storing all kinds of fuels, and then he went in search of Gary.

Abram found him working on one of the metal shutters. It must have been one from the back of the house, as he was pretty sure all the shutters from the front of the house were in place.

"It's too big," Gary said, holding the tool he was using to grind the edge. "I must have gotten the measurements wrong. But not by much, another couple of passes and it will be perfect."

"You went right to work," Abram said. "Not feeling secure?"

"Our defenses need bolstering," Gary said. "Before long, people are going to get desperate, and some people know we're here. The neighbors certainly do. The guy to the north was driving by as I pulled in."

"Where should I start?" Abram asked, looking around the workshop. There were rolls of razor wire, and fencing, among other things.

"I think we need to finish the fence along the far side of the property," Gary said, "but before we do that, I think razor wire needs to go along the top of the existing fence, starting at the gate. However, that will take two of us, and I want to finish this shutter first. Why don't you check to see that the cement boundary we laid under the fence line survived the winter? If we need to work on that, we'll have to get in supplies."

"I'll get changed," Abram said. "Will you need help remounting that shutter?"

"No, I've got a pulley system rigged for the shutters. Go get started inspecting the fence, and I'll find you when I'm done."

Abram walked back to the house and found the women in the kitchen, inspecting the supplies and brewing tea.

"I'm going out to work on the fence," he said. "If you need me, I'll carry a two-way radio. The other is stored in this cupboard." He opened a cupboard and took a radio, showing them where the other was sitting in its charging cradle. "Gary is here, but if you see anyone else, call me immediately."

Shelly came and kissed him on the cheek. "We'll be fine. Now go work on that nasty fence you've got surrounding us. You can have some tea when you get back."

He left them chatting in the kitchen and changed into his work overalls and boots. Then he walked up the hill, past the garage and along to the barn. He walked into the barn, checking on the chickens, who were sunning themselves in their chicken run on the far side of the building. The Guinea fowl were inside, out of the afternoon sun, sitting on their perches. The animal pens were empty but cleaned and ready for their inhabitants. They'd paid in advance for the animals and would need to collect them soon before people became so hungry and scared that they forgot the arrangements they'd made.

He exited the barn and walked up the drive to the gate. The concrete strip ran under the gate, and the wheels of the gate panels ran along a groove in it so that there was no space under the gate for anything much larger than a spider to squeeze under. It looked as good as it had the day it had been installed, so no problems there.

He walked the fence to the right, keeping an eye on the curb they'd had poured under the fence line so that no one could easily dig a hole under the fence. A determined soul might still be able to dig under, but it would take a bit of time, and hopefully, their perimeter sensors would catch the movement and alert them. He ambled along and only had problems where brambles had grown back into the area they'd cleared when they'd installed the fence. Blackberries grew quickly and could easily fill in a gap in the space of a season.

They'd cleared both sides of the fence, six feet on either side so that no one could use the brush as cover, or climb a tree and drop down over the fence from an overhanging branch. He thought they'd been smart about it. It had taken a lot of work, and in the case of the cement boundary that reached a foot into the ground, a lot of money. Some of it to keep the workers from talking.

He heard the sound of the ATV coming up the hill from the outbuildings and retraced his steps to meet Gary at the gate. He pulled his leather gloves from his rear pocket and pulled them on. Installing the razor wire was going to be tricky, and they'd be lucky if they managed it without ripping their skin to shreds. He hoped Gary had some experience in the best way to work with it, since he did not. He understood the need, but he wished he never regretted the decision to use it.

9

Corey was tired. His feet hurt more with every step, and his legs ached. He had Rae's suitcase tied to his backpack, and it was bumping against his thighs with every step. His shoulders were sore from the straps of his bag, and he really just wanted to stop walking and lie down somewhere.

It was so quiet here in the woods that it was almost spooky. He couldn't remember anywhere ever being this silent. He remembered always being able to hear cars or airplanes. There were generators at campsites, and motorboat engines on lakes.

There was something about the air too. It had a fragrance like dirt and trees. Kind of damp, like after it rained, but not like rain in the city. Rain in the forest. And he could smell water, too, when the wind shifted. There must've been a river or a lake nearby, and every so often, a whiff of it came his way.

"Can I walk again, Daddy?" Rae Ann asked. "My legs hurt from riding on your shoulders."

Corey's dad stopped and set Rae Ann on the road so she

could walk, but she was limping. Corey thought it wouldn't be long before she was asking to be picked up again.

He pulled his cell phone from his pocket and checked for a text from Emma, stopping himself when he remembered that there was no service. Emma couldn't text him any more than he could text her. He wondered how many more times he'd pull his phone from his pocket automatically before he lost the habit. One hundred times? Two hundred? Life was sure screwed up.

"Pick me up, Daddy," Rae Ann said.

Five minutes, Corey guessed. A new record. But he kept his thoughts to himself. He didn't want to start a fight with Rae Ann out here. Neither of them had a room they could stomp off to, and an argument could go on for days.

His dad picked up Rae Ann without saying much of anything. Corey had noticed he'd gone quieter and quieter as the day progressed. He was probably worrying about where they would spend the night.

Corey was wondering about that himself. No soft bed in a hotel for them tonight. Not a hotel to be seen for miles and miles. Besides, Dad's credit cards wouldn't work. Electricity was what made everything run. Did his dad have enough cash for a room if they could find a hotel? He supposed they'd have to sleep in the forest under a tree. Or in the grass at the side of the road. All he really wanted was a bed.

He looked around: trees everywhere. How long would it be before they came to civilization again? He'd never realized there was so much undeveloped land in New Hampshire. He should have, he supposed, but it had just never occurred to him.

A noise caught Corey's attention. Was it an engine? He

lifted his head and glanced over his shoulder. Was something coming?

"Come on!" his dad yelled, grabbing Corey's arm and pulling him up the slope into the woods, Rae Ann bouncing on his shoulders. Branches snagged their clothes and roots made the going treacherous.

"Hide behind a tree," his dad commanded.

"But, Dad," Corey said, trying to look down the road in the direction they'd come, "they could help us. Maybe give us a ride."

"We can't risk it," his dad said. "We'd be at their mercy. They could take the food we have left. What if they wanted to hurt Rae?"

"It will take us weeks to walk to Vermont, Dad," Corey said. "We have to chance it. Didn't you tell me that most people in the world are good?"

"No, Corey. We'll look for a ride when we're in a more populated area, where we aren't so isolated." He set Rae Ann on the ground. "Sit down here next to the tree, Rae Ann, where you can't be seen. Don't move until I tell you to." He leaned against the trunk next to Corey.

Corey could see through the branches to the bend in the road that they'd just come around. Cold sweat sprang out on his brow, and his heart was pounding hard. He glanced over to see his dad had his head resting on the bark, eyes closed. He returned his gaze to the road. The engine noise was getting louder, and it was knocking. Mr. D had taught them in shop class that a knocking engine might need oil, but that wasn't the only reason engines knocked. If it was old enough to still run, maybe that's why it was so loud. Old cars weren't affected by solar storms.

As it came around the bend, Corey was able to see it was a 1960s Oldsmobile. Bronze, with a white roof and a chrome bumper. He watched it rumble in their direction, looking to see who was driving. Then, Corey spotted the lone man driving the car.

This is it, he thought. There might not be another car for hours, and by then, the sun will have set. They'd be in the pitch dark, alone.

Corey shot a quick look at his dad, and saw his eyes were still shut. Then he stared back out at the road. Soon, the car would be speeding past them. In the next second, he'd made up his mind about what he had to do.

While waiting for the car to pass, Nick closed his eyes and let the exhaustion wash over him. He regretted leaving home with an intensity that hurt. Whatever happened, if they'd been at home, they'd have been safe and warm, with a roof over their heads. Now, they would be exposed to the elements until they found someone to take them in. And he doubted they would make it all the way to Vermont on foot, and certainly not up into the hills, where the Pattersons' hideaway was.

He dreaded the conversation, or rather argument, that he'd have with Corey when the boy realized they weren't going to end up with his girlfriend. There would be recrimination and bad temper, and truthfully, Nick did not want to deal with that right now. This was enough of a nightmare without dealing with a sulky teen.

The engine was getting louder, and Corey tensed beside

him. He reached out his hand to lay on his son's shoulder, but the boy was gone. Nick's eyes flew open. Corey was running for the road, set to intercept the Oldsmobile Cutlass that was coming up the street.

Nick pulled Rae Ann to her feet and ran after Corey.

He couldn't move as fast as he wanted to with branches snagging his hair and tripping his feet, plus Rae Ann struggling to keep her own feet as he pulled her along. He was too late: Corey had reached the road, and the driver of the car had seen him waving his hands frantically. Then Nick sucked in his breath as Corey tripped and almost landed in the way of the vehicle, but he caught himself at the last second and Nick breathed again.

Nick reached Corey, and hoped the car wouldn't stop, that it would just go on by.

Instead, the car slowed to a stop and the driver leaned over to roll down the passenger window. "You okay?" he asked from the driver's seat. "I thought I was going to flatten you."

"I'm fine," Corey said, "except we've been walking for hours after we were carjacked."

"What a crappy thing to do," the man said. "How could a person steal a car from a man with two children? That's just wrong."

Nick stood there with Rae Ann by his side, nodding. He couldn't ask this man for a ride to Vermont, but the thought of putting Rae Ann back on his shoulders made him want to weep.

"You look worn out," the driver said to Nick. "Do you want a lift? I'm headed east."

"I don't want to inconvenience you," Nick said.

"No inconvenience, if you're going my way; you're welcome to come along. There's plenty of room in the car. And your little one looks as if she could sleep for a week."

Nick studied the man. Slightly chubby with pale, freckled skin, he appeared to be in his mid-forties, his blond hair thinning on the crown of his head. He wore a pleasant smile as he waited expectantly for Nick's reply.

"I'll go get our bags," Corey said, and he leaped back up the bank on the side of the road.

"I guess I've got no business turning down a ride," Nick said. "It's not fair to the kids."

"Hop in." The man leaned over and opened the passenger door, pushing it wide.

Nick wasn't sure what to do. If he put Rae Ann in the car, the man could take off before he slid into the front seat. But he didn't want to seem suspicious, like he didn't think the man was trustworthy. Nick waited until Corey was back with the bags, then slid into the front, dumping his bag on the floorboards. He kept his door open, watching as Corey helped his sister into the back seat, close by the entire time. Corey leaned over and buckled her in while the man waited at the wheel.

Once everyone was settled in the car, the driver reached his hand out to Nick. "I'm Joshua, by the way."

Nick hesitated, but then shook the man's hand. "I'm Nick."

Joshua smiled, and it seemed to Nick that it was a warm, genuine smile.

But only time would tell if his first impressions were correct.

10

"Emma! I need you!"

Emma groaned as her mother's voice reached her. She was upstairs, sitting on the window seat in her room, wondering what had happened to Corey. Had he gotten her message? Had he been able to convince his father?

"Emma!"

"Coming, Mom!" She hurried down to the stairs and found her mother in the kitchen.

"I need you to go out and collect the eggs from the chickens," her mother said, gesturing to the wire basket on the table. "I don't want those hens going broody on me."

Emma wasn't sure leaving eggs in the henhouse would make a chicken go broody, but she picked up the basket anyway and headed up to the barn. If her mother wanted the eggs in, she'd better get it done. But as she was passing the garage, she heard voices inside. Gary and her father were talking. She told herself it wasn't eavesdropping if she happened to listen to what was being said as she passed by, and then slowed her steps until she was barely moving.

"I think we did well," her father was saying. "We have enough food to get us through. The storerooms in the upper barn, the basement, and the cellar under the lower barn are full to bursting. That's enough for even a prolonged blackout."

"I can't agree, Abram," Gary said. "There's never enough food. We both know the grid is going to be down at least two years, probably five, and it could be even longer than that before the power and communications infrastructure is fully up and running again."

"Even if that's true," her father said, "we can farm. That's why we bought all this land—so we could cultivate it. We could start now, this year. It's early enough in the season to plant. We could have fresh tomatoes this summer, corn in the fall. Heck, runner beans yield in just a few weeks."

"Sure, we can plant," Gary said, "but what if our crops fail? Can you ever really have enough?"

"If you are feeding everyone in your house, then you have enough," her dad said, "and we have enough."

"Abram, you aren't thinking far enough into the future. We didn't do enough to prepare—but don't worry, I have a plan that will set us up really well."

There was a tap on her shoulder, and Emma whirled around, startled. Maggie was standing there.

"Oh, Maggie, you scared me."

"Your mom wanted me to check and make sure you were finding the eggs okay. Shall I come up to the barn with you?"

"I know how to gather eggs," Emma said, somewhat taken aback. "I've done it every summer since I was six."

"Oh, I know that. I just thought you might like company."

"If you want," Emma said, wishing she'd heard what

Gary's plan was. What would he do that would set them up really well?

They walked into the upper barn, the barn where the animals would live, that housed the chicken boxes and the stalls. The wooden floorboards creaked beneath her feet as she strode toward the laying boxes.

"Can you hold up the lids to the laying boxes while I gather the eggs?" Emma asked Maggie.

"Sure thing, doll," Maggie said and lifted the nearest lid. A chicken who'd been resting there squawked and hopped into the primary enclosure.

"Aunt Maggie, do you think we're going to be here for a long time?"

Maggie looked at her thoughtfully. "I think it depends. If the power infrastructure was badly damaged, then it could be a while. They'll do the cities first, and then eventually the entire country. But, the thing is, they'll have to manufacture a lot of the parts, and that's not going to be easy without power. I'm not saying we'll be here that long, but it could be a few years before we're caught up again."

Emma was quiet as they searched for the remaining eggs, some of which were in the henhouse proper, and not in the laying boxes. As they left the barn, walking side by side, it occurred to Emma that she might be old before she saw Corey again.

"I guess that means we'll both be old maids," Emma said. "That's a disturbing thought."

"Communities of people will spring up around the old towns," Maggie said. "We'll just have to introduce ourselves to our neighbors. There's bound to be a lonely farmer or two."

Emma pulled a face, and Maggie chuckled.

"You never know, Emma, you might find that you like farming." Maggie grinned at her. "And then I'll be the only old maid."

Nick began to relax as the miles flew by. They weren't speeding by any stretch of the imagination, but it was so much faster than walking; it felt as if they were flying.

"I didn't see many people I was tempted to give a lift to," Joshua said to Nick. "Saw a lot of people who seemed like they were looking for trouble, and I avoided them. I don't need any more trouble than I already have."

Nick nodded. "And it seems like it's only going to get worse out there."

"Yeah, what a day..."

"Pretty close to my worst day ever," Nick said with a short laugh. "Never been held up at gunpoint before."

"Close to my worst day ever, too," Joshua said.

"What was your worst?"

"The day my wife died," Joshua said, somberly. "That was the very worst. How about you? What was your worst day?"

Nick focused his gaze on Joshua, seeing the grief cast upon his face. "Same as you. The day my wife died."

"How did she die?" Joshua asked.

"Cancer."

"Yeah, me too," Joshua said. "It's a terrible thing."

Nick gave one sullen nod.

Joshua's lips compressed and he kept his eyes on the road.

The men were silent for a few minutes, and Nick was eager to change the subject.

"So, anyway, why do you think some cars will run and others won't?" Nick asked. "Computer components?"

Joshua cleared his throat. "Actually, according to the science, a solar storm shouldn't have stopped any cars from running. It did, of course, but if the owners had taken the time to disconnect the battery and reconnect it again, they probably would have been fine until they'd run out of gasoline." Joshua shrugged. "Some people that think they were stranded weren't. Unlike you. A carjacker is a sure way to get grounded."

"Tell me about it," Nick said. "Not an experience I want to repeat. I'm grateful to you for picking us up."

"Sure, no problem. So, where are you from?"

"Manchester. Though we're on our way to Central Vermont. If you'd just drop us when you're no longer headed that way, I'd appreciate it."

"You are traveling from Manchester to Vermont? Why? Won't there be a better chance of getting resourced in Manchester? The cities will have multiple FEMA sites. I doubt the whole of Vermont has more than two. They just don't have the population."

"We have friends in Vermont." Nick shrugged. "Actually, I planned on staying in Manchester, but Corey convinced me we should leave, saying it would be safer to be out of the crowds. I've been regretting that decision since my car was stolen. So, where are you headed?"

"Canada—Montreal, to be exact," Joshua said. "I can drop you right at the doorstep of where you are going, if you want.

It's probably not more than thirty minutes out of my way, if that."

"That's not necessary," Nick said. He really didn't want anyone to know exactly where they were going. "If you just set us at the nearest exit, we'll be fine."

"I'm not leaving you at the exit. You'll be sitting ducks. I'll take you to town, at least."

"That's kind of you," Nick said, wondering if it really was or not. Could he keep Joshua from following them?

"We're coming into Lebanon, New Hampshire now," Joshua said. "Keep your eyes peeled and your door locked."

Nick trained his eyes on the back doors, but evidently, Corey had locked them when he'd gotten in. He pushed down the door lock on his own door. He wasn't interested in living through another carjacking.

They drove past a shopping center with a grocery store, separated from a movie theater and some other shops by a parking lot with a medical clinic on the corner. The medical clinic had "closed" scrawled across the windows in red ink. If the urgent care clinics were closed, then where were people going to get treated? A minute later, they were passing a church, and then a donut shop.

A man was chasing a boy down the sidewalk, and as the boy glanced back, Nick could see panic on his face.

"We need to stop and help that boy," Joshua said as they drove past.

Nick wished they wouldn't, and immediately felt guilty. He'd been rescued by Joshua, but he didn't want to return the favor by helping this boy. He was a hypocrite and a coward, and he hoped that Joshua couldn't see it in his face.

Joshua pulled the car over to the curb, and the boy rushed

toward them. Nick would have to unlock his door to let him in.

Hadn't Joshua told him to keep his door locked?

Before he could reach to unlock his door, a gunshot rang out. The window next to his head shattered, glass exploding into the car.

11

Corey awoke to the sound of a gunshot, and the window next to his father's head exploded, sending glass spraying through the car.

"Corey!" Joshua said, his voice urgent. "Open the door!"

Corey caught the urgency and leaned over Rae Ann, unlocking and pushing the door open, and then jerking backward toward his door as a boy dove into the car, landing on the floorboards.

"Go!" Corey yelled, leaning over to pull the door shut but keeping his head low in case another bullet hit the car.

Rae Ann was yelling for him to get off her.

"Stay down, Rae. And you too," Corey said to the startled face looking at him from the floor.

"Is everyone okay back there?" Joshua asked.

"Yeah, we're fine," Corey said. "Is Dad hurt?"

"I've got a few cuts," his dad said, "but they're superficial. It looks worse than it is."

"You can sit up now," Joshua said. "We're out of gunshot range."

Rae Ann sat up, and Corey helped the boy up off the floor and onto the seat, scooting closer to Rae Ann so he was sitting between her and the boy, who seemed to be about Corey's age.

"Thanks," the boy said, "but can you drop me off now? I need to get back to my mom."

"Why was that man chasing you?" Joshua asked.

The boy was silent, and Corey watched him as he stared out the window.

"What's your name?" Corey asked.

"Nathan," the boy said.

"What happened, Nathan? What did that man want?" Corey watched him intently. "We might be able to help you, you know?"

"You already did," Nathan said and sighed. "I don't know where Billy is."

"Who's that?" Joshua asked.

"My downstairs neighbor. He went with me to get medicine for my mom, and we got separated." Nathan's gaze shifted to his hands.

"Medicine?" Corey asked.

"My mom has diabetes," Nathan said, "and she needs insulin. She gave me her credit card, and Billy and I went to the pharmacy on our bikes. But the pharmacy couldn't take the credit card because there's no electricity. Billy thought we should get cash, but no ATMs are working, and the bank wouldn't give us money because we needed to have an account. They wouldn't let me take money out of my mom's account, or maybe there wasn't enough money in it. They wouldn't tell me anything, and they couldn't call my mom to ask."

Nathan stopped speaking for a full minute, and Corey was about to nudge him when he took a deep breath. "We thought we'd either have to rob a store to get cash, or just steal the medicine. It seemed simpler to just steal the medicine, and Billy's dad has a gun, so we went and got it. We held up the pharmacist with the gun, but the owner was in the store and told him not to give us the medicine."

Another moment of silence.

"And?" Joshua asked.

"Billy shot up the store," Nathan said.

"Shot up the store?"

"Yeah, I don't know why he did it. But I ran for my bike, and rode away as fast as I could. The man followed me in his car, and I had to ditch my bike and run between the buildings. Only, he was faster than me, and he almost caught me—then you showed up. But I don't know where Billy is. I think they must've caught him."

"You should have told the pharmacist that your mother needed her insulin. They might have let you have it," Joshua said. He pulled the car over to the curb. "Go on home to your mother."

Nathan got out of the car. "Thanks," he said, waved, and jogged away.

"He was bad, wasn't he, Daddy?" Rae Ann asked.

"He made some bad choices, Rae Ann," their dad said, "but he was in a tough spot. He was trying to keep his mother alive."

"I'm glad he's gone," Corey said. "He doesn't seem like he makes very good decisions."

"Yeah, he'd probably just bring trouble down on all of us

if we let him come with us," Joshua said. "Luckily, he's got a family, so he's not alone."

"Kids who make decisions like that are dangerous," Corey's dad said. "He should have gone back to his mom. She could have figured it out."

"Not if she was sick, Daddy," Rae Ann said. "She might not be able to help if she didn't feel good."

"You could be right, Rae Ann," their father said, "but he still should have found an adult to help him."

"I know that, Daddy," Rae Ann said. "I'd know to ask."

"What I hope is that you'd know to always have Corey with you to keep you safe," their dad said. "You shouldn't be out in public alone. From now on, you are not to go anywhere on your own. Do you understand?"

"Yes, Daddy," she said with a sigh.

Corey wrapped an arm around her shoulders and gave her a squeeze. "Don't worry, Rae," he said quietly, "it's going to be a while before there's anywhere any of us can go."

As they drove along, Nick thought of the boy they'd saved a few miles back. Boys like that worried him when he thought of his own kids. What if they fall in with the wrong kind of people? Hopefully, they would be insulated from all that at the Pattersons' compound. Corey had a head on his shoulders, but Rae Ann could easily be led astray, and if anything happened to Nick, Corey might one day be in a position to do whatever it took to keep her safe. Even make bad decisions.

Life had gotten pretty bad if boys were holding up drug stores for their parent's medications. Pretty soon, there wouldn't be any medicines available at all. Hospitals would have to close down as the fuel ran out for their generators, food would become scarce as the supply chain was disrupted. How long would it be before the US government ran out of fuel to supply the FEMA shelters? How would they keep water running in the pipes without pumps? He hoped Abram had considered that.

In another hour or so, less maybe, they'd be dropped off and on the last leg of their journey. He hoped they didn't run into any lawlessness before they reached the end of their trek. It all seemed so dicey, so unsafe. But then he realized that Joshua couldn't be the only good person left in the world. There would be other people who maintained their integrity, who didn't steal people's cars or shoot at young boys. The wind coming through the broken window reminded him that the owner of the drugstore had been willing to kill not only Nathan but the random people who stopped to be sure the boy was okay.

Still, he would not give up hope. There were good people, and he'd be willing to bet that there were more good folk than bad. They would stick with the people that made good role models for his children. People who would protect them and keep them safe.

Nick glanced into the back seat to see if his children had gone back to sleep, but no, they were huddled together, Corey's arm around Rae Ann's shoulders. Their eyes were wide open and watching the road in front of them, and Rae Ann looked scared. The incident with the gun and the boy had obviously spooked her.

"Are you okay?" he asked her.

She nodded, though her eyes betrayed her.

He wanted to ask Joshua to pull over so he could join her in the back seat, to help sooth her, but he didn't want to ask the man to stop the car. Instead, he reached his hand back and held onto hers.

"Everything's okay," he said, and he saw the tightness in her jaw dissipate.

It wasn't too much later when they turned off the state route and crossed a bridge into the small town. There was a town green, and across from one side, a block of stores and restaurants. The grocery store, Nick noticed, was boarded up, and it didn't look hastily done. Perhaps the owners had taken precautions and secured the windows and door before the power went out. There was a deli toward the end of the block, and it was boarded up too. The coffee shop and the restaurant on the corner were unblemished, but Nick wondered how long it would be before someone was desperate enough to shatter the windows and steal whatever food was still unspoiled.

"I think we have to walk another forty-five minutes to an hour," Corey said, "but we're almost safe now."

"Safe?" Joshua said.

"Yeah, we have friends with a bug out location near here," Corey said.

Nick could have kicked himself for not telling Corey to keep his mouth shut.

"Not really a bug out shelter," Nick said. "It's just a farmhouse a neighbor owns."

"Still, it sounds safe," Joshua said. "Can I come with you?"

"I'm sorry, but it's not my place. And I'm not even sure we'll be welcome."

"I'll only stay the night. I've got a long way to go, and it's going to be dark soon. I'd rather not have to sleep in my car in an unsecured location. Why don't you let me drive you all the way there?"

"I'm sorry, Joshua," Nick said, trying to be firm and kind at the same time, "but I really can't bring you. I was serious when I said I didn't know how we'd be received. If I bring a complete stranger with me, I'm sure they'll turn us all away. You do see that I have to keep my children safe?"

"Yes, of course," Joshua said, stopping the car. "Go ahead, then. I wish you well."

"And I, you," Nick said. "You were very kind to bring us this far." He felt some regret at leaving the man behind. He had, after all, saved them from a night in the open with no blankets and little water or food.

They walked away from the car, Rae Ann looking back and waving to Joshua.

"Dad," Corey said, "Joshua saved us. We should have let him come."

"Listen, Corey, I feel bad for him—I do. But I know that Abram Patterson has no idea that we are going to show up on his doorstep. There's no way I could bring a stranger."

"But Emma said—"

"Emma said what she needed to, to get us to come. But I don't for a moment believe Abram asked us to come. He would have talked to me, son. Not sent a note from his daughter." Nick shook his head.

"But then why did you agree to bring us, if you knew he might turn us away?"

"I thought it was our best chance of surviving this emergency intact. I'm hoping your friendship with Emma—and the fact that she wrote a note telling us to come—will be enough to get us in the door. After that, we'll have to prove our worth. Which means working hard. Are you ready to work hard?"

"I am," Corey said.

They walked along in silence after that, and when Rae Ann started to lag, Nick picked her up and placed her back on his shoulders. Nick hoped he was right, that the fact that Emma had asked them to come would sway Abram into letting them stay. He was sure that Abram wouldn't turn them away this evening. He wouldn't be as cruel as that. But would he let them stay? Like he'd told Corey, they would have to prove their worth by working hard and pitching in. Three extra people would put a burden on their food stores, so he'd have to prove himself willing to do what it took to replenish those supplies. He'd be out in the field planting crops, and he'd probably have to fish and learn how to hunt.

And he'd do all those things and more, if that's what it took to keep his kids safe. He'd tell Abram that he was willing to do whatever it took so that they could stay at the compound.

Nick said a silent prayer that it would be enough.

"How much longer, Daddy?" Rae Ann asked from over his head. Even with the nap in the car, she was exhausted. He could feel her drooping.

"Not long now, sweetheart," he said. "Just hold on, and we'll be there real soon."

12

"Abram," Shelly called to him as he came back into the house, "what do we have to do to get hot water here? You promised me hot water."

"It's the pilot light," Abram said. "I have to go up and light it."

"Why don't you show me how?" Shelly asked. "In case it goes out when you aren't around."

"I'll come too," Maggie said.

The women followed him up the stairs to the second floor and stood out of the way as he pulled the attic ladder out of the ceiling. They climbed the ladder one at a time and walked the dusty planks laid out over the open floor joists to the platform that held the water heater.

Unlike every home Abram had ever lived in, where the water heater was in the basement, the one in this house was in the attic. This was because the system was gravity fed, and there was no pump to push the water up into the house. If they wanted hot water, it had to be able to run down the pipes into the building below, just as the water in the tank on the roof ran down to the heater, or to the pipes supplying the house if it didn't need to be heated.

"First, you have to make sure the propane tank is turned on," he said, taking in a breath of the stale air. "There's one extra tank at the far side of the attic, but the rest are down in the lower barn. We've stockpiled several hundred full tanks, so we shouldn't run out."

He bent down and opened a small metal door in the bottom of the water heater and reached for a long, thin, metal pipe with an alligator clip welded onto the end.

"This is an old car antenna," he said. "I put a clip on the end so it would hold a match. You light the match and put it in the clip, then you can guide the match into the pilot light and turn this knob"—he pointed to a round knob on the side of the water heater—"to light. Once the pilot light is burning, turn the knob to the 'on' position. And you are set. It's very straight forward, and there's a panel here with the instructions." He pointed to a metal plate attached next to the tiny door. "But if you forget to turn on the propane tank, you'll be out of luck, and that step is not printed here."

"Hang on," Shelly said, rummaging in her pocket. "I have a permanent marker." Shelly knelt down beside him and printed "Turn On Propane" above the instructions. "There, now I won't forget."

"I was wondering," Maggie said, "where are the food stores kept? I might want to check if we have certain ingredients. Shelly and I are going to share meal prep, and it would be helpful to know what we have."

"There's the pantry of the kitchen," Abram said. "That

should be pretty well stocked, as we just got here. Then there's a cold room in the basement where a good many things are stored. Any fresh food, like vegetables, should be stored there until they are eaten. Next to that is a root cellar with things like potatoes and carrots. There is a locked room in the lower barn with canned and dry goods, and a much smaller stash in the upper barn."

"So, we're pretty well set?" Maggie asked.

"We've also got dairy and beef cows coming, as well as some goats. I think Emma should be charged with taking care of them. They'll need to be milked, but that will mean dairy products like butter and cheese are achievable."

"That's a relief," Shelly said. "When I realized we could become a permanent part of this community, I worried we'd go hungry."

"Actually, Gary doesn't think we have enough stored. He thinks we need to bring in more food," Abram said.

"How does he think we are going to get more?" Shelly asked.

"He says he has a plan," Abram said. Inwardly, he doubted the feasibility of any plan that waited until now to acquire more supplies.

"I hope he's not planning on doing anything reckless," Maggie said.

"He's a farmer, so it's something along those lines, most likely." It occurred to Abram that Gary had gotten off topic and never told him what his plan was. They'd been sidetracked by the beef versus dairy argument.

"But we already have farming as a core part of our plan," Shelly said. "What else does he want to do?"

"I don't know," Abram said.

"I don't trust him, Abram. I wish you hadn't invited him here," Shelly said.

"He's my best friend, Shelly. And he has survival skills that we'll need to get by. We won't be able to make it without him. Gary is a skilled survivalist." He noticed Maggie had turned and was making her way back to the ladder. He thought she must be embarrassed by the argument. Or, perhaps she was afraid he would bring her up. But she was family, and was always going to be included in any bug out plan.

"Something about him just doesn't sit well with me," Shelly said. "I don't trust him."

"I do. Sure, he's rough around the edges, but he understands the value of life and friendship. He would never do anything to harm us."

"I think you'll find that he's not as high minded as you think, Abram. This is just the kind of situation his love of lawlessness rejoices in."

"Love of lawless—"

"There's no law that can't be broken, because there is no longer unified law enforcement."

"Nonsense." Abram tried to make his tone light—he was ready to steer the conversation away from Gary. "Fenton has a police chief and two officers. They may not be able to communicate with Montpelier, but they can keep peace in their town. And, for now, they even have vehicles. I'll go down to town tomorrow and make sure they know that their cars can be restarted if they disconnect and reconnect their batteries. And when the gasoline runs out, I'm sure they'll ride bicycles or horses. There are plenty of horses in this area. Would you like a horse?"

"A horse would just be another animal to feed. Unless you are going to use it to plow the fields, I don't see needing to go very far. A bicycle would do very well."

"Do you think we need a horse for plowing the fields? We have a lot of gasoline put aside for the tractor, but eventually, we will run out. I suppose it depends on how soon that happens. We could prolong the use of gas if we did some of the harvesting by horse, I suppose."

"But then you still have to feed it," Shelly said. "That means making sure you have enough hay in for the winter for one more animal." She moved toward the ladder. "We could bring in the hay by hand and save gasoline that way. There are five of us, after all. It should be possible."

Abram didn't know what Gary's plan for harvest was, but he wasn't going to mention his friend's name again now. Shelly had let the argument slide, and he was grateful. Gary could stay in the background until dinner, when Abram would warn him to keep his conversation civilized. Eventually, the women would get used to Gary and realize he wasn't such a brute, as he seemed.

Then, to his surprise, as he was descending the ladder, the gate bell rang.

The walk from town to the Pattersons' compound hadn't been easy for Nick. Rae Ann's sparkly red shoes had rubbed her heels raw, and she had to be carried the entire way, as the road grew progressively worse. It had turned to dirt as soon as they had navigated off the route that led along the river, and it was a steady uphill slog. On top of that, the farther they traveled, the more like a track and less like a road it became. It was rutted, potholed, and riddled with rocks that would twist your ankle if you weren't careful.

Finding himself standing at the gates to the compound was a relief. There was even a mailbox with the correct house number on it. That was a minor miracle out here in the middle of nowhere, miles up a dirt track. How did the mail carrier even navigate this road?

The problem was, now that they were here, how would they get the Pattersons' attention?

He studied the gate. It was padlocked, and there was a cement strip under it, so there was no digging a trench and going under. There was no house in sight, although he thought he could see a barn through the trees.

Corey gave an exclamation and moved to where a rope hung near the latch. Nick hadn't even seen it hanging there, but Corey grabbed and pulled, and a bell rang clear and loud from under a small wooden structure he'd taken for a rather large birdhouse. A few minutes later, they heard footsteps crunching on the drive, and a man appeared from around the bend.

He was a short man and stocky, with squinty eyes and a mouth that drew down. But the thing that made Nick's heart drop was the rifle cradled in his arms. This was not the welcome he was imagining. Not that he'd assumed Abram would be glad to see them, but this man was positively hostile.

"Go away," he said. "We can't help you here."

"I'm looking for Abram Patterson," Nick said. "Is he here?"

"I said, go away." The man cocked the rifle.

Corey stepped in front of his dad. "Is Emma here?" he asked, his voice high and reedy. "She invited us to come."

The man raised the gun, pointing it straight at Corey's head. "I won't repeat myself again," he said. "Go away, or I'll shoot."

"No, Gary. Stop!" It was Emma's voice, coming from behind the man; she was running fast. "Put the gun down, Gary, that's my best friend."

Behind Emma, Abram, Shelly, and a woman Nick didn't know appeared, walking quickly. When Abram recognized them, his face flushed beet red, and if Nick had had any doubt about the "invitation," it was gone. Abram had not invited them to join him at the compound, and he was not happy they were here.

Emma was tugging at Gary's arm. "Lower the gun! Those are my friends."

Gary glanced at Abram, who gave him a small nod of agreement. *Well, at least we aren't going to be shot*, Nick thought, as Gary reluctantly lowered his rifle. And Nick was only slightly comforted. The weapon was still loaded and cocked, and the man's eyes were focused back on Nick's face. They weren't out of danger.

"What are you waiting for?" Emma said. "Open the gate."

Gary glanced at Abram again, and this time there was the merest hint of headshake. No. He wasn't throwing the gate open to welcome his neighbors. He really didn't want them here. Nick wished now, more than ever, that they'd stayed home. He could have coped in his own home, but this was beyond the ability to absorb.

"Can we at least spend the night?" Nick asked. "Rae Ann needs some first aid."

Shelly started forward, but Abram caught her eye, and she stopped.

Emma looked from Gary to her dad and back again, her face showing the disbelief she was feeling. "Dad," she said, "you have to let them in. They can't stay out there on the road all night."

"I made it perfectly clear that we weren't including any of your friends, Emma," Abram said. "That hasn't changed."

"But you have to." She grabbed his arm. "I invited them. They wouldn't be here if it weren't for me. You've got to let them in, Dad, because if anything bad happens, it will be my fault."

"I'm sorry, Emma, I really am, but you need to learn to live with the consequences of your actions." He was staring at Nick, not even looking at Emma as he talked to her.

Emma's face flushed. "Dad! Please?"

"You heard me, Emma, now go back to the house," Abram said. "Now."

But that was the wrong thing to say to a modern young woman. Nick watched her face grow hard, her chin jutting out.

"Fine," she said. "Then open the gate and let me out. If you don't let them in, then I'm leaving with them."

Shelly made a sound that might have been, "No!" but it was hard to tell because Gary produced a key and said, "Fine with me."

"Gary," Abram barked, but the man ignored him.

"Let her go, Abram," Gary said. "Girls aren't much use, and this one won't take orders. We don't need her." He opened the gate and let her slip through.

"That's my daughter, Gary," Abram said, giving Gary a look that would have melted a lesser man. "And this is my property."

"And you told these people to leave," Gary said. "If she wants to go with them, I say let her."

"But I say let them in," Shelly said, stepping forward. "If girls aren't much use, then you should be happy to get another man and a boy. I'll put Emma and Rae to work in the house, and you can have Nick and Corey." Eyes locked on Abram's, her face was set. "Let them in, Abram, or I'm going with them too. And I can't speak for Maggie, but I imagine she'll want to come with me."

Maggie stepped forward. "That's right, Shell, I'm with you. You go, I go."

"What's it going to be, Abram?" Shelly said. "Are you and Gary going to spend the duration alone together?" She took another step toward the gate.

"Shelly," Abram snapped, his face a mask of rage, "stop playing and go back to the house, now. And take Maggie with you."

"If that's how you want it," Shelly said, and she took Maggie's hand. The women walked past Abram and Gary to the gate and slid it open again to walk through.

Nick watched as Abram caved. The rage that was holding him together dissolved, leaving his face slack with despair. His hands were shaking at his sides.

"Come back, Shelly," he said. "Nick and his family can

stay. But they will have to work for their living, is that understood?"

"Let me make sure you understand something, Abram Patterson," she said. "If you ever talk to me like that again, if you ever order me to do something like that, I will be gone. Do you hear me?"

"I'm sorry, Shelly," Abram said. "I thought a national emergency made me responsible for your safety. But you are an adult and responsible for yourself. It won't happen again."

"Oh, come on, Abram," Gary said, shaking his head.

Shelly walked back through the gate and got right up in Gary's face, making him lurch back. "If you ever think you can break up my family, you're wrong. Pull that crap again, and you're gone. You'll be on the other side of that gate before you know what happened. Do you understand me, Gary?"

"Yes, ma'am," he said, straightening up. "My apologies, ma'am."

"Good." She regarded Nick and his family. "Emma, take Corey down to the house and put him in one of the downstairs bedrooms, the one with twin beds. If Nick doesn't mind, they can share."

Nick shook his head; he didn't mind.

"Rae can sleep in the little room next to yours," Shelly continued. "It's just the right size for a six-year-old girl. Gary, lock the gate."

Nick started forward, but something he heard made him look back. Was it a car? What he saw surprised him. Joshua's car was crawling up the rocky track a ways behind them.

Nick stepped quickly through the opening in the fence and Gary locked it behind him. He dismissed Joshua as not important, thinking he'd just seen Shelly go from inferior housewife to commanding officer in the little man's eyes, and it amused him. Nick was going to get on Shelly's good side just as soon as he could. If one thing was clear, it was that Shelly and Maggie were the moral backbone of this group, and it would pay to have their approval.

13

"Do you know that car?" Abram asked Nick as Gary locked the gate behind him. Joshua had increased his speed as they walked through the gate, rocking and bumping up the road.

"Yes. He gave us a ride to town when our car got stolen."

"Do you mind if Shelly takes Rae Ann down to the house without you? We may need you for this."

"Sure, that's fine."

Shelly came and took Rae Ann from Nick's shoulders. Rae Ann wrapped her arms around the woman's neck and her legs around her waist as Shelly took her, holding her close. "Come on, sweetheart."

"My feet hurt," Rae Ann said, "and I have blisters."

"Goodness, yes," Shelly said, walking toward the house with her burden. "Those are magical shoes, but I don't think they were made for walking."

"And Louise is hungry, and I lost my clothes…"

"That's okay, sweetheart. I think I have some of Emma's old clothes. We'll get you all set up." Shelly eyed Corey, and said, "Come on, you look like you could use a nice, hot meal too."

Maggie, Corey, and Emma followed Shelly back to the house, Rae Ann looking over the woman's shoulder as they went, trying to see what was happening at the gate.

Nick shifted his attention back to the approaching car, which had arrived at the gate. Joshua was sitting behind the wheel, watching them, and Nick wondered what he was waiting for, then noticed that Gary had his rifle pointed at the car.

"You don't need to do that." Nick said. "That guy isn't armed. He's harmless."

Gary glanced at Abram, who nodded, and he lowered the gun.

The car door opened, and Joshua lumbered out, carefully raising his hands in the air to show them he wasn't armed. He strolled to the gate, and Nick thought he seemed relaxed and friendly until he saw that Joshua's knees were shaking. He was scared, but also desperate enough to face his fear.

"I'm only looking for a safe place to spend the night," Joshua said. "I'll go first thing in the morning."

"We're not a flop house," Gary said, sneering. "Find somewhere else to stay."

"Like where? Is there a B&B down this road?"

"Not one that would take you in." Gary laughed. "You look a little down and out, man. I'm surprised Nick got in the car with you."

"Come on, Nick, the only reason you are here is that I brought you," Joshua said through a tight jaw. "Doesn't that mean anything to you? Your kids are safe because of me."

Nick thought Joshua was acting more on edge than he

should be. "Why don't you drive on through to Canada, like you said you were going to?" he asked.

"What if they aren't letting people through the border? I don't want to be stuck up there all night with no gas. Come on, man. Let me in."

"It's not my call. I'm lucky they let me in."

"If we let you in," Gary said, "before long, every lost soul this side of the river will be asking us to take them in. Abram knows Nick. No one knows you. I hear there's a FEMA shelter set up in Burlington. You could go there for the night. It's only another hour; you could be there before dark."

"I'm tired of driving. Let me in, and I'll help you out with some work or something before I leave. I'm a good mechanic." Joshua smiled, but it was strained.

"What do you think, Abram?" Gary asked. "You don't want this stranger in your house, do you?"

"I could stay in that barn," Joshua said, pointing. "I'd be fine in an outbuilding or on the porch. I won't even ask for food or to use the bathroom."

Smart, Nick thought. Joshua had seen the women and probably realized they'd insist on feeding him. They might even offer him a bedroom for driving Corey and Rae Ann here. Shelly took a stand for Corey and Rae Ann, he was pretty sure. If it had just been him standing on the other side of the gate, he'd probably be headed back into town now. But she wasn't going to turn children away, and Nick was lucky enough to belong to them. She wouldn't separate children from their father, either.

Abram was quiet for a long time, and Nick could see his thought process reflected on his face. Should he do the humane thing and let the man stay, or should he protect what was his and make Joshua go away? His jaw tightened, and Nick thought he was going to say no, when Joshua spoke up again.

"I can chop wood," he said. "I know you don't need it now, but you will in the winter. I can help clear a field for planting."

He watched Abram's face transform again. These were tasks that needed doing, and it couldn't hurt to have help.

"I'm a good man to have around," Joshua continued. "Besides, it's only one night. I'll give you three hours of solid work just to sleep in your barn overnight."

Gary turned to look at Abram. "You can't be thinking of letting this joker spend the night in the compound," he said. "The next thing you know, there will be people ringing our bell every day, looking to work for a safe place to stay. We just acquired two able-bodied men."

"It wouldn't hurt to have extra help for a day," Nick said. "I'm sure Joshua would keep quiet about the compound if you asked him to."

"No one asked you," Gary said. "We went to a lot of trouble to keep people out. What was the point of that if we're just going to let people in?"

"I'm sorry, Joshua," Abram said. "I can't let you in. Gary is right. What's the point of all this security if we are just going to open the gates to everyone who comes by?"

"You let him in," Joshua said, nodding to Nick.

"We know them," Abram said. "I can't, in good conscience, turn away my neighbor. You should go now."

Gary had the nose of his rifle pointed through the links in the gate now.

Joshua turned away, but when he reached the car door, he

glanced back over his shoulder. "I'm afraid the day will come when you will regret turning me away," he said. "I could have been a friend and an ally."

He got in his car and backed it out of the drive, traveling back the way he came.

"What a nut job," Gary said. "I'm glad you finally came to your senses, Abram. And now we will really need to fortify our supplies. Teenaged boys are bottomless pits when it comes to food. And everything else, for that matter. We will have to be much more careful about food now."

"If you say so," Abram said, turning away and heading back down the drive to the house.

Nick followed him, leaving Gary at the gate on his own, the rifle still pointed down the road, as if he was afraid Joshua would come back. Nick felt terrible about Joshua. He'd helped Nick and the kids out of a difficult situation, and Nick hadn't been able to return the favor. Regardless, he had to watch out for his own family. Abram could have changed his mind and sent Nick packing if he'd pushed for Joshua to join them. He couldn't take that risk.

As they walked down to the house, Nick realized he was relieved that there were women here. Rae Ann would not be his sole responsibility anymore—she would join the women in the household activities while Nick and Corey joined the men. There would be proper mother figures in her life, something she hadn't had for years. Perhaps Shelly or Maggie would be able to pry Louise from Rae Ann's arms for more than a moment or two each day, and the girl would grow up to be normal. Although, that seemed like a lot to ask. She hadn't been right since her mother had died.

Nick took a deep breath as he approached the house, and a smile crept onto his face.

Against all odds, they had made it to their new home in one piece.

When they'd been dismissed from the scene at the gate, Emma took Corey by the hand and dragged him down the drive to the house. They left Rae Ann to walk down with Emma's mother and aunt, so that when they reached the house, they were alone. She pulled him through the living room and past the kitchen, down the hall to a large bedroom with two twin beds, two dressers, and two night tables.

"This is your room," she said. "You should take that bed"—she pointed—"because it's more comfortable and doesn't squeak when you move. My dad and mom have the bedroom across the hall, so if you go wandering, do it quietly. My dad's a bear when he gets woken up at night. He's an extremely light sleeper."

Corey plopped his backpack down on the bed Emma indicated, and she pulled him back out of the room.

"Come upstairs, and see where my room is," she said, pulling him along, "and then I'll give you the tour."

"Okay," Corey said and followed her up the stairs.

She stepped to the right when they reached the top of the stairs and led him down the hallway to the room at the end.

"We can't be in here alone when my father is in the house," she said, "but I wanted you to see which one it was." She sat on the bed and bounced. "It's the best room in the house, but don't tell my father I said so." She jumped back up and grabbed his hand, pulling him out into the hall, carefully closing the door behind them. "I was afraid you wouldn't come," she said, opening a door that led into one of the rooms next to hers. Because her room spanned the width of the house, there was a bedroom next to hers on one side and a bathroom on the other.

"This is Rae's room," she said, stepping back and letting him see into the cupboard-sized room. "I think it used to be a sewing room. That's what the man who sold the house to my dad told him."

"I didn't think my dad was going to come," Corey said. "I had to talk him into it. And then, when our car got jacked, I had to talk him into it all over again."

"I'm glad you did." She closed the small room and opened the door into the bathroom. "The power went out before we got here, and I couldn't share my location with you. It's a good thing you could read the map."

"No, your instructions were good," Corey said, "but it was a long walk from town. I thought it was closer."

"I couldn't really remember how far it was," Emma said. "I'd only been driven here once. I had to guess." She opened the other doors in the hall, displaying five more bedrooms and a bathroom near Aunt Maggie's room.

"You've got two bathrooms up here?" Corey asked. "That seems kind of unusual for an old farmhouse."

"Dad wasn't sure how many people might end up living with us," Emma said, heading back down the stairs, "so he put another bathroom in."

She showed him the kitchen, with the giant kitchen table, the dining room, the living room, the downstairs bathroom, and the mudroom out the back of the kitchen, before leading him outside.

"That's the biggest house I've ever seen," Corey said. "The rooms are huge."

"I know, right? Like you could have an epic house party or something. And guess what? There's hot water. The water tank is on the roof, and the hot water heater is in the attic, so it's got gravity-fed water pressure. There's a spring up the hill that fills the water tank, so it's all really efficient, and the water heater in the attic should keep the tank warm enough that it doesn't freeze in winter. It's genius. Come on, I'll show you the animals."

She'd taken him out the back door on purpose, so that they'd missed her mom coming in the front with Maggie and Rae Ann, and if her luck held, her dad would have taken Corey's dad and Gary to look at some project that needed doing and she could be alone with Corey for a while. They walked back up the drive, and she was pleased when they reached the barn without running into the men.

She took him inside to see the birds. "These are the hens," she said, standing at the enclosure, "and those are the Guinea fowl over there. They are noisy birds, but they eat a lot of bugs, so they are good to have on a farm." She walked him over to the stalls. "These are where the goats are going to live, and this stall is for cows. I'm hoping we'll get donkeys and ponies and maybe a horse, but my dad says we can only have animals that work for a living. You and I will probably end up milking the goats and the cows. I hope you like animals."

"I like animals well enough, but I've never milked one. Have you?"

"The dairy farmer down the road taught me when we

came up here last summer, but I probably need a refresher. Let's go up to the hayloft," she said pulling him to the ladder.

They climbed up, and Emma led him to the back of the barn, where you could sit on the bales and look out the door where they brought the hay into the barn. "See those big, round, marshmallow-looking things in the field out there? Those are round bales. They use them to feed cows. My dad had to find a farmer who would do square bales for us because he wanted to store them up here, and the round bales weigh like a ton. There's no way to get them up here."

"How did they do it? Did they have to carry them up the ladder?"

"They used a hay elevator. I never knew there was such a thing."

"We'll learn a lot living out here, being farmers."

"Some of it's fun, but it's a lot of hard work, too. You are going to sleep like a rock and eat everything in sight. I did, when we were here."

"Em," he said quietly, "I was really scared I was never going to see you again. When we were walking, I was afraid we'd be stuck in the forest forever and starve to death."

"I was worried about you too, Core." She reached up and touched his face. "I almost died when the power went out, and I hadn't been able to text you. My dad said we had to save the phones for emergencies, and I didn't dare text you in the car. Aunt Maggie would have seen me, and she might have said something."

"Why did you tell me that your dad wanted us to come, Em? I think my dad is furious about that."

"Because I knew you wouldn't be able to convince him to come if he thought he didn't have an invitation. So, I invited you." She flipped her hair back.

"He figured it out, but I convinced him to come anyway." Corey leaned in toward her and gave her a hug.

"Emma!" her father's voice roared from below them. "Where are you?"

Emma jumped back, her eyes wide. "We're up here. I'm showing Corey the marshmallow hay in the field."

"Close the hay door and come down here right now." She could hear the anger in his voice.

"Yes, Dad."

She closed and latched the door, and they returned to the ladder and climbed down.

Her father was pacing back and forth across the barn floor, from one side to the other, but stopped when they were back on the first floor.

"I don't want you two going off by yourselves, do you understand?" he said. "It's a bad example for Rae Ann, and it will make your mother worry. In the future, if you have somewhere to go, you will tell your mother where you are at all times, and you will bring Rae Ann with you."

"Yes, Dad."

"Yes, Mr. Patterson," Corey echoed.

"Good, now go back to the house and help your mother make dinner. Corey, you can come with me and help with mending the fences." He gave Corey a severe look, and Corey ducked his head. "Off you go, Emma."

Emma left the barn reluctantly, and as she left, she heard her father's muted voice: "I don't want you alone with my daughter. Do I make myself clear?"

Corey's voice was barely audible: "Yes, sir."

14

NICK FOLLOWED Abram and Gary to the house, where he was passed off to Shelly and Maggie, who promised him a tour of the house and grounds. Gary had bypassed the porch and gone down to the lower outbuildings. Abram, after asking the women to look after Nick, went back up the hill in the direction of the garage and barn. Maggie took Nick into his bedroom.

"Oh, too bad," Maggie said. "Looks like Corey already claimed the best bed."

"You've been here long enough to know which beds are the most comfortable?" Nick asked.

"Oh, yeah. Almost the first thing Emma and I did was to try out all the beds. And there are a bunch in this house. It's bigger than it looks. If you want, I'll give you the house tour while Shelly is busy in the kitchen."

"Sure. Why not?"

Maggie took him upstairs and opened all the doors, pointing out Rae Ann's room. He was grateful that she made such a point of showing him his daughter's bedroom, and he was amazed by the number of rooms on the corridor. The house could support a lot more people, even if the food stores could not.

When they finished the tour of the house, Shelly took off her apron, and they went to head outside. But before they did, Nick noticed there was a door in the kitchen that wasn't opened for him, and he wondered why not. He'd put money on it being the basement and was curious as to what might be hiding down there.

When they reached the lower barns, Nick discovered a well-equipped repair shop, fuel storage, a woodworking shop, and a garage full of utility vehicles such as ATVs, tractors, and dirt bikes. There was also a shed with farm supplies like cowlicks, rolls of fencing, and building materials. Abram had obviously been planning this for a while. A lot of thought had gone into the items that might be needed to stay alive without electricity or communication. There were snowshoes and skates hanging on the wall, and fishing rods in a metal locker. There weren't any firearms down here, but maybe those needed to be closer at hand.

Gary was working on an ATV in the metal shop, and he called Nick to come in for a minute. Shelly said she wanted to check on something and said she'd meet him in the next barn, so while the women moved off, he stepped in to see Gary.

"You know you'll need to pull your weight around here," Gary said, glancing up from the quad bike.

"Of course," Nick said. "I think that was made perfectly clear." He wondered why Gary felt the need to repeat this information.

"I've got an important mission coming up that you can

help me with. Something that will help make up for the food you'll be eating."

"Of course, I'll help if I can. Does Abram know about it?"

"It's a bit of a surprise for Abram. An act of good faith on both our parts."

"Great. Whatever you need," Nick said, wishing Gary meant what he said. He didn't trust Gary; there was something about a person who could casually cock a gun and point it at another person that made Nick uneasy.

"Do you know how to fire a weapon, Nick?"

"I've fired a gun, yes."

"Can you hit what you fire at?"

"I have no idea. It's not like I've ever done any target shooting."

"Hmm. We may need to work on that."

Nick wondered if he should tell Gary that he wasn't interested in shooting at human beings, but it seemed a bit inflammatory. Maybe Gary was thinking of hunting deer and turkeys. Saying something about killing people could sound a bit insulting.

"I better catch up with Shelly," Nick said. "She's waiting for me."

"Okay. I'll catch up with you later."

Nick found Shelly and Maggie leaning over a wooden box at the back of the next barn, and when he joined them, he heard the sound of mewing. He peered over their shoulders to see a kindle of kittens that couldn't have been more than a few days old.

"Their mother left them," Shelly said, "and we don't know if she's coming back. We were just debating how long they can survive, or if we should take them up to the house. Good mousers are invaluable in the country."

"She might just be catching a mouse for her own dinner," Maggie said. "They should be okay for an hour or two, as long as they are warm enough." Maggie turned to Nick. "Don't you think?"

"I'm not really an animal expert," Nick said, "but I could check back in an hour if you want."

"Would you?" Shelly asked. "And if the mother isn't back, could you bring them up to the house?"

"Sure. That sounds easy enough."

"Hang on," Shelly said, and she took off the cardigan she was wearing and tucked it around the kittens. "Come on, I'll show you the garage and the upper barn, where the animals will be housed."

"Will be?" Nick asked. "They aren't already here?"

"No. We had someone come in and take care of the birds, but it didn't make sense to feed animals that weren't being used. The goats will be delivered tomorrow, and the cattle guy is going to walk the cow up with her calves later this week. We're waiting for a litter of piglets to be old enough to leave their mother. The kids are going to have plenty to do." Shelly flashed a wicked smile. "They won't have time to miss their electronics."

"Didn't you say you were getting rabbits too?" Maggie asked.

"We thought about it, but we thought it might be tough on Emma when she realized we were going to eat them. And now we also have Rae...I just don't think it's a good idea, and Abram is absolutely dead set against pets. No feeding animals that don't contribute."

Maggie placed a finger on her chin. "We could have a cat, then. To keep the mice population down."

"I might be able to convince him a cat was pulling its weight. I know he's talked about a guard dog, as well."

They walked up the hill, past the extended garage, which housed the cars and what appeared to be a four-wheeler with a plow attached to the front, and walked on up the hill to the barn that housed the chickens. There wasn't much to look at, just empty stalls, and an enclosure for the birds that had some laying boxes attached to it. There was an opening to an outdoor run, and most of the birds were sunning themselves in the evening light.

"What are those big birds?" Nick asked, eyeing the larger birds. They weren't turkeys, he knew that much.

"Guinea fowl," Shelly said. "They are really good at eating the insects in your garden. And they are really low maintenance."

"Are they good to eat?"

"I've never eaten one, but I assume you can. It shouldn't be much different than eating turkey or duck."

"I'm not sure I could eat a chicken I'd been feeding every day," Maggie said.

"And that's why I'm not putting you in charge of the birds," Shelly said. "I'd hate for you to starve to death."

Maggie furrowed her brows. "You don't think I could kill a chicken, do you?"

"Nope. You'd end up trying to live off chicken feed before you'd kill an animal you were responsible for. Don't worry, unless we all die of the plague or something, you won't have to. But my advice is not to hang out up here with the animals. Abram will be killing them, and we will be eating them.

That's how we are going to survive in this electricity-free world."

"When we were growing up, Shelly, I would have never guessed that you'd turn into a pioneer woman. It's kind of amusing."

"You're going to be very happy I did, when you're eating fresh blackberry jam. Oh, and we have blueberries too. I might put you in charge of those. We need to put up a deer fence, so they make it through the summer." Shelly smiled at Nick. "Come on, it's time to get back to the house and finish dinner. Those kids are going to be starving."

As he followed Shelly, Nick spotted Abram in his peripherals. He was walking from the barn, his face scrunched up in a scowl.

"Nick, a word?" Abram said as he closed in on Nick. He motioned for Shelly and Maggie to continue on.

"Sure," Nick said. "What's going on?"

Abram cleared his throat as the women moved out of earshot. "Listen, Nick. You need to keep your son away from my daughter."

"What happened?"

"Just keep him away from her. If I find them alone together again, you are all out of here. Am I clear?"

"I'm not sure I—"

Abram's voice cut through Nick's. "I said, am I clear?"

Nick nodded, trying to keep himself calm. "Clear as glass."

"Good," Abram said, then strode toward the house, where Shelly and Maggie had gone.

Nick took a deep breath, still struggling to understand what was going on. Corey and Emma had been best friends since they were little. They had been going places alone together their whole lives, without much complaint from Abram.

So, what had changed?

Obviously, Abram's opinions of Emma and Corey's friendship had changed the moment the lights went out. Perhaps he figured that when kids got bored, they got into trouble. Of course, there wouldn't be much time to get bored now... they'd all be working from dawn to dusk every day, fighting for their survival.

Regardless of what Abram's reasons were, he'd have to ensure his boy complied.

Nick steeled himself and stepped toward the house, keeping an eye out for Corey. He'd have to talk to him as soon as possible. The last thing he needed was to be kicked out—they'd only just arrived.

15

ABRAM WAS WALKING toward the house when he heard Gary's voice coming from near the barn.

"Abram?"

"Yeah?" Abram called back. "What's up?"

"Walk the fence with me. I think we need to talk."

They walked the drive to the gate and veered right, walking the brush- and tree-free zone on the inside of the fence. It had taken them weeks to clear the path, and they were keeping it clear, at least on the inside, so they could keep an eye on its condition.

"We really need to finish the backside of the fence," Gary said. "Anyone with persistence will follow the fence all the way to the back of the property, and then they'll be able to walk this easy path we've made for them right back to the house. I think we've got maybe two or three weeks before people start to get desperate. And that man we turned away—Joshua, was it?—he could be in town bringing us to people's attention right now."

"That's true, but you argued against letting him stay. We

can get started on the fence in the morning, if you'd like. We could put Nick and Corey to work putting in fence posts."

"Truthfully, I think it's more important to get in more supplies. We've got three more people to feed."

"We have two years' worth of food. Even with the additional mouths to feed. I think we can leave it for now. We should focus on plowing up a garden plot and a field for corn and hay. I'm not sure there's enough hay in the barn to get us through a year of feeding livestock."

"Yes, we should plant crops, but so much can go wrong in farming. We can't count on it sustaining us through two winters. I say we get in more food."

"And how are we going to do that?" Abram asked. "Where could we go that would sell us large amounts of food now?"

"People aren't buying anymore. They are looting."

Abram slowed his pace. "You aren't suggesting we do that, are you?"

"No, but—"

"Listen, Gary, we'll be able to plant more with the extra labor we have. Yes, there are more mouths to feed, but they'll work off what they eat. We'll make the garden larger. We'll plant more corn. We'll breed the cow again. No reason to take any unnecessary risks."

"Okay, but sooner than later, we'll have to start taking risks in order to survive the long haul." Gary stopped picking his way along the path and turned to Abram.

"What are you talking about?" Abram asked. "We're prepared. We have two years' worth of provisions. Two years, Gary. If the power isn't on in two years—and I realize it could be longer than that—but in two years, we'll be in a groove. We'll know what it takes to survive, and we'll be able to grow or barter for what we need. It's by working with our neighbors that we'll pull through."

"Right," Gary said, nodding. "Working together..."

Abram could hear the lack of enthusiasm in the man's voice. Something else was on his mind, apparently. He followed Gary along the fence to the end, and then along the path they'd already made for the remaining fence sections that must be erected. Gary occasionally stopped to whack back a bush that was encroaching on the track, taming the overgrowth.

On their way back toward the house, Abram couldn't shake the thought that Gary was intent on taking more risks than necessary to achieve their goals. Abram made a mental note to keep an eye out on Gary, to keep him in check before he jeopardized them all.

After dinner, Emma found Corey sitting on his bed in his room. She could see he was unhappy and went to sit next to him.

"You shouldn't be in here," Corey said. "Your dad told me he doesn't want us alone together."

"He's just really stressed right now. He'll relax in a few days, and we'll be back to normal."

"Until then, you really shouldn't come in here. We could never get back to our home if he kicks us out. We can't risk it."

"He's up at the gate right now." Emma pursed her lips.

"Your dad doesn't seem like he's fooling around."

"I told you, he'll relax. He'd never make you go away, because he knows how sad it would make me." She tried her confident smile on him, but it seemed lame, even to her.

Corey looked at her as if she had lost her mind, and she belatedly wondered what her father had said to him in the barn. Had her father threatened him?

The door banged open, and both Corey and Emma jumped, and Emma backed away from the bed, but it was only Rae Ann.

"Your dad is coming down the hill," Rae Ann said, plopping down on her dad's bed.

"That's okay, as long as you stay in here with us, Rae," Emma said.

"He's with Gary."

Emma shrugged. "I'm glad that guy's not staying in the house with us."

"He's not?" Corey asked.

"No, he converted one of the outbuildings into a little cabin. Mom said he won't even eat all his meals with us, so we shouldn't see him too much. Thank goodness."

"Do you want to play Go Fish with me?" Rae Ann asked, interrupting. "I've got a deck of cards." She reached into her back pocket and produced the cards.

"Sure, I'll play with you," Corey said. "What about you, Em?"

"No, I don't want to play. We're not at sleepaway camp."

A wrinkle creased Rae Ann's brow. "You can't play Fish with just two people. It doesn't work right."

"Sorry," Emma said. "I don't want to play."

"We can play War, Rae," Corey chimed in. "That works with two people. Come sit over here with me."

They heard the door open at the front of the house, and Emma noticed that Corey tensed. Okay, so he was afraid of her dad, she realized. She was going to have to get around that somehow, but she'd better not push it, or he'd completely shut down.

The door opened again, only this time it was Corey's dad. "Here you all are. I'm just looking for a sweatshirt; it's a little chilly, now the sun's going down." He smiled at Emma, and then rifled through his bag and pulled out a sweater. "Oh, and Corey, can I have a word with you?" he said, and he and Corey left the room.

Emma smiled at Rae Ann, shuffling the cards. "Once he gets back, we'll start."

Rae Ann smirked, obviously excited for the game to begin.

Corey followed his father out into the hallway, shutting the door behind him. His father had his sweater draped over his arm and his hand on his hip.

"What's going on, Dad? Emma, Rae, and I were about to play War."

"Listen, son. Tell me what happened."

"With what?"

"Mr. Patterson just got done talking to me. Said he doesn't want you and Emma alone."

"I know. He told me the same thing."

"What happened up there in the barn?"

"Nothing. We're just friends, Dad. Mr. Patterson didn't mind us being alone last week at the library."

"I know. It's not you, Corey. Just don't be alone with her until he calms down. Give it time, son."

Corey nodded, though he could feel his fists tighten at his sides. "Okay. Now can I go back and play War? Rae's there with us, so we're not alone."

His father appeared hesitant, and Corey waited for him to reply.

"Dad," Corey continued, "we wouldn't be alone, so it's not a big deal, right?"

"Right. Have fun, son. Just remember what we talked about, okay?"

"Yeah," Corey said, then opened the door to his room, leaving his father alone in the hallway.

16

After breakfast the next morning, Abram led Nick and Corey to the back of the property, where a stack of metal fence posts and several rolls of chain link lay on the ground. There were two post hole diggers, two pairs of work gloves and a pair of shovels leaning against the stack of fence poles.

"Gary tells me these fence posts need to be eight feet apart, and the holes thirty-six inches deep," Abram said. He reached into his pocket and pulled something out. "Here's a tape measure. I suggest that you measure eight feet and then sixteen feet so you can both work on a hole at the same time. I don't expect people to be desperate enough to walk all the way back here and find their way to the house, at least not yet. But soon enough, people will come looting, and we don't want a gaping hole in our security."

Nick nodded, somewhat dismayed by the amount of physical work he and Corey were expected to take on.

"I'll be up near the gate securing razor wire to the top of the fence up there if you need anything," Abram said, giving a short nod and turning to walk back the way they'd come.

"Dad," Corey said, "I've never dug a fencepost hole. What if I do it wrong?"

"We'll have to do the best we can, Corey. If they don't like our work, then they'll have to teach us. I think we're being tested. They want to know we can withstand hard work without complaining."

"I'm sorry, Dad. I don't think we should have come here."

"Is it about what we talked about yesterday?"

"Yeah. I thought about it, and it doesn't make sense. I think Mr. Patterson is just looking for a reason to kick us out. He won't let Emma and I be alone together, like he's afraid something's going to happen. But he doesn't mind her being alone with that creep, Gary. I don't like him, Dad."

Nick had taken the tape measure and was measuring the first eight-foot stretch. "Gary? No, I don't trust him, either. But he has Abram's ear, so we should try to stay on his good side. Or at least out of his way."

"I wish I could. He's everywhere."

"He's not down here, thank goodness, but you're right—he pops up unexpectedly, so you'd better help me measure out these lengths."

Corey helped his dad measure the eight- and sixteen-foot lengths, and Nick started the first hole. He showed Corey how the post hole diggers worked. Corey took his to the sixteen-foot mark and got started, while Nick dug his own hole a few inches at a time. The ground was rocky, and every so often he had to lie down on the ground to wiggle out a rock that was in the way. He didn't know what he'd do if there was a rock in the very bottom of the hole.

He measured the depth of his first hole with the

measuring tape, then realized there was a better way. He measured the post hole digger from the tip of the blade to thirty-six inches up and used the shovel to carve a narrow notch in the handle at that point. Then he did the same for Corey's.

"That will make it easier to know when you've reached the correct depth," Nick said and continued to work on his hole. He finished his hole first and went to help Corey complete his. The boy was strong, but he wasn't used to this kind of labor—he'd tire quickly. When they'd finished both holes, Nick looked at the stack of poles. Should they seat the posts?

"Corey, can you find Abram and ask him if we should go ahead and put up the poles as we go, or should we wait?"

"Okay, Dad, I'll go."

Nick could hear the reluctance in his voice.

"You're faster, is all," Nick said, "but if you want me to come with you, I will."

"It's okay. I can manage." Corey took off at a trot.

Nick ambled toward the existing fence to see how the poles had been anchored. Interestingly, they'd been cemented, and there was a concrete trench running under the wire. Abram obviously didn't want anyone, or anything, burrowing under his perimeter. Out of curiosity, Nick walked a couple of hundred yards along the fence to see if it was the same all the way around. He was just about to turn around and go back to the work site, when he heard a hissing sound from the other side of the fence.

He looked up and saw nothing, his brow furrowing. What had he heard? But then the hiss changed to "Nick," and he spotted a figure standing just on the other side of the fence, half hidden by a tree.

"Joshua, what are you doing here?" Nick asked.

"Nick, you have to convince them to let me in," Joshua said, standing on the other side of the fence. "Please."

"Joshua, I'd like to help you," Nick said, "but I don't have any pull with these people. The man who owns the land, Abram, is my neighbor, but I don't think he considers me his friend. He's angry that we came, and I don't think he would have let us stay, except his daughter was upset and threatened to never speak to him again."

"Come on, Nick. Can you at least ask again?"

"I thought you were on your way to Canada."

"I'm low on gas, and none of the gas stations are open now. I won't make it far on what I've got. I had to sleep in my car last night in town."

"Maybe I can get them to give you some gas if they don't let you stay, but I can't guarantee anything."

"It's that other dude, isn't it? The one with the gun. He's calling the shots."

"He seems to be. It's Abram's place, but Gary is his friend, and he relies on his advice. He has a lot of skills when it comes to farming, apparently."

"Tell him I'm a skilled rifleman, and I grew up on a farm. That might convince him I'm worth having around." Joshua's eyes darted toward the front of the property.

Nick twisted around to look. He spotted a figure, but

couldn't tell who it was. "Someone's coming," he whispered to Joshua. "You need to go."

"You'll regret this," Joshua muttered. "I'll be back, I promise you."

Nick watched as Joshua faded back into the woods.

A moment later, Corey came trotting along the fence.

"They are going to cement the poles in, and run a line of concrete under the fence, like here," Corey pointed to the fence. "They want us to dig all the post holes, then we'll dig a trench as a form for the cement. Then, when that's all done, they'll come down and help with pouring the concrete. So, we'd better get to work. They want to put the poles in this afternoon."

Nick knew it was unlikely that they'd get all the way across the bottom of the property in a day. But he didn't say that to Corey. They'd just have to do their best. He was happy Joshua hadn't made it all the way to the end of the fence. It wouldn't do for him to know that he could just walk right in. Not that he'd want to be caught hiding out on Abram's property—Nick figured what Joshua really wanted was to be part of the community. He wanted to be safe.

Nick worked with Corey, digging holes and thinking about the best way to create a trench until Emma came to find them for lunch. They walked back to the house, and Nick couldn't help but think it would be more efficient to carry their lunch with them in the morning.

They washed and went to sit at the large dining room table with Abram and Gary. The women carried the food in from the kitchen before they joined the men. It made Nick uncomfortable. There was something about the division of labor that bothered him. Corey looked miserable, and Nick thought he was embarrassed about it too.

"Abram," Maggie said when they'd all filled their plates, "why don't I come out with the rest of you and help with the farm work? Shelly, Emma, and Rae have meal prep and housework down pat, and I'm strong. You should put me to work."

"We decided on a clear division of labor," Gary said, "to keep things clean."

Maggie shot Gary a look. "It's unclean to let a woman pull her weight? That's ridiculous. Let me help Nick and Corey with the fenceposts, at least. They'll be days getting them all dug. What if it rains and washes them out?"

"Are we expecting rain?" Abram asked.

"How could we know?" Maggie said. "It's not like there's a weather service anymore. It's spring in Vermont; I'd be surprised if we got through a week with no rain."

"Perhaps it would be a good idea for you to help," Abram said.

Gary pushed his chair back from the table, grunting. "I thought we were in charge here," he said, before walking out.

"Why do you put up with that man?" Shelly asked.

"Because he is very knowledgeable," Abram said. "He's made a lot of improvements here. And he understands the need for security."

"Well he doesn't know a thing about the division of labor," Maggie said. "And I'm going to help. You can only make the beds so many times a day."

"It will be different when the harvests come in. You'll be busy with canning and preserving food for the winter."

"And I'll expect everyone who's not out there milking

cows to be helping with the harvest and the canning. When you've got a big job, you throw as many people at it as you can. The fence is a big job."

"Do I have any say in the matter? This is my land, after all. Mine and Shelly's."

"Well, Shelly is happy for me to get out and help. Aren't you, Shelly?"

"I don't mind if Maggie wants to do some more physical work, Abram. She wants to stay fit, and what better way than to help with the chores? Why shouldn't she? This is the twenty-first century."

"We were just trying to protect you," Abram said. "People sometimes get hurt doing farm work."

"I promise not to shove my hand in the blades of a harvester," Maggie said. "And I'm far more likely to burn myself on the oven than hurt myself digging a hole."

Emma, who'd been watching this exchange, spoke up. "Can I dig fencepost holes too?"

"No, Emma, you should help your mother," Abram said.

"Actually, Em, the animals will start arriving today," Shelly said. "I'm going to need you to assess their condition, set up a feeding schedule, and figure out which of the ewes need milking."

"Does, Mom. Female goats are called does. And why are we getting goats, again? And why not sheep?"

"Goat milk products are very healthful," Maggie added, "and you can spin their hair into yarn."

"They'll help keep areas clear of grass and unwanted shrubs, as long as we can keep them out of the garden and the cornfield," Abram said.

Rae Ann beamed. "And their babies are cute as anything. Can I help with the goats?"

"We'll see," Nick said. "Maybe you could help with the baby goats. They call them 'kids.'"

Rae Ann wore an excited smile, and Nick knew she'd be delighted to help with the baby goats.

17

Corey was on his way back to the back of the property after lunch when Gary approached him. Corey took a look around, hoping someone else was nearby, but he was alone with him. He didn't like Gary; the man made him very uncomfortable and, if truth be told, a bit scared.

"Hey, kid," Gary said, "do you know how to shoot?"

"No, I've never handled a gun," Corey said, hoping that would be the end of it.

"We're going to need you to step up and help with perimeter control. If you want your dad and little Rae to stay here, you are all going to need to pull your weight." Gary spoke deliberately, as if he wanted his words to sink in. "But don't worry—I'll train you, kid. Why don't we get started now?"

"My dad is expecting me to help with the fence. He'll wonder where I am."

"Maggie's helping him this afternoon. He won't need you. Come with me."

Corey didn't dare defy Abram's best friend, so he followed him to one of the sheds near the lower barn. Inside, the walls were lined with gun lockers, and a huge wooden table scarred with many years of use sat in the middle of the room. Other than that, it was bare. Not even a stool or chair to sit on.

Gary pulled the keys from his pocket and opened one of the lockers, pulling out a handgun and a rifle, and set them on the table. "First, I'm going to teach you how to do basic cleaning on a semiautomatic handgun." He opened an unlocked cabinet at the end of the room, pulled out a towel, and draped it over the end of the table. Then he pulled out a caddy with two bottles and some tools. He pulled the items from the caddy and set them on the towel.

"This is gun cleaner, lubricating oil, cleaning patches"—the cleaning patches looked like little cotton squares to Corey—"a bore brush," Gary continued, "a cleaning rod with two attachments, a cleaning brush, and a cleaning jag." There was also a toothbrush and some cotton swabs, but Gary didn't name those. Hopefully, he thought Corey was bright enough that he didn't need to.

"First, you need to disassemble the gun," Gary said. "Watch me. I'm removing the magazine first, and I'm clearing the firing chamber. Got that?"

"Yeah."

"Now, I'm taking the gun apart."

It seemed to Corey that the gun just came apart in Gary's hands and he wasn't sure how that had happened, but he was afraid to say so. Gary reassembled the gun and handed it to Corey, and he quickly removed the magazine and checked that the chamber was clear.

"Now," Gary continued, "pull back on the slide and down on the two levers on either side of the barrel." He showed Corey how to hold the gun in his hand so that he could move the slide with one hand and depress the two tiny levers with the other.

Corey pulled the slide back, depressed the levers, and was able to remove the slide by moving it forward off the body of the gun.

"Set the frame aside and pull the spring and then the barrel off the slide." Gary raised his eyebrows at Corey, and Corey did as he was told. "Now you are going to reassemble the gun."

"Do I just do everything in reverse?" Corey asked.

"Yes. I'll let you know if you are doing anything incorrectly."

Corey reassembled the gun and Gary made him take it apart again. The second time, Corey tried to put the spring in backward, and Gary set him straight while giving the impression that Corey was an idiot. At least, that's how it seemed to him. Finally, after the third time, Gary had him leave it in pieces so he could clean it.

He first wiped the magazine with a cleaning patch. Then, he was instructed to soak a cleaning patch in cleaning fluid and push it through the barrel with the cleaning jag attached to the cleaning rod.

"Okay, set that aside," Gary said. "Now take the toothbrush and clean the frame."

Corey brushed the body of the gun with the toothbrush until Gary told him it was good enough.

"Now brush under the rails on the slide," Gary said.

Then he had to take a dry patch and wipe the front of the

slide, working it into the barrel hole and inside the slide. Then a toothbrush and cotton swab inside the slide, making sure to get the back corners. And then he used his fingernail to push the patch into the grooves under the slide rails. Then he brushed the spring.

"Now pick up the barrel and wipe the outside with a dry patch. Then put the wire brush on the cleaning rod and put it through the barrel ten times."

Corey was starting to wonder if he'd be able to remember all this the next time Gary asked him to do it. "Should I be taking notes?"

"I expect you to memorize the steps, kid. Not today, this is the first time. But within a week, you should have the steps down blind. Now put the jag on the rod and push patches through until they come out clean. And make sure you wipe the breach."

Corey pointed to what he hoped was the breach, the back end of the barrel, and was relieved when Gary gave him a nod of approval. Then he taught Corey how and where to oil the gun, and to clean off the excess oil, then had him reassemble the weapon again. Corey was just about to sigh with relief when Gary said, "Right, now the rifle."

The thing that Corey took away from taking apart the rifle was to not try and remove the tiny screw that held the barrel to the gunstock. It only had to be loosened, and if you took it all the way off, you would ruin the gun. Also, Gary did not want the wood scarred by the crossbar safety, and he'd better remember to hold it in the middle as he was removing the barrel. Oh, and no gun oil was to come into contact with the stock wood. Ever.

He assembled and disassembled the rifle several times,

cleaned it with a bore snake instead of a rod, and put it back together. When Gary seemed satisfied, Corey waited to see what would be next. A machine gun? A bazooka? Corey wouldn't put it past him. And he had glimpsed what looked like a gun that soldiers carried. Some kind of automatic machine gun.

"Right," Gary said. "It's time to learn to use them. First, you learn to load them."

He made Corey load the magazines for both the pistol and the 10/22 rifle, and as usual, he had to do it three times before Gary was satisfied. Then, he gave Corey the magazines for the pistol to put into his pockets, and the gun itself to carry. Corey wasn't sure how to hold the weapon. It was empty, Gary made him double-check it, even though Corey had just cleaned it and knew it didn't have any bullets in it. He held it as if he was ready to shoot it, but with his trigger finger alongside the barrel rather than on the trigger, and pointed down at the ground beside him—that's how he'd seen it done in the movies. He glanced at Gary, but he didn't seem bothered, so Corey assumed he must be doing the right thing. Gary picked up a sack from next to the door, and they strode outside.

The firing range wasn't far from the gun shed, a couple of hundred feet at most. There were hay bales stacked at the front of the firing range, and Gary set the 10-22 and magazines on the stack, so Corey did the same with the pistol. At the other end, there were rows of bales stacked three high in front of a row of targets mounted between fence poles.

Gary taught Corey how to stand with his body facing the target, two hands on the gun and careful not to put his left-hand thumb around the back of the handgrip where it could get caught in the slide, but alongside his right thumb. It was uncomfortable, and he found his left thumb automatically wanting to slide around the handle.

"If you leave that there," Gary said in disgust, "you're going to end up hurt. But I'm tired of telling you, so it's on you now."

Corey moved his thumb back to where it belonged.

"Okay, put the gun down for a moment," Gary said. "We're going to discover which is your dominant eye."

Corey set his gun down, the barrel pointing down range, hoping that was correct.

"Turn around and look at the tree behind us," Gary said. "Do you see that mark on the trunk?"

Corey studied the trunk. "Yeah."

"Take both your hands and create a diamond by touching your thumbs and forefingers together."

Corey did as he was told.

Gary glanced at him. "Yes, that's right. Now, look through that hole at the mark on the tree with both eyes."

Corey squinted, peering through the diamond-shaped hole his thumbs and fingers made.

"Now close your left eye. Can you still see the spot?" Gary asked.

"No, it disappeared."

"Okay, that means you are left-eye dominant, and that's the eye you need to use when you are sighting your target." Gary turned back to the guns.

"But I'm right-handed," Corey said. "That doesn't make any sense."

"They aren't related. Just trust me on that. Now put on your ear protection."

Gary reached into the bag he'd brought from the shed and tossed a set of big orange ear protectors at him. They looked almost like headphones, but they didn't have speakers, just layers of sound-blocking material.

"Pick up the pistol, kid. It's time you learned to shoot."

18

Nick was worried about Corey. His son had not shown up to help with the fenceposts after lunch, and he wished he knew where he'd gone. Abram did not seem at all keen for Corey to hang out with Emma, so he hoped the boy wasn't out in a barn with her somewhere. They'd all end up on the street if that happened.

"Let him have a break," Maggie said from where she was digging a fence post hole. "He dug with you all morning. He's got to be exhausted."

"It's not like him," Nick said. "He usually would have at least checked in with me."

"It's not like he's going anywhere, and Emma is smart enough not to get caught alone with him. Abram's just being a typical dad. Wait until Rae is old enough to date."

"I hope you're right." Nick dropped his post hole digger down into the hole he was working on. It was almost deep enough now. Just a couple of inches more.

Gunfire sounded from the direction of the house, and they both froze. *Pop, pop, pop, pop*—the noise continued until seventeen rounds had been fired. Nick left his tools and ran for the house. He hadn't gotten more than a few yards when the noise started up again. *Pop, pop, pop.* He counted another seventeen rounds as he ran, Maggie not far behind him.

He nearly collapsed with relief when he came upon the firing range, until he realized that the man firing the gun was Corey, and then anger flared in him. Still, he waited until Maggie had come up beside him and the boy had finished shooting before he said anything. The last thing he wanted to do was startle Corey while he had a gun in his hand.

When Corey ejected the magazine, Nick spoke up. "What's going on here?"

Gary regarded him. "I'm teaching your son to fire weapons."

Corey pulled off his ear protectors. "Look, Dad, I hit the target every time."

Nick eyed the target that was hanging a quarter of the way down the range. Clearly, Gary was starting with a doable distance. "Nice work, son, but I don't remember giving Gary permission to teach you how to shoot a gun."

"One of us has to be able to protect Rae Ann, Dad. And Gary had time to train me. I even learned how to clean them." Corey gestured to the handgun, and Nick took in the rifle that was also on the bale of hay.

"It's not your job to protect your sister, Corey. It's mine." Nick's mouth thinned.

"But you couldn't protect her, could you?" Corey asked. "If you'd had a gun, that guy wouldn't have been able to steal our car."

"Or possibly he and I would both be dead. Firearms are

dangerous, Corey. You can't just go shooting your way out of tough situations."

"You just say that because you don't know how to fire a gun. You could have taken that guy out as soon as you saw his gun."

"There are more to guns than just pointing and shooting. And you can't go around killing people because they are trying to steal your vehicle." Nick knew as he said this that the conversation wasn't going anywhere. It would just escalate until Corey stomped off, but he didn't know how to stop it.

"You're weak," Corey spat, "so I have to be strong."

"Hold on, now," Gary said. "Don't be so hard on your dad, kid. He heard unanticipated fire, and he was probably worried about what was going on. I'll tell you what: your dad has to learn too, so why don't we go back to the gun storage and you can teach him how to field-strip the weapons. In fact, why don't you teach him everything you've learned today, and I'll correct you if I need to."

"Yeah," Corey said, turning his shining eyes on his dad. "That would be great. Will you, Dad?"

Nick considered the fence that needed to be erected and wondered what Abram would have to say. Still, the hope in Corey's eyes was impossible to ignore. He'd deal with Abram when the time came.

Nick wore a warm smile. "Yes, Corey, I'd like you to teach me."

His son's face shone with pleasure. He watched the boy eject the magazine from his pistol, and check to see that there weren't any bullets in the chamber. Then he picked up the magazines and slid them into his pockets. "Can you bring the rifle?" he asked Gary.

"Wait," Maggie said, "can I learn, too? I'm going to have night watch soon, and I'd feel more comfortable if I knew what I was doing with a gun."

Corey glanced at Gary.

"What about the fence?" Gary asked. "That needs to go up, and soon."

"We can work on it after," Nick said. "All three of us."

"You might as well," Gary said. "You all have to learn sooner or later, even that little Rae Ann."

"Rae Ann is too young to learn to use a handgun."

"Nick, she should at least learn to use the rifle. She can help keep varmints away, and shoot rabbits for food."

"I don't think Rae would shoot a bunny," Corey said. "Not until she's a little older."

"We can start her on target practice so that she'll already be a good shot when she's old enough to understand," Gary said. "No one gets off free here."

Nick was thinking there was no way in hell his six-year-old daughter was going to learn to shoot firearms, but he was smart enough not to say anything now. They'd cross that bridge later, and for now, she could be kept busy with the animals.

He followed Corey and Gary back to the buildings that were grouped around the lower barn and remembered about the kittens. He'd spotted a cat in the barn yesterday evening, but he thought he should take a moment to make sure it was the kittens' mother.

"I'll be right back," he said. "I just need to check on something in the barn."

"Dad," Corey said, disappointment thick in his voice, "you promised."

"It'll only take a minute, Corey, I promise. I'll be back before you are ready to get started." He jogged away, feeling Corey's eyes on his back. Thankfully, the mother cat was in with the kittens. He took a moment to watch them sleeping contentedly and ran back to the others.

"Did I miss anything?" he asked as he burst in through the door.

"That was quick," Gary said. "What did I tell you, kid? He probably just needed to take a piss after all that running."

Nick mentally rolled his eyes. Gary couldn't get through fifteen minutes without saying something crude. Well, maybe Nick could tame him down some, given enough time.

There were three pistols on the table, and Nick took up position next to the empty spot at the table. Corey began to talk them through breaking the gun down, and Nick was proud when Gary didn't have to correct him. They were instructed to take apart and reassemble the guns three times before Corey taught them how to field-strip their weapons.

"What does field-strip mean?" Maggie asked, to Nick's relief.

"It means to take apart a weapon so you can clean and oil it," Corey said. "Get it ready to fire."

Once the pistols had been successfully cleaned and oiled to Corey's exacting standard, they started on the rifles, which turned out to be strikingly similar, and before long they were carrying magazines in their pockets, a shotgun over the shoulder, and an empty pistol in their other hand. Nick was amazed at how competent Corey had become in one afternoon and hoped he would be able to match his son's newfound ability.

Abram was on a slow burn. He'd spent the afternoon attaching razor wire to the top of the fence, on his own. Where Gary was, he didn't know for sure, but the sounds coming from the direction of the firing range gave him a good idea. Gary had blown him off for target practice, leaving him to work with the dangerous and challenging task of reinforcing the top of the fence on his own.

He wasn't happy.

When Nick approached him a little before dinner, he felt his face falling into a scowl. His daughter had used emotional blackmail to get him to allow Nick's family to stay at the compound, and that irritated him. He wished Nick and his kids would stay out of his way for a while—every time he saw them, his resentment toward Emma flared. It was another reminder that he was weak when it came to that girl. He'd learned to set aside Shelly's feelings for the most part, but he couldn't seem to get around Emma.

Abram had just returned the ladder to the upper barn, not where it belonged but to the storage area closest to where he was working. It could live there until one of the other storage areas was closer to the section of the fence he was currently reinforcing. He walked out of the barn to find Nick coming up the drive, walking with purpose. He sighed.

"Abram, I'm glad I found you," Nick said. "Can we talk?"

"What is it you need, Nick? You can't be ready to start pouring concrete?"

"No, not yet. I just wanted to talk to you about Joshua."

Abram made a sound of negation, but it didn't stop Nick from continuing on.

"You know we really could use him—Joshua, I mean," Nick said. "He'd be another set of hands, and we have a lot to do. He's skilled, too, and knows how to use tools."

"I'm sure he has plenty of skills, but we don't know him. Where's his character reference? I don't want a man in my house, around my wife and daughter, that I don't know. His worth as a worker doesn't outweigh the threat a strange man brings."

"I'm his character reference. He picked us up in the middle of nowhere and brought us right to town. How many people would do that? By all rights, he should have left us at the freeway exit."

"Be that as it may, he's an outsider and I'm not letting him in." Abram stood firm on this.

"Could we at least give him some fuel so he can reach his family in Canada? Can we spare a few gallons of gas?"

"Everything we give away is something we'll run out of eventually. I don't think it's wise to give the man a commodity that we'll be needing. Everyone will run out eventually. No, Nick, if you want to help him, you'll have to find a way to do that without including me. I owe this man nothing."

"No. Of course not. Sorry to have bothered you." Nick turned and walked back down the hill toward the house.

Abram followed more slowly. They wouldn't begin dinner until he arrived, so he could take as long as he wanted and not have to make small talk with Nick on the way down.

After dinner, Abram asked Gary to join him on the front porch and discouraged anyone else from joining them.

"Where were you this afternoon?" Abram asked Gary once they were settled on the Adirondack chairs with a beer each. "I was counting on you helping with the razor wire."

"I decided it was time to teach the kid to use a weapon."

"That was more important than securing the perimeter?" Abram asked, putting a lid on his anger.

"I mean, why not? I don't expect we'll be seeing looters for a few weeks yet."

"You could have let me know, Gary. I could have worked on something easier to do without a partner."

"You figured it out, didn't you? You're an intelligent man, Abram, so I didn't think you needed me to hold your hand."

"I'm talking about common courtesy. You've known me long enough to know that communication is important to me."

Gary shrugged and sipped his beer, which Abram took as a signal he was done talking, and Abram wasn't going to get an apology.

"What did Nick say when you asked to teach Corey to shoot? Oh wait, you didn't ask, did you? And Corey just didn't show up for his afternoon work duty." Abram pursed his lips.

"Nick came running when he heard us shooting, and I convinced him to let Corey teach him how to handle guns. So now they both have some experience, and Maggie too. Corey's got a good grounding because he had to teach the others. It was a productive afternoon. You should be happy."

Abram took a swig of beer. "I'd be happy if we could make a plan and stick to it instead of just doing what we feel like doing."

"It's early days yet, Abram. You shouldn't worry so much. Let me tell you my plan for the fields."

Abram listened to Gary's grand plans until it was time to go to bed. He stood up and stretched, watching Gary head down the path toward his cabin. A crashing noise came from the direction of the upper barn, and then a cacophony of squawking Guinea fowl and bleating goats. Abram sprinted down the stairs, joining Gary on the path up past the garage and up to the animal barn.

Gary, who always carried both a flashlight and a gun, had both out and aimed the torch at the entrance to the supply storage room. The hasp that held the padlock had been ripped out of the wood, and the door hung open lopsidedly. A figure ran from the black hole of the doorway, a bag over their shoulder, and headed into the woods.

Abram ran after them while Gary hurried into the storeroom to check if anyone else was there. Abram kept the figure in his sights and crashed through the undergrowth, zigzagging around the birch trees glowing white in the moonlight. He tripped over a log or a root, he couldn't really tell which, and nearly fell. When he'd steadied himself on a maple, he saw the intruder go over the fence in an area they hadn't strung with razor wire yet and disappear into the woods on the other side.

Gary reached him, panting with the effort of running up the hill, and Abram realized his breathing wasn't exactly even either.

"He got away?" Gary asked, hands on his knees, catching his breath.

"Yeah. Went over the fence like a monkey. It barely even stopped them."

"Judging by the amount of stuff that was stolen, there had

to be more than one. Still, we got off easy. I'll sleep up here tonight in case they decide to come back."

"Are the animals okay?"

"I didn't look," Gary said, finally standing upright.

"Let's go check," Abram said, and they made their way back through the woods to the barn.

The animals were all there, although the goats were skittish, and the birds were complaining about the disturbance. The chickens, while not as deafening as the Guinea fowl, were cackling as well, distressed by the feeling of being in danger.

"They're fine," Abram said, "they just need some time to settle down. All the goats are here, and the hen house is still locked, so I doubt they ran off with any birds."

"Still, I'll keep an eye out," Gary said.

"Who was supposed to be on watch this evening?"

"Either Shelly or Maggie. We'll have to check the roster in the morning."

"I'm surprised they haven't shown up here. You'd think they would have heard the noise."

"Do you want me to go looking for her, Abram?"

"No, the looters could come back, and we'd be unprepared. We'll talk in the morning."

He headed back down the path, wondering if he should be worried about whoever had been on watch. But there was no point in searching for them now. You could walk right past them and not know they were there in the dark. It would have to wait until morning when they could see. And anyway, he didn't think anything had gone wrong—they'd heard no screams and seen no sign that any harm had come to the night watch.

19

Abram was up at first light and spotted Shelly and Maggie in the kitchen making breakfast.

"You'll never believe what happened to me last night," Maggie said from her position at the propane-powered stove. She was stirring oatmeal.

"What's that?" Abram asked.

"I heard a noise in the woods, and I followed it out past where we are putting the fence up. I thought I saw a figure, a person, but they kept disappearing just out of sight. Then I heard a noise up at the animal barn, but I was blocked by this huge thicket of brambles, and by the time I got around it and back up to the house, everything was quiet."

"Yes, we were robbed last night. Someone looted our stores at the upper barn. Sounds like they got you out of the way before they broke in."

"I fell into their trap," Maggie said. "I should have stayed up here, close to the buildings, rather than chase someone through the forest where there's nothing to be stolen. Except for fenceposts. They could have stolen those."

"We will all be working on getting the fence up and fortified. That will take priority until it's done. And then, yes, we need a strategy for when we are on watch. Clearly, we need to protect the buildings. We could have lost all our animals last night."

"That would not have been good," Shelly said. "And how did they know where the supplies were kept? Who would have told them?"

"That's where we unloaded all the deliveries," Abram said, "wanting to keep the location of the bigger store caches a secret for just this reason. So, anyone who knew anything could only spill the beans on the small storeroom. It's our dummy. A safeguard."

"Too bad it's so close to the animals. I don't want to lose them."

"Actually, it's good. They made a lot of noise and helped alert us to what was going on." Abram stepped toward the door. "I'll be back for breakfast. I need to see what the damage was."

He walked out of the house and up the hill to the barn, where he found Gary working on repairing the broken door.

"What's the damage?" Abram asked.

"The door is an easy repair," Gary said, "but we've lost maybe a week's worth of food."

"It could have been worse. Do you know they lured Maggie into the forest and got her lost? That's why she never showed up."

"They're smart. We'll have to be more prepared."

"You know, Nick has been encouraging me to let Joshua join us here. I'm beginning to think he may be right. We could use help defending our perimeter."

"We have enough people, Abram. You don't need more mouths to feed. Once we have the fence finished, it will be a lot harder for anyone to breach the boundary."

Abram rubbed his face. "Yes, we need to focus on that. No more weapons training until the fence is finished. We're vulnerable here."

"I beg to differ. I think weapons training is just as important."

"If we need weapons to protect ourselves, then that just tells me that we need more people and I should let Joshua in. If we had a strong fence and enough people, we wouldn't need firearms."

"What have you got against firearms training? With weapons to use, we can survive with fewer people. Fewer mouths to feed. I'm already worried enough about having enough supplies."

"There isn't any way to get fresh supplies without violence. I mean, besides farming and bartering. We'll just have to live with what we have and what we can grow."

"They looted us, so we loot them. It's small scale warfare, and they expect it."

"No, Gary. No looting."

"No looting, no extra people. Joshua is a no-go."

"But we need more bodies. We should have at least two people on watch at night. Corey and Emma are too young, so that leaves us with just five adults. And the days after they take watch, two people will be unavailable to work. I think it makes sense to add to our numbers."

"Corey and Emma can pair with an adult. As long as they have someone to take orders from, they should be fine.

Everyone takes two nights a week. It works out fine." Gary tested the door by swinging it back and forth.

"That only leaves five of us to finish the fence, plant the garden, seed the corn fields. Then there will be the harvests," Abram said. "I think Joshua could be helpful."

"Joshua is an unknown quantity, a stranger. And he'll need to eat, and sleep in the house near your wife and daughter." Gary raised his eyebrows at Abram. "Is that what you want?"

"We could set him up in the rooms above the garage. Or in one of the sheds."

"I'm still saying no unless you let me bring in more supplies."

"And, I'm saying no to that. Absolutely not, Gary. I'm putting my foot down. If you go looting, I'll send you away and replace you with Joshua. Do you understand?" Abram could feel the anger burning through him. Why must Gary always push for his own way?

"Then I want to do an hour of target practice with the boy, his father, and Maggie before we work on the fence. Just give me an hour. Then it's all-hands-on-deck for the fence project. Rae's too small and Shelly needs to work on meals, but everyone else on the post holes. Can you give me that?"

Abram pursed his lips. It wasn't what he wanted, but it probably wouldn't do that much harm. One hour of daylight spent shooting.

"Okay," Abram said. "But no blowing me off. That person we saw last night went over the chain link like a monkey. We need to get this place secured."

"It's a deal. Why don't you come and take a look at what we lost yesterday?"

Abram nodded and followed him into the storeroom. There was a cot set up against one wall where Gary had slept the night before. Abram noticed a rifle on the floor underneath it and pursed his lips.

The shelves closest to the door had been ransacked. It looked like they'd taken bags of flour and rice, as well as canned vegetables. Like Gary had said, a week's worth of food. Well, they'd be fine without it. What was a week or two when you were looking at several years or longer with no power? They were going to have to be able to grow their own food to survive, in any case.

"We'd better go down to breakfast," Abram said, "get our day going."

"My day has been going since dawn. I planted bear traps around the area where they climbed the fence, so be careful walking out there. That's what I did before I started on the door."

They left the storeroom and Gary closed and padlocked the door behind them. "Just so you know, Abram, I'm not wasting any daylight hours."

"I already said you could have an hour for target practice. What more do you want?"

"I want you to trust my judgment. When I say we need more supplies, I want you to believe me."

"It doesn't matter if I believe you or not—the avenues for obtaining supplies have been closed to us. And I'm serious about no violence."

"In times like this, violence is the language of trade," Gary said. "We either dominate, or we are dominated."

"I don't believe that the world is that black and white. Outside these walls, alliances are being made, communities developing. We have separated ourselves from those groups of people, but if we threaten them in any way, we're putting ourselves at risk. We need to tread carefully. We want to be self-sufficient, yes. But we also want to be seen as a community of reasonable people. Not a gang of outlaws who shoot before they ask questions. Law abiding people don't want outlaws living near them. If we are benign, they'll let us be, but if we are seen as killers, then they'll happily wipe us out. Remember that."

"But that is black and white," Gary said. "Us and them."

Corey was at the table eating breakfast with Rae Ann, Maggie, and Emma when Gary stuck his head through the doorway.

"Weapons training after breakfast at the range," Gary said. "Authorized by Abram. We'll work on the fence after."

Rae Ann clutched Louise, eyes excited. "Me too?"

"Sorry, kid. You are still too young."

"But when will I be old enough?"

"You'll have to ask your dad that," Gary said, then disappeared.

Corey finished his breakfast and headed down to the firing range to find Gary and Emma already there. Emma had her eye and hearing protection on and was shooting at a target that was positioned twice as far away as the other two targets that had been placed on the range. Corey grabbed his gear and walked to a position in the middle, but Gary motioned for him to set himself up at the far end of the range.

Corey wondered if this was because he was the worst shot, but when Emma put down her pistol and started his way, Gary stepped in front of her and sent her back to her end of the range, and Corey understood. Gary was in on the plot to keep Emma and Corey apart. Anger blossomed in his chest, and he shot all seventeen rounds in quick succession. A few of them even hit the target.

Of course, Gary had to come over then. Corey kept his eyes on the ground, ready for the telling off he knew was coming.

"You'll get better faster if you take each shot deliberately," Gary said. "I know it's fun to just let off a whole magazine all at once, but it's not going to improve your aim, so it's a waste of bullets. You'll have to work that off."

"I thought I was working everything off," Corey said, his anger overflowing. "Or isn't manual labor good enough?"

"Never mind. I can see you aren't mature enough for what I have in mind, so I'll have your dad do it. Meanwhile, take each shot slowly, and remember to hold your breath while you are pulling the trigger."

"My dad has enough to do. Tell me what you want."

"No, kid, I can't. I shouldn't have said anything. I forgot how young you are. Don't worry about it. Just get in your practice and go back to work on the fence. That's the priority."

Corey concentrated on aiming, holding his breath, and squeezing the trigger slowly for the next several rounds, then his dad showed up, and he was so clearly agitated that Corey couldn't focus on his target. He put his gun down and listened.

"But what did we lose?" his dad was asking Gary as Corey took off his ear protection.

"A couple of weeks' worth of supplies," Gary said. "It could be worse. Remember to watch out for the bear traps I hid around the area of the fence they breached."

His dad's brows rose. "But you didn't put any down where we're working on the fence?"

"No, they didn't come from anywhere near there. Although, it seems someone lured Maggie that way, so they must know the back of the property is not secured."

"All the more reason to get it done, then. Tell me, why are we out here putting holes in paper when we were robbed last night? We should be concentrating on perimeter defenses."

"Because you are no use to me if you can't use a gun," Gary said. "That's why. Stop wasting time and get your gear on."

Corey's dad did as he was told, and Corey followed suit, but five minutes after Emma had gone to clean her firearm, he hurried after her. No one could object to him taking care of the pistol; after all, Gary taught him to clean it after every use. And, as an added bonus, Gary was busy helping his dad with his aim and didn't seem to notice that he was going to be alone with Emma.

"This is a conspiracy," Corey said as he placed his gun on the towel Emma was using to protect both the table and the gun. "Everyone is working to keep us apart."

"Gary is dad's best friend," Emma said. "They tell each other everything. So, of course, Gary's going to keep us from talking. I'm surprised he isn't in here right now."

"What are you talking about?" Gary asked, walking in through the open door.

"Nothing," Emma said, rolling her eyes at Corey. "I was just proving my superiority."

"At shooting? There can be no doubt."

"Not just shooting. Everything else too." She winked at Corey behind Gary's back.

"Is it safe to leave my dad out there on his own?" Corey asked.

"Safer than leaving you two alone in here," Gary said.

"I don't know what you think we're going to get up to while cleaning guns," Emma said. "Really, Gary, it's a public place. Anyone could walk in here."

"I know your father doesn't want the two of you to be alone. That's good enough for me."

"But we're not alone," Corey said, feeling he should support Emma, "we're here with you and Dad."

"We can't see you in here, though, can we?" Gary said in a singsong voice that set Corey's teeth on edge.

Corey figured Emma felt the same way—she disassembled her firearm with brutal efficiency.

"Anyway," Corey said, "we've been friends forever. Why would we change now?"

Gary grinned. "Hormones."

"What are you guys talking about?" Corey's dad was standing in the door.

"Ask Gary," Emma said. She'd finished cleaning her firearm and reassembled it, storing it back in the locker. She placed the magazines in a separate drawer and turned around. "Can you put the supplies away, Corey? I need to get to work."

"Sure. I'm still cleaning my gun; I'd have to put it all away when I was done anyway."

She shot Gary a look. "You heard that, right?" she asked before she stomped from the gun shack.

"She's not happy with you," Corey's dad said.

"I'm just honoring Abram's request," Gary said, then gestured to the guns and cleaning supplies on the table. "Make sure all this is put away properly before you leave. I'll be checking it later." He turned and left as well.

"How are things going?" his dad asked, disassembling his gun now.

"Fine."

"You'd tell me if anything was wrong, right?"

"Yeah, of course," Corey said, though his tone nearly deceived him.

Corey finished assembling his gun. Then he picked up the slide of his father's pistol and started cleaning it. As he helped his father put away the cleaning supplies, he wondered what the future would hold during their time at the compound. He wondered what Gary had in mind, but quickly shook those thoughts from his mind before he drove himself mad.

Corey sighed to himself as they walked down to the end of the fence. Maybe it would have been better if they'd stayed at home.

Nick's shoulders and arms ached after a day of digging. They'd finished the last fencepost hole with the help of Maggie, but now they were digging the ditch for the strip of concrete that was going in under the chain link. It was brutal work for a man who spent most of his time on the computer. The three of them—Nick, Maggie, and Corey—walked back to the house, where they were offered hot showers. Nick told Maggie to go first and went in search of Rae Ann.

She was in the kitchen helping Shelly and Emma prepare the evening meal, standing on a chair in front of the propane-powered stovetop and stirring something in a large pot. When she spotted him, she gave the spoon to Emma and jumped down, running across the kitchen for a hug.

"You've been gone a long time," Rae Ann said. "Why didn't you come back for lunch?"

"We had sandwiches with us," Nick said. "We have a lot of work to get finished, and it made more sense to work through. What have you been doing all day?"

"It takes a lot of work to keep the house running, Daddy," she said, so obviously repeating what Shelly had told her that it made him smile. "We made the beds and swept the floors. After lunch, we planted vegetables in the raised beds, and flowers in front of the porch. It's important to keep beauty in your life, that's what Shelly says. She says beauty reminds you of the finer things, so you don't feel like a drudge."

"Shelly is very wise." Nick caught Shelly smiling from the corner of his eye.

Corey came in, his hair wet and spiky. "It's your turn to shower, Dad."

Nick hugged Rae Ann once more and moseyed out of the kitchen. He showered quickly, relieved that the grime was washed away. After his shower, he changed into clean clothes from his suitcase, then folded his dirty things and stacked them in a pile. He didn't know what the laundry routine was yet, and he made a mental note to find out. When he arrived back in the kitchen, Maggie and Abram had joined the others.

"Where's Gary?" Nick asked.

"On watch," Abram said. "We'll have to send someone out to relieve him soon."

"I can go," Nick said. "I'm too sore to sleep tonight."

Abram glanced at Nick. "If you are sure. We really should take watch in pairs, but I'm not sure we can manage it and get everything done during the day as well."

"We should carry whistles," Maggie chimed in. "So, if something goes wrong, the people in the house could be alerted."

Corey's brow furrowed. "Why not the two-way radios?"

"We can use those until the batteries die," Maggie said. "But those rechargeable batteries don't last forever, and I'm afraid the solar chargers only work when it's sunny. A whistle is pretty indestructible."

"Do we have any whistles?" Nick asked.

Abram's spoon scraped the bottom of his bowl. "I think there are one or two in the survival kits in the basement. I'll go down and check later."

Shelly handed Nick a bowl of chicken stew. "You should eat this before you relieve Gary. It'll get you through the night. And don't forget to take a water bottle. I've filled half a dozen and left them just inside the door, so you can grab one as you leave. When you come back at the end of your shift, leave the used bottle on the sink. I'll wash it and refill it."

"Thanks. This smells really good." Nick took a spoonful of stew, blew on it to cool it down, and tasted it. "Oh yeah. This will really hit the spot."

"What are we going to do about security?" Corey asked.

"Even if we have two people on watch, what if they come in a group like they did with Maggie? They lured her into the forest and raided the barn."

"Don't remind me," Maggie said. "I didn't know how stupid I could be. They won't catch me out like that again."

Abram said, "If you find yourself on watch, which you won't for a good long time, remember what we are protecting are the upper and lower outbuildings and the house. If you have to make a choice, protect the lower barns. That's were the most valuable things are stored. The animals and stores in the barn can be replaced. Those of us in the house can protect each other, but if we lose the fuel, supplies, and ammunition stored down there, we'll be in trouble."

"Do we shoot on sight?" Corey asked.

"No, we shoot over their heads if words don't send them packing, unless they are aiming at you, then shoot to kill. Gary is afraid we'll become an easy mark if we let too many people get away with supplies."

Nick raised an eyebrow. "So, if they don't run away, we kill them?"

"No," Abram repeated. "Shoot over their head, shoot them in the arm or leg, only shoot to kill if you are in danger. And most important of all, blow your whistle when you first realize we're being raided, so the rest of us can come to your aid."

"Not all of us," Shelly said. "Someone has to stay in the house to protect the children."

"True," Abram said. "One person at the house, one to the upper barn to help prevent huge losses, and the other two down to the barn to help whoever is on watch. That seems reasonable."

Nick scanned the table. "I hate to repeat this, but it does seem as though we could use another person or two. If someone is ill or injured, we won't be able to cover all the bases."

Abram gave him a sharp look and frowned. "You should be out there looking for Gary now."

Nick rose from his chair and took his bowl to the sink. Returning to the table, he placed a hand on Rae Ann's shoulder. "Rae Ann," he said, "Corey is in charge. Both of you are to do what the adults in this house tell you, but when it comes to bedtime and washing up, Rae Ann, you do what Corey tells you. I don't expect Shelly to have to tell you to go to bed, understand?"

"Yes, Daddy," Rae Ann said and hugged him tightly.

"Goodnight, sweetheart."

"Goodnight, Daddy."

Ending their embrace, Nick glanced at his son. "Corey, if I hear you are abusing your authority, you know what will happen."

"Yes, Dad."

Nick said goodnight to his son, grabbed a water bottle from beside the door, and headed out into the night to find Gary. He was easy enough to locate—he'd settled himself on an empty wooden crate on the backside of the garage, overlooking the lower barn buildings. Nick sat down beside him.

"Hey, Gary. Chicken stew for dinner. You should go in."

"I will, but I need to ask you a favor. I need to run into town a little before dawn, and I could use your help."

"Whatever you need," Nick said, knowing he'd regret it but wanting to ingratiate himself to Gary.

"Good. I'll come to get you when it's time to go. I think it unlikely that anyone would try to loot us at that time of day, so we won't tell the others." Gary got up.

"Whatever you say, Gary."

"Good. See you later."

Gary lumbered into the house, and Nick was alone with his thoughts.

Nick would have liked to put the man out of his mind, but he could not. Abram trusted Gary, and that should have been good enough for Nick—after all, this was Abram's farm. Still, something about Gary bothered Nick. The whole idea of leaving the place unguarded while they snuck into town during the night seemed underhanded. Gary was Abram's righthand man, so he couldn't go to Abram with the knowledge. Hiding behind Gary's back would be a death blow. Gary would convince Abram that the Caulfield family was dead weight if he thought Nick was undermining his authority. So, he'd just have to go with Gary and hope for the best.

20

A COUPLE OF HOURS LATER, Corey was making the rounds of the lower barns and other outbuildings, looking for his father. "Dad, are you down here?" he shouted into the darkness.

"I'm here, Corey," his father replied. "Near the shooting range."

Corey shone his light in the direction of his dad's voice and came to stand beside him in the gloom. "Hey, Dad. I just came to tell you that Rae Ann was excellent tonight."

"That's good to hear."

"Yeah, I thought you might like some good news. I'm sorry I brought us here. I know it's been weird." Corey was examining the ground at his feet, wishing he didn't feel like he had to apologize.

"It's weird, yeah, but I think I'm glad we're here. At home, we'd be at the mercy of government programming, and it's possible that they'll run out of food and water before things get back to normal. Here, we can grow food. And it won't all be such hard labor. Once the fence is in, and the cornfield and vegetable gardens are planted, it will be weeding and maybe watering. Harvest will be a lot of work, but winter should be easier."

"Except for watering the animals. Emma told me that keeping fresh water available at sub-freezing temperatures is hard."

"Well, it won't be an easy life, but it won't all be as hard as it is now. My guns are killing me."

"That's because you don't have guns, Dad." Corey smirked. "People who work at desks all day don't develop biceps."

"You may be right." Nick paused a moment. "Don't worry if I'm not in bed when you get up in the morning, okay? Gary wants me to go with him on an early morning trip into town. I don't know when we'll be back."

"Don't go. That guy is a maniac. I don't trust him." He couldn't see his dad's eyes in the dark, couldn't tell what he was thinking.

"I have to go, Corey. Gary is in tight with Abram, and I need them both to feel like I'm an asset. I need to be willing to do anything, go anywhere, until they stop talking about kicking us out."

"They can't kick us out, Dad. There wouldn't be enough people to get the work done." Corey scuffed the ground at his feet. "I know they threaten us with it all the time, but I don't see how they could manage without us. Especially if they decide to have two people out on guard all the time."

"I think they should let Joshua join us. An extra adult wouldn't be a bad thing."

"He did seem like a nice guy. He got us here, but we don't really know him."

"You have to take people at face value, son. I mean, you could just distrust everyone, but I think the way humanity is going to survive this is by creating alliances. He helped us, and we should help him. But I can't convince Abram. Every time I think he's about to change his mind, Gary butts in and changes it back. I'd do more for Joshua if I could, but I don't want to risk our position here. The same reason I'm going to town before dawn. I don't dare say no."

"I wish you didn't have to."

"Yeah, me too." His dad wrapped an arm around Corey's shoulders. "You should head back up to the house. It will be a long day tomorrow. I think we're pouring cement in the trenches and placing the fenceposts."

"All right, Dad. Be careful, okay? Don't let Gary get behind you. You want to keep him in your sights at all times."

His dad laughed. "Okay, I'll do that, but he's going to think I'm strange."

"No, he won't—he's going to be trying the exact same thing on you. Goodnight."

Corey walked back up to the house, but instead of going inside, he eased into one of the chairs on the front porch. He was worried about his dad, and he wished he wasn't going into town before daylight. Obviously, whatever Gary was going for, it wasn't above board. Nobody went into town before anyone was out of bed for legitimate business.

He sat in the dark on the porch as the night stretched on. Soon, he'd discover what Gary's real plan was. Until then, all he could do was wait and see.

It was going to be a long night.

The night sky had lightened from black to dark gray when Nick heard Gary coming up the drive. Nick had been patrolling the fence—he'd heard noises, but it could have been deer or a bear, coyotes or foxes. He hadn't seen anything on his walk along the inside of the fence, so it probably was wild animals scared away by the scent of him.

He met Gary on the drive outside the upper barn, the animals there still deep in sleep.

"Got your pistol?" Gary asked.

"Yeah."

"Follow me," Gary said, and they walked side by side up to the front gate.

Nick wasn't surprised when Gary produced the key that let them out through a door-sized gate not far from the drive. Of course, Gary would have the keys. He was trusted with everything. He waited until Gary had reattached the padlock and the two of them continued up the drive toward the road.

"What are we doing in town at this time of day?" Nick asked.

"You'll see." Gary played his flashlight on the road ahead of them.

The sky was brightening, but not yet enough to illuminate their way. Nick could make out the horizon, but the stars were still visible overhead. He hadn't thought to look at the sky while he was keeping watch and he regretted it now. It must have been brilliant in the dead of night, if it was this wondrous now.

They passed a farm a mile down the road. The house was dark, but there was a light in the barn, and they could hear the lowing of cattle and the voices of the people tending to them. Nick wondered why they had to begin their day so early. Did they have so many cows to milk that the chores took them all day?

The next farm they passed was the same, except that there was also a flickering light in one of the downstairs farmhouse windows. The world here was stirring, but when they finally came down to the small town, it was still swathed in darkness. Only the farmers got out of bed in the middle of the night.

"Where are we going here?" Nick asked. "No one is awake yet."

"You'll see. Just stay alert," Gary said shortly, motioning for Nick to follow him across the road. There was a row of shops on Main Street. All dark, many shuttered. Three of them were restaurants, Nick noticed, and he wondered if they would remain closed until electricity returned to their world. Or would they learn to cook on an open fire and feed people anyway?

They came to stand before the small grocery store, the windows shuttered with plywood. When Gary walked to the door, Nick said, "I don't think they're open yet," and heard how stupid he sounded. Of course, the store wasn't open.

"You're a bright one," Gary said, pulling a small tool from his pack.

"What are you doing?"

"What's necessary. Stand back."

After making short work of it, Gary gave a grunt of satisfaction, and the door swung open.

"Come on," Gary said, his voice a mere whisper. He handed Nick a backpack as he stepped through the door. "Take food. Stuff that won't go bad."

"Couldn't we have bartered for what we needed instead of stealing?"

"There's no guarantee that they would have bartered with us. We'll take what we need. Same as those people that looted us. Now get going."

Nick took the backpack hesitantly, nodding somberly. Though he wanted to leave upon learning of Gary's real plan, something inside him urged him to advance further into the small store.

Nick's chest tightened, and his forehead gathered sweat as he wandered down an aisle that had vegetables in open coolers on one side and canned goods on the other. There was a ten-pound sack of potatoes still sitting in the produce section. He remembered the taste of mashed potatoes and picked up the bag, then he started tossing baking goods, flour, baking soda, salt, cornmeal, whatever he could see into the bag that Gary had given him. The whole time, one side of his brain was telling him how wrong, immoral, and stupid this was, while the other screamed that if he didn't do as he was told, he'd end up on the street with his children.

There were tins of evaporated and condensed milk on the bottom shelf, and he bent down to shove the cans in his bag. He had the idea that milk was important. They didn't have a cow for milking yet; they would need milk. Then there were boxes of milk. Not dried—he'd seen his mother buy dried milk—but these were full of liquid. He began to reach for them when he considered the weight. No. He'd grab the dried milk, and they could reconstitute it. It was lighter, and they'd get more in the long run, even if it maybe wouldn't taste as good.

At the end of the short aisle—it really wasn't much larger

than a gas station store—there was an endcap with pre-baked cupcakes and pies. He thought of Rae Ann, who loved junk food, and picked up three, one for each of the kids. Emma would like those too.

"Hey!" It was a shout from the back of the store. No wonder there was still stock on the shelves—the owner was guarding it.

Nick backed down the aisle, looking for a place to hide. With the backpack in one hand and the bag of potatoes in the other, he didn't even consider pulling his gun from its holster. He slid into a space between a cooler full of rotting food and the wall. Maybe they wouldn't see him there, and he could sneak out when they went back to bed. He made himself as small as possible, resting the potatoes and backpack on his feet so he could pull the pistol from its holster. But he couldn't cock it. If he pulled back the slide, they would find him, and he'd never get out of here alive.

He could hear at least two people moving through the store, getting closer and closer to where Nick was hiding. His heart pounded in his ears, and his breathing sounded so loud that it seemed everyone in the store must hear it. He held the gun pointed at the ground, his hands shaking so badly that he couldn't have aimed if he'd wanted to, and wondered if he would get out of this alive.

Corey, I'm sorry, he thought, *I should have listened to you.*

The little bit of food he'd managed to pick up was not worth his life. Who would take care of his kids? Would Abram kick them out? No. Maggie wouldn't let that happen. She had a clear head and would make sure they were okay.

"Nick, where are you?" Gary's voice hissed in the darkness. "Get up here and back me up."

Nick stood frozen. Gary had betrayed him. Now the owner of the shop knew there were two of them and he wouldn't be able to hide until they went away. Anger flared, making red dots dance in front of his eyes in the dark. This reckless lunatic was going to get him killed.

"Nick, get out here now." Gary's voice held a level of command he didn't dare disobey.

He couldn't afford to be on Gary's bad side, so he left the backpack and the bag of potatoes and stepped out of his hiding place, slipping up the aisle between honey and chocolate chips, unseen in the darkness, until he came to the front of the shop, where Gary stood with his back against an endcap.

Gary gave a nod when he saw Nick in the faint light coming through the door. "Cover me," he said and held his weapon at the ready. Before Nick could protest, there was a movement at the other side of the store and two flashlight beams caught them full on.

21

Nick froze, his gun pointing uselessly at the ground. Even if he wanted to fire, he wouldn't have time to cock it before the strangers were upon him. Maybe that was better. If he wasn't killed, they could see that he wasn't prepared to fire, and they might spare him.

"Get out." One of the flashlights swung toward the door, illuminating the exit. "Get out, now!"

Nick made a move toward the door, but Gary raised his firearm in one smooth motion and shot the guy who had ordered them out. Nick, shocked, ducked back into the aisle behind him and pulled the slide back, cocking his gun. He'd be lucky to make it out alive now.

The uninjured gunman returned fire, sending Gary back down an aisle one over from where Nick was now crouched.

"Why aren't you firing?" Gary growled at him. "You are supposed to have my back."

"You were in the way. I didn't want to hit you."

"I'm not in your way now," Gary hissed. "Get out there and shoot 'em."

Nick slinked his gun hand around the corner and shot without aiming, and the bullet hit something made of glass and shattered it. Thank goodness it hadn't impacted a human being. A projectile hit the shelf near him, and he scooted back down the aisle.

The gunman was talking to her partner, and Nick was surprised to realize it was a woman. He'd just shot at a woman. He knew it shouldn't matter—he really wasn't that keen on killing anyone—but somehow this made it even worse. He glanced out to see the woman trying to pull her partner toward the back of the store, and then Gary stepped out and fired on her again, causing her to let go and run out the door in the rear of the store.

Nick ran to the man on the floor, feeling for a pulse, but he couldn't find one. The pool of blood the man was lying in made his stomach churn, and he backed away. He was heading for the door when he remembered his loot in the corner next to the cooler. He should go back for it, or this would have all been for nothing. The thought bothered him. Nothing could make up for this...what did it matter if they got a day's worth of food? A man had paid for it with his life. He gagged and moved toward the door.

"Finish filling your bag and let's go," Gary said. "It'll be full light soon."

Nick crept to the back of the store and picked up his backpack and bag of potatoes. Holding both in his left hand, he picked random items from the shelves as he walked to the front of the store, not even bothering to look at what he'd stolen. He just wanted out of here and to never come back. His stomach roiled at the thought of having been involved in the death of a man, and despair washed over him.

"Hurry up," Gary snapped. "We don't want anyone to see us here." He jogged away from Nick, who hefted the backpack onto his shoulders and ran to catch up.

As they passed the muddy alley that backed up onto the row of shops, Nick spotted a car parked in the shadow of the building. It was familiar, and it crossed his mind that it could be Joshua's. But Gary had begun to run, and Nick turned his attention to keeping up with the other man.

They slowed down once they were off the main road, walking in the concealing shadow of the tall trees. Nick's heart began to beat at a more normal rate, and his fear transformed to anger.

"Why did you shoot that man back at the store?" Nick asked. "We could have bargained with him."

"I don't bargain. We needed supplies. So, we took what we needed."

"How can two backpacks full of food justify taking a life? That's ridiculous."

"I didn't kill him for the food. I killed him for the reputation. They'll know we're ruthless, and they won't dare mess with us. That's worth the life of one man."

"How can you say that? They don't know who we are, so how can they attribute us with a reputation? I think you killed him because you could. Because you wanted to." A thought flashed through his mind: Perhaps Gary had been waiting his entire life for the opportunity to kill with impunity. The lights going out had provided that opportunity...Nick's stomach churned once again.

"What if I did?" Gary asked. "It suited my purposes."

"You killed an able-bodied man," Nick snarled. "Somebody's son, maybe somebody's husband or father. You may have left a family without protection, and without someone to keep them fed."

"Fewer people putting a strain on the resources is a good thing. You don't think the old and infirm are going to live through the coming winter, do you? Because they will not. Some will go hungry, and others will die of the cold. It won't matter if they lost a father or a son come winter. The weak will die."

"And are you going to help them along?" Nick's rage was just below the surface now. "Sit on the hill like a sniper and take out whoever you deem weak?"

"I don't need to waste my ammunition on the ones who are going to die anyway. I'm saving my bullets for my true rivals."

"And the man you killed in the shop? Was he a true rival?" Nick asked. He wondered if Gary could hear himself talking like a madman.

"No. I don't think so. He was in my way. But he'll make a decent messenger." Gary hiked his backpack higher onto his shoulders.

"And the message?" Nick asked, kicking a rock out of the way.

"Stay out of my way or die."

"In other words, you've just declared war on the village, and not just for yourself, but for everyone in Abram's compound. Thanks for that." Nick bit back the vulgarities that were on the tip of his tongue. He didn't want to antagonize Gary for fear he'd turn around and shoot him.

"Don't worry. It's a war we'll win. We are more prepared for this emergency than ninety-nine percent of Americans.

They can't win a war they aren't prepared for." Gary spat into the undergrowth.

"And what if we need people to help us? What happens then?"

"What could we possibly need, Nick? Maggie is a trained nurse. She can handle anything medical. We've got three and a half strong men for everything else."

"And if one of us needs surgery? Or to learn a new skill? Who would we ask to help with that?"

"Abram and I have been preparing for this for years." Gary drew out the word "years." "Between us, we can do just about anything. Plumbing, welding, harvesting, birthing cattle—you name it. We aren't going to need anyone else."

"Until we do, and then we'll have no one to ask because you will have killed them all." Nick kicked another rock.

Gary stopped and turned to face Nick. "Let me tell you something," he said. "Your adrenaline is pumping through your body, messing with your emotions. So, I'll cut you some slack this time. But the next time we go out on a raid, you'd better be ready."

Nick bit back a retort. He didn't plan on there being a next time. There was no need to make enemies of their neighbors. And he wasn't going to shoot anyone over a few cans of food. He didn't care what Gary said. He would not be turned into a killer.

Gary narrowed his eyes and stared straight into Nick's face. "And you are not to say a word about this raid to Abram, do you understand? I'll tell him when the time's right, but you will keep your mouth shut." He had his pistol in his hand and was caressing the trigger guard.

"Of course," Nick said. "It's not like I'm proud of what we

accomplished today. What are we going to do with the supplies we picked up?"

"For now, we'll store them in the upper barn. Then, later, I'll tell Abram we were able to pick up some extra supplies. He'll be pleased."

Nick thought that was stretching it. If he were the leader of the farm, a meal's worth of canned food wouldn't really register as worth the time. And that was not knowing a man had been killed for it.

Joshua sat bolt upright from a dead sleep. Had that been gunshots? Another shot rang out, and he thought it must have come from the grocery store. It was still mostly dark out, which made him think someone had been robbing the store. He tried to calm his breathing, but it was hard. He was scared all the time now. He hadn't made it to his family in Canada, and didn't dare try to even reach the border—in all likelihood, he'd run out of gas before he made it there.

He was stuck in this town, hoping beyond hope that Nick would be able to convince the man who owned the farm to allow him to stay there. If Nick could use his influence on the man, then Joshua could join the farm and be safe. Otherwise, he was afraid he'd either starve or freeze to death in his car once winter set in.

There was a movement at the end of the alley where he was parked. Two men running with backpacks. He'd been right—they were looting the store. One of the men shot a glance down the alley, and Joshua recognized his face. It was Nick. Nick with his two lovely children, who he claimed he needed to protect. And who, apparently, wasn't as law-abiding as he made himself out to be. Joshua had assumed the farm was already well provisioned. Why then, was Nick out filling his backpack with goods that other people would need?

Joshua remained still and counted sixty seconds ten times. Ten minutes should be long enough. He unlocked the car door and got out, stretching and pulling his clothes back into alignment with his body. Then he walked down the alley and around the block to the front door of the grocery.

The bell jangled as he opened the door and stepped in. There, in the early morning light that entered the shop through the window in the front door, was a man lying in a pool of blood. The copper odor was strong, and Joshua didn't bother checking for a pulse. The man's face was gray, and the amount of blood on the floor was more than any person could live without. He bowed his head. Just yesterday, this man had given him a loaf of bread.

Footfalls on broken glass sounded from behind him, and he raised his hands into the air.

"Turn around." The woman's voice was grim. "And keep your hands up where I can see them."

Joshua turned slowly, careful not to make any sudden moves.

As she caught sight of his face, the expression in her eyes turned from hatred to confusion. "You aren't one of the men who killed Ron."

"No," Joshua said, "but I saw them leave, and I know who they are."

"How do you know them?" The suspicion was back in her voice.

"I picked one of them up in my car and brought him and his kids up here."

"And you disliked them enough to rat them out?" Her jaw was tight, and the expression in her eyes was hard again. "Why should I believe you?"

"Because I don't have any reason to steer you wrong. This man"—Joshua motioned to the dead man—"Ron? He gave me food yesterday. He was a kind man and didn't deserve to die. I'm frankly surprised that Nick was in on it. I mistook him."

"People change in hard times," the woman said and lowered her gun. "What can you tell me about the people who did this?" she asked.

"They have a bug out base camp a few miles from here, to the north of town. In fact, I begged them to let me stay there. But they turned me away. Now, I'm sleeping out of my car."

The woman's curly, brown hair bobbed as she nodded slowly. "Listen, I'll make you a deal," she said, gritting her teeth. "I have a place you can crash, but you have to do one thing."

"Sure. Name it."

"Show me on a map where this camp is, and tell me everything you know about it."

Joshua took a deep breath, letting it out slow. He considered the woman's offer, seemingly too good to pass up. He'd considered continuing along toward Canada, but how many miles further could he get before his car was completely empty of fuel? Where would he be stuck when it ran dry? No, it seemed better to stay here.

A sudden wave of empathy struck him as he considered Nick's children, Rae Ann and Corey, who were also at the camp. "They have children there," Joshua sputtered, unable to contain his thoughts.

"We aren't in the business of hurting children. You have my word."

Joshua considered the offer again, and weighed it against the woman's promise that she wouldn't harm any of the children. He hoped she was sincere.

The woman shifted her weight. "And I can sweeten the deal—we've still got plenty of food, so you won't have to scrounge."

Joshua pursed his lips. He opened his mouth to speak before he could talk himself out of the deal that could very well save him from being out on the street and starving. "Okay," he muttered, "we have a deal."

The woman nodded somberly. "Good. So, what's your name?"

"Joshua. May I know yours?"

The woman held out a hand. "Cindy. Cindy Hammel."

22

ABRAM WAS JUST COMING out of the upper barn where he'd been feeding the animals with Shelly when he spotted Gary and Nick coming down the drive. He'd wondered why he couldn't find Nick when he'd come out at dawn, and now he knew why. Gary had gone on a supply run without his permission. His jaw tightened with exasperation when he noticed Nick's expression. Clearly, something had gone wrong.

"Where have you been, Gary?" Abram asked, moving to meet them on the drive.

"You can see where we've been. It doesn't suit you to play dumb."

"You took Nick on a supply run."

"We've got another day's worth of food, but that's all. We'll have to go again."

"I'd rather you stay here and get the perimeter secure. Supplies can wait." From the corner of his eye, Abram noticed that Nick's jaw was tight, and he kept his eyes on the ground. *He doesn't want to meet my eyes*, Abram thought. *What happened?*

"We're back before breakfast," Gary said. "We've got all day to work on the fence."

"Nick's been up all night," Abram said. "He needs some sleep before we put him to work again."

"But that would be the case anyway. It has nothing to do with our supply run. That's just what happens when you have night watch."

Abram clenched his jaw. Gary always had a comeback. He was always right. He would never capitulate. Abram took a deep breath. "All the same, I want the fence done before you go out again. You left the farm unguarded."

"Are we pouring the cement today? Securing the fenceposts?"

"Yes, but we have to let the concrete harden before we can hang the chain link. And I really want everyone present on the farm until the fence is up."

"We can come to a compromise," Gary said. "Come on, Nick, let's put this stuff away and you can help me plan the next supply run."

Nick's face went ghost white, and Abram thought he was going to be sick.

"Let the man get some sleep, Gary," Abram said. "You always push too hard."

"People need pushing," Gary said. He walked away to the storage room on the far side of the barn and Nick followed.

Abram stood and watched them go before turning back to the barn to see why Shelly hadn't come out yet. He found her with the baby goats, one in her lap and another with its front hooves on her shoulders, trying to eat her hair.

Shelly grinned up at him. "They're so funny," she said,

feeding a handful of hay to the kid in her lap, and as if to emphasize her point, one of the others did a funny little stiff-legged hop in a circle and made her laugh. Then she peered at him. "What's wrong, Abram?"

"I'm not sure. Gary took Nick on a supply run, which I had asked him not to go on, and from Nick's face, I'd say something went very wrong." Abram pursed his lips. "Neither of them are talking, so it had to be bad."

Shelly lifted the kid out of her lap and got up, staring hard at him. "I've told you time and time again that I don't trust Gary, don't feel safe around him." Her jaw flexed with anger. "Now you have a concrete example of him going against your wishes. You told him not to go out for supplies, and he did it anyway. Who knows what he did…Get rid of him, Abram."

"I can't turn my back on the man, Shell. We've been friends for years."

"It's misguided loyalty, and it's going to get us killed."

"That's ridiculous. You've taken your distrust for the man too far." He turned his back on her and walked out into the sunlight.

"I haven't, you know," she said from just behind him. "Gary is the opposite of everything you stand for. And he's undermining your authority and digging the foundation out from under our lives. We will be pariahs in the community for harboring him. You wait and see."

"Gary knows how to stay alive during this regression. I don't agree with him on everything, but I think his instincts will save us in the long run. If you want, I could talk to him about consulting me before going on another supply run, but I won't send him away."

"Supply run? Is that what we're calling looting now, Abram?" She crossed her arms. "Is this what we've come to? Someone loots us, so then we turn around and loot someone else. We planned this place so that we'd be self-supporting. We were to grow our own food, and trade peacefully with our neighbors—not raid other people's supplies." She started off, down the drive toward the house, and Abram followed her.

"Don't speak to him, Shelly," Abram said urgently. "I'll take care of it."

"Oh, don't worry, I won't. He's dangerous."

"Dangerous?"

"I wish I could get you to see that. He's a threat to all of us."

"That is an overreaction," Abram said, taking a few quick steps to catch up to her. "I would never—"

"I'm done talking about this, Abram." She turned and put her hand up. "You find out what happened on that 'supply run' and decide if you can tolerate whatever brutal act he perpetrated on the people he stole from." She picked up her pace and moved down the hill toward the house, leaving him on the path.

He stood for a long minute, watching her disappear from sight on the slope. She didn't understand. As much as Gary had changed for the worse, he was the one person in the world that knew everything there was to know about Abram, and that meant he knew things that Abram didn't want the world to know. Things he didn't wish for Shelly or Emma to know. And he was afraid that if he sent Gary away, Gary would retaliate by telling Shelly everything. He didn't know what Gary had done down in the town, but he really didn't want to know. He didn't want to be forced into taking action that could result in the ruin of his marriage.

"You aren't making this easy, Gary," he said to the empty landscape.

Corey was on his way to breakfast when he heard someone retching in the bathroom. The door was partly open, so he checked to see who it was. His dad was hunched over the toilet, throwing up, or maybe it was more like dry heaving—there didn't seem to be anything coming up. He stuck his head in the door.

"Are you okay, Dad?" Corey asked, wondering what he should do to help.

His dad waved him off. "I'm fine, Corey, just not feeling myself right now."

"Can I help?" He found a washcloth and dampened it before handing it over.

"No, bud, I'll be better after I've had some sleep. I was on watch all night." His dad mopped his face with the washcloth.

"But everything is okay?"

His dad stood up, but his face was still kind of green. "Yeah. Yeah, it is. What are you doing this morning?"

"Target practice and then we're going to pour concrete. It's going to take all of us, I guess. Abram even asked Shelly and Rae to come down."

"What does he expect Rae Ann to do?" His dad cupped his hands under the faucet and rinsed his mouth.

"I think he said she could hold a fence post upright while

the cement set. I guess you don't have to be too strong to do that."

"As long as it doesn't tip and fall over on her."

"Those holes are three feet deep; I don't think a fencepost could fall out of it. More likely, she'll get bored, and it'll end up wonky." Corey positioned his forearm perpendicular to the floor and then tilted it to demonstrate what he meant.

"I suppose Abram knows what he's doing," his dad said. He lowered the toilet lid and sat. His hands were shaking.

"Shouldn't you eat something before you go to bed, Dad?" Corey knew people sometimes got shaky when they didn't have enough to eat.

"I'm not ready to eat yet, but I will when I wake up. Keep an eye on Rae Ann for me, son, will you? I hate to keep asking Shelly to watch her."

"I think Shelly feels like watching Rae is part of her job, Dad. She spends most of her day in the house, and Rae helps her do the chores. She was planting seeds in the garden yesterday." As well as sweeping and helping to bake cookies in the old gas oven. Shelly had explained that modern stoves had electronic components and wouldn't work without electricity, but the oven at the farm had a pilot light that could be lit by hand. They were lucky that Abram had thought these things through ahead of time—at least, that's what Shelly said.

"That's nice of her, but Rae Ann is our responsibility, so please go check on her for me, okay?" His dad looked so gray in the face that Corey felt sorry for him.

"I'll go now and make sure she's doing okay. I hope you feel better."

"I'll be fine," his dad said. "I'll see you down at the worksite this afternoon."

Corey went upstairs and found Rae Ann sitting on her bed, clutching Louise to her chest. The poor stuffed bear's head was lolling.

"Something's wrong with Daddy," she said when Corey had closed the door behind him. "He's sick."

"He's just had a long night," Corey said. "He'll be better after he's had some sleep. Are you coming down to breakfast?"

"What if he dies, Corey? What if Daddy is so sick, he dies?" Rae's eyes were wide with worry.

"He's fine, Rae, you goof. Dad's not going to die just because he threw up a couple of times. He probably just ate something that didn't sit right. You know, like when you ate too much pizza that time."

"What did he eat? There's no pizza." She had a look of calm curiosity on her face that would have made him laugh if he hadn't known she was worried sick.

"I don't know. But he's fine." He held out his hand to her. "Come downstairs to breakfast."

She sighed. "If I have to. But it doesn't seem right to eat without Daddy."

"He doesn't want you to go hungry. And you have to keep your strength up for work today." He took her hand and pulled her up off the bed. "I'm hungry, anyway," he said, hoping that would get her hungry too, and then as if on cue, his stomach growled. "See?"

"Okay." She let herself be towed into the hall and down the stairs to the kitchen.

Emma was already there, eating scrambled eggs, toast,

and bacon. Corey and Rae Ann said good morning to Emma and Shelly, and then plopped down across from her and waited to be served. The plates, when Shelly brought them, were laden with food.

"Wow," Corey said, shoveling eggs in his mouth. "This is awesome."

With Louise resting in her lap, Rae Ann crunched on her bacon and smiled for the first time that morning. Emma was ripping pieces from her toast with her teeth, holding it with one hand and doodling in a notebook with the other.

"Is that your sketchbook?" Corey asked her. "I didn't know you brought it with you."

"Of course, I did," Emma said. "I can't go anywhere without my drawing pad. I have to draw now because we all have to help with the fenceposts today."

"And don't forget to go to the firing range and shoot a hundred rounds before you go to the back of the property," Emma's mom, Shelly, said.

"Is Dad okay with that? I thought he wanted us right after breakfast."

"It will take some time for them to mix the concrete, so it should be okay."

"I hope so."

"I'll keep Rae with me. I'll take her with me when I'm ready to go, so you two just do your target practice and then head straight back."

"We have to clean our guns first, Mom."

"Yes, yes, I didn't mean you weren't to clean your weapons. Just don't dawdle."

"Corey isn't allowed to be alone with Emma," Rae Ann

chimed in. "I should go with them." She'd finished with her bacon and started on the eggs.

"Rae, honey, the firing range isn't a safe place for you to be," Shelly said. "Emma and Corey can be alone for a few minutes. I trust them to do their target practice and then go straight to the worksite. It's not like they've ever been much for making trouble." She plunged a stack of plates into the sink full of soapy water.

"But Mr. Patterson said—" Rae Ann began.

"Doesn't matter what my brother-in-law said," Maggie said, coming into the kitchen. "Everyone knows my sister is in charge." She grabbed a plate from the stack on the counter and served herself from the food on the stove. "Are we all ready for fencepost sinking day?"

"Morning, Maggie," Shelly said, smiling.

"Morning," Maggie said through a mouthful of food.

"But we're putting the fenceposts up," Rae Ann said. "Not putting them in water."

"We're sinking them in their holes," Corey said, coming up for air. "We're putting the bottom third of the fencepost in a hole, and that's called sinking it. Right?" Corey looked to Maggie for confirmation.

"That's right," Maggie said, smearing jam on her toast. "Do you know what your job is going to be, Rae?"

"Keeping them straight?" Rae Ann asked.

"You are going to hold the level that tells us when the posts are straight up and down. It's an essential job. I hope you can manage it."

Corey had to bite his lip to keep from grinning. He'd seen the tiny, six-inch level that Rae Ann would have to hold. She would have no problems.

"I can," Rae Ann said. "I can focus good, and I can hold still for a long time for my age. My teacher told Daddy that."

"Good," Maggie said. "Then I want you on my team. I only like workers with excellent concentration." She took a gulp of coffee, and Corey could see she was hiding a smile. She liked Rae Ann and wanted her to feel important.

"You two should finish up and get down to the range," Shelly said. "You don't want to miss any of the fun."

Corey caught Emma's eye. What that really meant was that they needed to be there before things got started so they'd be available when they were wanted. He drank down the last of his orange juice and carried his plate and glass to the sink.

"Would you like me to wash my dishes?" he asked Shelly.

"Thank you for offering, Corey, but I really think you should get going." She took the dishes from him and placed them in the sink. "Go on, now."

He waited while Emma cleared her plate and kissed her mother on the cheek, then they walked together down the path to the firearms shed.

"You know," Emma said when they were away from the house, "I heard gunshots at first light this morning. Do you think it had anything to do with what Gary and your dad were doing? I heard Dad say they came back just after dawn."

"My dad was in the bathroom throwing up this morning," Corey said. "He said he was under the weather, but I've never seen him look like that. I think he's hiding something."

"You know Gary and guns. I wonder if something happened in town. Why would they go before daylight? They had to be doing something wrong. I think they were stealing supplies."

"My dad wouldn't steal. It can't be that."

"Not even if Gary told him he'd make my dad kick you guys out if he didn't? I bet he would, if it meant keeping you and Rae safe." Emma opened the door to the shed.

"I guess you could be right," Corey said, opening the gun cabinet and taking out two pistols while Emma pulled open the drawer that held the magazines and started setting them on the bench. He grabbed a box of bullets from another drawer, and they began loading the magazines. They loaded six each, and Corey shoved the gun in the back of his waistband so he could carry them out to the range. He set them on the hay bales at the far side of the firing range and went to move his target back. His aim was improving, and his goal was to match Emma's distances by the end of the week.

He returned to the hay bale and loaded a magazine into the handgun. He aimed, both eyes open using his dominant eye, held his breath, and eased the trigger back. The bullet hit the target, but it wasn't anywhere close to the center. He glanced over at Emma, who was on the other side of the range, popping off shots one after the other and consistently hitting the center ring of her target. He groaned inwardly and aimed again.

This bullet struck closer to the inner ring, and he kept it up, shooting round after round until the magazine was empty. Emma was replacing her target when Corey finally emptied his magazine, but there was still plenty of paper left in his. He discharged another magazine before he bothered to replace it. His aim improved from the first shot to the one hundredth, and he was feeling pleased with himself when he joined Emma in the shed.

"I'm getting better," he said, putting the empty magazines

back in the drawer. "My last twenty-five shots were all within a half inch of the center if they didn't hit it."

"Good for you," she said, pushing a patch soaked in cleaning fluid through the barrel. "You've got the focus to be a good marksman. But do you have the focus to find out what your dad and Gary were doing in town this morning?"

"Do you really think you could hear shots from town all the way up here? It's miles away."

"Sound echoes up the valley. I can hear the train, so why not gunshots?"

"I don't know. It just seems too far away."

"We can do an experiment sometime. I'll go into town and bang on a drum at dawn, and you can tell me if you hear it or not." She giggled. "That would be kind of odd, wouldn't it? To get woken to the sound of a drum on the green. I'd probably end up in the stir."

"You mean the rubber room, Em. The stir is prison."

"Neither one is where I want to end up." Emma finished cleaning her pistol and began reassembling it. "Are you going to find out what happened, or not?"

Corey hurried to catch up with his cleaning. "He won't tell me. So how do I find out? I'll keep my ears open, though. Maybe Gary will tell Abram. I know they like to talk down here in Gary's cabin so no one else will hear them."

"Don't let them catch you eavesdropping, Corey. You'd be in so much trouble."

"I don't intend to. But I'm going to try."

They locked the now clean handguns in the cabinet and left the shed, turning to walk to the back of the property. There was the beginning of a path from the shooting range to the fence because it was traveled every day now. Corey and his dad both had to shoot and then work on the back wall every day. Not today, though—today his dad was asleep.

They had reached the perimeter fence and were walking the path that was cut along the inside. There were roots and stones, but it was much easier than trying to make their way through the woods.

"Tomorrow we should go the other way," Emma said. "Through the corn and hay fields and along the fence next to the creek."

"Wouldn't that take longer?" Corey asked. "That's a lot of acreage to cover."

"Yeah, but we'll be working closer to the other side by tomorrow, don't you think? Or maybe we won't get that far."

They walked on a couple of minutes before she spoke again, lowering her voice. "Remember, Corey, be careful not to get caught listening in on Gary's conversations. He's a suspicious little weasel, and he's mean."

"Emma! You can't go around calling your dad's friends names."

"Why not? He is. He never gives anyone the benefit of the doubt. He'll skin you alive if he thinks you are spying on him, so be really, really careful. Okay?"

"Okay, I'll be careful. But I can't help if I'm passing by and I hear something, can I?"

"You'll have to do better than that. You'll need a real excuse. Something someone else can back up. And not me, because he knows I would lie for you. And not Rae, because he knows you can manipulate her. It would have to be an adult, and preferably not your dad."

Corey's eyebrows rose. "Not even my dad? That's going to make it almost impossible."

"Your dad might work if it's obvious that it's not something he'd lie about." She stopped in the path, and Corey realized they were almost at their destination. "Like we needed eggs for breakfast, something normal like that. Something that, if he questions you, he's going to look like an idiot."

"Something one of us would normally do, only it just so happens it takes me past where he's talking with your dad. This isn't going to work. You know that, don't you? Either I'll find nothing out, or he'll catch me, and I'll be good as dead." He pulled a finger across his throat.

"Don't be melodramatic, Corey. He wouldn't out-and-out kill you—you'd have a fatal accident. That's why you have to be so careful; he'd kill you and everyone but me would think it was the slip of a foot."

23

Nick crawled out of bed in the early afternoon. He'd been exhausted and had fallen asleep quickly, but he'd been plagued by nightmares. Zombies, of all things, coming up out of the ground to pursue him. It would be laughable if it hadn't hit so close to home. He told himself that the dead would be chasing Gary, as Nick hadn't killed anyone, but he'd been party to it, and it weighed on him.

There was no one in the house, so he showered and found his breakfast waiting for him on the counter. Cheese and bacon in thick-cut homemade bread, wrapped in brown paper. He slipped it into the pocket of his hoody. His stomach wasn't feeling up to eating yet, so he drank some water and headed outside.

He knew he should be with everyone else down at the end of the property, pouring cement or holding posts upright, but he didn't want to deal with people at the moment. They'd managed all morning without him—they could survive a little while longer. He walked up the path to the drive and then past the garage and around the bend to the upper barn.

The Guinea fowl were making a ruckus in the outdoor pen; they sounded like a dozen rusty gates being opened and closed over and over again. The hens who were sharing a pen with them paid them no attention. They were sunning themselves, spreading their wings, and a couple were rubbing their wings in the dirt. Nick took a second look. One hen was actually rolling around in the fine dust in the corner of the coop. He shook his head—who knew that birds were so amusing?

He meandered inside the barn where the baby goats were gamboling around in their pen, making funny four-legged hops and jumping over everything, the water trough, the feed buckets, and even the other kids. Nick's heart began to lighten a little. Such carefree little creatures, how could he not smile at them? He climbed the ladder into the loft to see the view that Corey had told him about. He walked to the large opening in the outside wall. It was the size of a double doorway, and the piece that could be used to close it was leaning against the wall, off to one side. It wasn't attached like a door with hinges, and Nick supposed that was so you could close it even when the place was packed to the rafters with hay.

He rested on a bale near the doorway window—there was probably a proper farming term for what that was. Hay door? He looked out on the world: one side was the drive surrounded in woods, and the other was open fields. He wondered which belonged to the farm, and then he noticed the fence. It ran along the nearest cornfield, which was huge, and was bordered on the far side by a creek or small river. He didn't know what the difference was.

The farmer on the far side of the creek hadn't bothered to

fence his property. And thinking of the places they'd passed on the way here, he couldn't remember any of the fields being enclosed. Only the pastures where the cows or horses grazed had fences. The people around here hadn't been preparing for the apocalypse. Wouldn't have had the time or money to prepare, had they anticipated its coming. Abram had known it was coming; why hadn't they?

Maybe they didn't think they needed fences around their land. Their neighbors were known to them, they were part of this community. They had the trust and assistance of their neighbors. A thing Abram would now never have, if what Gary had done came back to haunt them. Gary had probably ruined that for him, and he would need his fences and razor wire to keep out the irate townspeople who would happily lynch them all for Gary's brutality.

Nick cursed his mind for coming back to the memories of this morning. His stomach had started to knot up again. He pulled his sandwich from his pocket and broke off a piece of the bread. He chewed and swallowed it to give his stomach something to digest besides its own lining, but immediately regretted it. It sat like a lump and his belly threatened to reject it. He kept it down but felt worse instead of better, and decided he probably should go help with the fencing. After today, they'd be more vulnerable than ever to attack from the outside. Would anyone know it was them?

As Nick descended the ladder into the main body of the barn, he remembered seeing Joshua's car in the alley behind the store. "Damn," he said, startling the birds. The goats ignored him, lucky creatures. If Joshua had seen them, then he would know who had killed the shop keeper. Would he tell? Probably. They'd never done him any favors. Leaving him to live in his car after he'd driven them here.

He left the barn and walked down the hill, past the lower outbuildings and the firing range, and along the newly made path to the perimeter fence. He moved slowly, drawing out the time before he had to come face to face with Gary again. He noticed Emma and Corey's footsteps in the damp earth—they'd traveled this way today as well. He felt slightly ashamed, leaving those children to associate with Gary when he couldn't face him. He was a coward, he knew. He'd never liked confrontation and didn't have the self-confidence to engage bullies. He was going to have to change.

When he got closer to the work site, Abram was shoveling wet cement from a black plastic garbage can into the molds in the ground. Rae Ann, Corey, and Emma were each holding a metal fencepost steady in its hole, and Maggie was busy smoothing off the top of the wet curb while Shelly came along behind and set broken glass upright into the damp concrete. They weren't kidding about keeping people out. Gary was nowhere to be seen, and Nick found himself relaxing. Of course, Gary would be skiving off work; he always had something better to do.

Emma and Corey were chattering across the eight-foot stretch between them, each claiming they would have the straighter fencepost. They were smiling and relaxed, more relaxed than he had seen Corey since they'd arrived.

He was just about to head down to where they worked when Gary came striding along the area they'd cleared from the other side of the compound.

Nick couldn't help it, he spun on his heels and started away, hoping nobody spotted him. How could he manage to live and work here if he was going to feel disgusted every time he set eyes on Gary? He glanced back and saw that Abram was handing the shovel over to the other man. Then Abram turned and followed in Nick's footsteps.

Nick kept going, not looking back now, hoping Abram wouldn't call his name. He quickened his pace, stumbling over tree roots and stones, climbing the hill that ran down behind the house. He should have gone back the way he came, but the cleared path would take him right past them. Branches snagged him and dragged through his hair as he ducked under tree limbs.

He glanced back to see if Abram was catching up with him, but the man was nowhere to be seen. Maybe he hadn't been coming after Nick, after all. Maybe there was some errand that he needed to do, and the fact Nick had been there was only a coincidence. He slowed his pace and walked up the hill sedately, letting his heart rate drop and his breathing slow. He tried to find some peace in the sunshine filtering through the branches, the leaves only just beginning to unfurl. Spring came late to Vermont, he knew that, although he wasn't sure how he knew. It was later here than it was at his home, just a couple of hours southeast.

As the farmhouse came in sight, he wondered if he'd ever see his home again.

Abram left Gary in charge of the concrete and followed Nick through the woods, but when it became clear that it wouldn't be easy to catch the man, he walked to the perimeter and walked along the fence line, where the going was much more accessible. No point in racing; there was only one place Nick could be going.

He reached the house in good time, but Nick wasn't there yet, so he adjusted one of the chairs on the porch to face the sun and eased into it. You had to take your breaks when they came out here on the land. He closed his eyes and waited; he knew he'd be able to hear Nick before he came in sight—the man didn't have the skill of quiet walking in the woods. A moose coming through the forest would've been quieter than Nick.

And he was right; a few minutes later, he could hear someone coming through the brush. He was muttering and breaking branches as he went, making Abram happy he wasn't walking through the orchard. He opened his eyes and watched Nick reach the path and climb the stairs without even looking up. He'd clearly had no military-style training at all.

"Nick," Abram said quietly, "have a seat."

He'd tried not to startle the man, but Nick jumped and nearly tumbled backward down the stairs. He righted himself and took a chair next to Abram in the sun.

"What happened this morning?" Abram asked.

"Not much," Nick said. "We just got some things from the general store in town."

"Don't lie to me, Nick. I could see by your face that something happened."

"It was nothing." Nick's eyes were fixed on the painted floorboards.

"It wasn't nothing. You were a wreck when you got back, and you're becoming more of a wreck as the day goes on."

Abram kept his tone in check. He might want to yell at Nick, but he didn't think that would help produce results.

"I'm sick, that's all. I must have picked up a bug." A leaf fluttered down from the gutter and landed on the armrest of Nick's chair. He flicked it away.

"You are not sick. Something happened out there."

"You can ask Gary—he'll tell you."

"I believe that Gary told you to keep quiet."

Nick looked up and caught Abram's eye. The sunlight hitting Nick's face made his eye look strangely transparent. "I would be signing my children's death warrant."

"I can protect you and your kids from Gary, but only if I know what happened." Abram put all the warm feeling into his voice that he could.

Nick shook his head.

Abram continued, "I don't care what happened, or what you did. We will take care of it. We'll do what's necessary to make reparations."

"Reparations?" Nick sounded hysterical. "How do you make reparations to a dead man's family?"

"You killed a man? It must have been an accident," Abram said. "They'll understand."

"It wasn't an accident. He gave us the option to leave. We could have picked up our bags and left, but instead, Gary shot him in cold blood. He wasn't even pointing his gun in our direction." Nick held his head in his hands, visibly shaken to his core.

"You must be mistaken," Abram said. "Gary would never shoot anyone. Not to kill."

"I am not mistaken," Nick said, shakily. "His finger wasn't even on the trigger, and Gary shot him in the head."

"Was there anyone else there?"

"Yeah. A woman."

"Is she still alive?"

"She fled."

Abram shook his head. If this was true, then Shelly was right—Gary could get them all killed. He leaned forward and asked, "Do you think anyone followed you from town?"

"I don't think so. We left quickly. I didn't see or hear anyone behind us." Uncertainty flashed across his features.

Abram was silent for a moment, then said, "We'll have to double our watch. Put two people on during the night, and maybe have one person patrol the perimeter during the day. We can't take the chance that they don't know who we are."

"What are you going to tell Gary? How will you protect my kids?"

"Nothing. I will tell him nothing, and neither will you. I'll take care of this when the time is right." Abram stood up. "I'd better go back now. Why don't you stay out here in the sun for a while? It will do you good."

He left Nick on the porch and walked down the hill, deep in thought. What if Nick was right and Gary had killed a man in cold blood? Gary would never admit to it. But then, his old friend would have never killed. He was famous for talking himself out of situations. When had he changed? What had changed him? Why hadn't he, Abram, realized that Gary was different?

Abram felt low. Lower than he had in many years. If Gary was a killer, then having him here was a mistake. And there was only one way to rectify that.

Corey and Emma had been released from their work duty and were on their way back up the trail toward the upper barn, where they were in charge of feeding the animals, when Emma stopped in her tracks and Corey ran right into her, knocking her over into the damp earth.

"Sorry, Em," he said, reaching over to help her up.

She laughed and accepted the hand up. "You never watch where you're going. I know that."

"Then why did you stop in front of me?" Corey brushed the dirt off her sweatshirt.

"I thought I heard something," she said, stopping to listen. "It's gone now."

"What did you hear? A bear?" There were bears and moose, deer and coyotes in these woods, or so Abram had told them when they'd arrived. And those were just the larger animals.

"Voices. I thought I heard voices."

"That was probably Rae and Dad up at the house. Come on, let's get our chores finished so we can hang out before your dad finds out that Gary sent us up here on our own."

Emma was staring into the brush on the other side of the fence. "What's that?" she whispered, pointing to a spot of bright red visible through the undergrowth. "I've never seen that before."

Corey peered through the fence and the bushes on the other side of the boundary. He could see a patch of color through the bare brambles whose leaves hadn't popped out yet. Spring came so late in Vermont. "It's probably an old Budweiser box. Or Coke. Coke boxes are red."

"Whatever it is, it shouldn't be there. I'm going to go check it out. There's no razor wire here yet, so this won't take me long to get over and back."

"No, don't. It's not safe, Em. Remember, we don't know what happened in town today." Corey caught her shoulder, but she shook him off. "At least go tell your dad first."

"Tell my dad?" she said slowly, elongating the spaces between the words. "Why would I do that? You were just worried about my dad finding out we were alone." She grabbed the fence with her right hand.

"Please, Em, don't."

"Corey, I haven't had five minutes of fun since we got here. What's it going to hurt for me to jump the fence and find the place the local kids come to drink beer? Maybe we can make a path so we can join them. My dad is always going on about community—we can make our own community. A 'let's get drunk and high' community." She grinned.

"I'm pretty sure that's not what he meant. And putting yourself in danger is not fun, it's reckless."

She locked eyes with him, smirking. "How am I supposed to know what it feels like to be alive if I can't be reckless? I'm rebelling, Corey. I'm sick and tired of being the good girl who doesn't make waves. My whole life sucks. And since we don't know when we're going to see our friends again, we might as well make some new friends and have fun while we wait for life to get back to normal."

"You won't be having much fun if you end up getting yourself killed. And you know they'll blame me if you get hurt."

"I do know, so I guess you'd better join me."

She turned and reached up to secure her left hand.

"Em. No," he said and caught her arm.

She shook him off. "I'm going." She climbed the fence, gripping the wire with her fingers and shoving the toes of her sneakers into the holes. She dropped down on the other side and pushed through the brush, staying well clear of the brambles.

"Crap," Corey said and hurried after her.

It took him longer to get over the fence—the toes of his boots were too big to fit in the holes in the chain link. He had to jump to catch the top railing and pull himself over using his arms. He fell flat on his back on the other side and scrambled up, searching for Emma in the undergrowth. He spotted movement and raced after her. "Em, wait up," he called.

"I found it," she called back. "It's a—"

Her words were cut off with a strangled cry, and there was a flurry of movement.

He ran forward and caught sight of two hooded figures hurrying away, Emma slung over the first person's shoulder. He started to cry out but stopped himself. He went into full stealth mode, bent on following them until he could rescue her. But they moved quickly, darting between the trees with a speed that kept Corey on the run to keep up. They clearly knew the lay of the land, because he would go around a tree, swearing it was the exact same path they had taken, but he'd come up against a thicket of brambles or a boulder blocking the way and would have to backtrack. Three of those missteps and he'd lost them completely.

Still, he ran on, tripping and falling, or sliding down a bank into a stream, soaking wet and covered in mud. He couldn't turn back—he had no idea which direction he'd been running. The way back looked the same as the way ahead. So, he kept on, hoping beyond hope that he'd catch them. That he'd be able to save Emma and bring her home. And trying not to overthink the fact that he had no idea which direction home lay in.

In the end, he came out of the woods onto the dirt road. There was no sign of the intruders, or Emma, in either direction, but when he'd walked a few yards up the street, he discovered fresh tire tracks in the muddy shoulder. He hadn't heard an engine, but maybe he'd been falling down the creek bank when the engine caught. Or perhaps it was a Prius, but he wasn't sure how it would still be working. Whichever, it was clear they had gotten away with Emma, and he hadn't helped at all.

He ran up the road. The drive to the farm could only be in one direction, and he moved as fast as his legs would carry him. He scanned for landmarks that might indicate he was nearing the compound, but everything seemed the same. Anonymous woods on both sides of the road. But then the far side opened up into pastureland, and he thought he remembered the land on the other side of the street from the drive being cleared. He could see it from the barn, couldn't he? There were the woods and the driveway, but also a view of the field, and beyond that, the creek and the road. With a clear pasture on the other side.

His spirits rose. He would be there soon.

He pushed harder, trying to run his fastest, but his boots were waterlogged and his legs heavy with fatigue. He dropped to a walk right before he came to the drive. He turned down it, running again until he reached the gate. He pulled the chain that rang the bell, and then kept yanking it. The noise clanged around the countryside and echoed back to him. He heard the birds in the barn, which he knew was just out of sight around the bend, squawking and kicking up a racket.

He remembered that they'd been on the way to feed the birds and the kids, and the cow with her calves, if they'd arrived. He wondered if he'd ever see Emma again, if they'd ever get to feed the animals together.

He pulled the bell harder and faster.

He heard voices yelling and finally feet on the drive, running up the hill. And still, he kept ringing—he couldn't stop. Emma had been taken, and he would ring the bell until she had been rescued. He would ring the bell until the whole damn world knew she was missing. Then everyone was there all at once, and Abram slid his arm through the gate to stop him from ringing the bell.

24

NICK HEARD the bell from where he was sitting on the porch and knew at once that Joshua had ratted them out. There could be no other reason that someone would be at the gate on the day he and Gary had robbed the general store. That would be too great a coincidence, and Nick didn't believe in coincidences. The woman behind the flashlight had seen his face; she would be able to identify him. And he didn't want to be identified.

But seconds later, he was running up the path to the drive and was joined by Abram running up from the direction of the lower barns. Abram glanced at Nick with eyebrows raised, but Nick shook his head. He didn't know for sure what they would find.

The birds in the barn were adding to the noise, croaking and clucking out their warnings, the Guineas in a flock at the fence, trumpeting at Nick and Abram as they ran by. There were footsteps behind them, and Nick swung his gaze to see Shelly, Maggie, and Gary coming up the hill, followed by a wide-eyed Rae Ann. Where were Emma and Corey?

Nick sprinted away. The absence of Corey had created a pit of ice in his stomach. Where was his son?

As he rounded the curve and the front gate came into sight, a wave of relief washed over Nick, and he nearly fell to his knees. He pulled himself together and finished the sprint to the gate. Corey was stuck on the far side, clinging to the fence, pulling and pulling on the bell.

"Corey, what is it?" Nick yelled over the sound of the bell, but it was as if Corey couldn't hear.

Abram reached through the fence and grabbed the bell pull. The noise stopped abruptly, leaving the world in silence but their ears ringing. It was then that Nick noticed the paper attached to the middle of the gate by wide gray tape. He raced over to it and tore it from the fence as Abram unlocked the gate and pulled Corey inside.

Give us half your food and the man who killed Ron, ALIVE. Deliver to Hammel's Grocery in two hours, or we'll kill the girl.

Nick's blood ran cold as he read the note. This was at least partly down to him. If he had refused to go with Gary, then maybe the man, Ron, would still be alive. And if Ron were alive, Emma would be here with her family, not held on pain of death.

The world spun around him, and he reached out to thread his fingers through the fence. The wire was cold and bit into his hand, and surprisingly, that steadied him. But the last four words of the note reverberated in his brain: *We'll kill the girl.*

He couldn't believe it; the words weren't registering. His heart raced as he tried to think through the panic.

"We have to save Emma," he muttered, though nobody heard him.

He knew they had to save Emma, and he would help. He needed to pull himself back from the edge and use reason and logic to rescue Corey's best friend. He closed his eyes and sucked in air. He needed all his skills he used as an engineer now. He needed to do as he was trained to do and use his brain.

"Dad?" Corey's voice snapped him back to the present. "Dad, Emma's gone, we have to save her." Corey was pleading with his voice and his eyes.

"We will, Corey. Take Rae Ann back to the house."

Corey turned and rushed toward Rae Ann, who stood there, confused.

In the next moment, Abram walked up and grabbed the note from Nick's hand, staring at it in disbelief. Nick cringed at the noise that emitted from Abram's throat as he read the letter.

The words on the page swam in Abram's vision. *We'll kill the girl.* His hands were trembling so hard that he could barely see the words, but their meaning was seared into Abram's mind. They would kill Emma. His only child was in the hands of people who would see her dead. He must clear his head. He needed to think.

His stomach heaved, and Shelly came to him and placed a cold hand on the back of his neck. She was sobbing and gulping air, but she did her best to comfort him.

"What's going on?" Gary asked from behind him. "What does the note say?"

Abram spun around, rage burning through him. He lifted his arm and pointed at Gary, his hand still shaking. "You killed a man? I told you we had enough food, and you killed a man for a handful of canned goods? How could you?" The words were little more than a hiss, quiet and menacing. "You...you put my family at risk." The world had narrowed to one person. He could hear Shelly talking to him, but the words were meaningless. This was all about Gary.

Gary had both his hands up now. "Easy, Abram. I didn't kill any—"

"What happened to you?" Abram asked. "You used to be a decent man, Gary. You used to value human life. Or was that all an act? A silly game for me to believe until the world fell apart and you could kill whoever the hell you pleased."

"Abram, listen to me, I didn't—"

"The hell you didn't," Abram cut him off. "Nick told me all about it. How you killed a man, who was giving you the option to walk away. He wasn't even pointing a gun at you."

But Gary's attention wasn't on Abram now. He'd turned, his eyes searching.

"Gary killed a man, and that's why Emma is gone?" Shelly's voice was shaking. "He killed a man? Abram, tell me this isn't true."

Abram shook his head. He wished it wasn't true. He wished his daughter wasn't in the hands of people bent on getting their revenge. But she was. His only child. Their only child. He turned to look at Shelly.

"You were right, Shelly. I should never have brought him

here. I'm sorry, I should have listened to you." He reached out to take her hands.

"We need to get moving," she said. "We only have two hours to get the food down, and him," she sent a venomous glance toward Gary, "to the store."

"So that's how it is now?" Gary growled low in his throat. "Everyone is against me?" He swung his head back and forth until his gaze rested on Nick. "This is your fault. If you'd kept your mouth shut like you were supposed to, they might have thought you were the killer. I could have talked myself out of this."

"It's not his fault, Gary," Abram said. "I made him tell me. How could you possibly think you would get away with killing a man in cold blood? What could it possibly gain you?"

"What it should have gained us was power," Gary said. "Fear. You want them to stop looting us? Then they need to fear us. All the razor wire in the world isn't going to do as much as a little healthy fear."

"And you killed a man to achieve that?" The loathing was thick in Shelly's voice.

"It's the quickest way, and I know you don't like it, but I'm establishing dominance in the community. It's the best way I know of to keep you all alive."

Shelly grunted. "That's abhorrent," she said and turned away to be comforted by Maggie.

"You do see what I'm trying to do here, right?" Gary was addressing Abram now. "You see the logic in it?"

"This is not what I'm looking for. I was hoping for a peaceful existence and harmony with my neighbors. I think that's lost to me now, Gary. You've taken that away from me."

Abram could barely look at his friend. How could Gary have betrayed him so thoroughly?

"I was protecting you! Why can't you see that? I was protecting your family from outside threats."

"Well, that backfired, didn't it?" Nick said. "You got Emma snatched, and now we have to give up half of our food. Not that I think you'll be any loss. They can have you, and good riddance."

Abram saw the blow coming and tried to stop it, but he was too late. Gary launched himself at Nick, striking him in the chest with his shoulder, and driving Corey's dad hard into the post that held the gate, smacking his head hard against it and then sending him to the ground. Gary swung a foot back as if to kick Nick and Abram grabbed his arm and swung him around.

Corey put Rae Ann down and rushed back to his dad, yelling, and Maggie was holding Shelly, preventing her from throwing herself into the fray. Abram landed two solid blows —one to the head, the other mid-body—before Gary came at him, arms swinging like pistons. Abram gave way, moved back to avoid the maniac who had possessed his best friend, and kicked Gary in the knee to break his mad fury. Gary grunted and nearly lost his footing, allowing Abram to land a few more punches.

But this just seemed to infuriate Gary more. He recovered his balance and came at Abram. Shelly shook Maggie off and launched herself on to Gary's back. He swung around first one way and then the other.

"Get the hell off me," Gary shouted, trying to pry her fingers from where they had taken purchase on his neck.

She was yelling and scratching the back of his neck,

fiercely unaware of the damage Gary was inflicting on her fingers. Abram saw Rae Ann watching with her eyes wide, hovering next to Corey, who was trying to rouse his dad.

"Corey," Abram yelled, "take Rae Ann back to the house."

"I can't," Corey cried. "My dad."

"We can't leave our dad," Rae Ann echoed her brother.

But then Gary pried Shelly's hands from his neck and brushed her off by slamming her against the gate, and he came straight for Abram again. Abram was able to land the first blow, but Gary overwhelmed him quickly, and the blows to Abram's head were staggering.

He had a vague impression that Maggie was once more holding Shelly back, keeping her out of the battle, and Abram was grateful. He launched another kick at Gary's knee, but only grazed it. Still, the man gave a grunt of pain that was satisfying to hear. But now he pushed into Abram even harder, making Abram backpedal, looking for a way to escape the punishing blows. The man was like a machine, fueled by his rage and unstoppable.

Shelly was yelling at Gary to stop, but he showed no sign of having heard her. Abram bent low, and ignoring the blows that landed on his head, he pummeled Gary's midsection, coming in close so that Gary couldn't land a blow effectively. Abram thought he'd gotten Gary calmed down—he was standing still, breathing hard, but not struggling to get out of Abram's embrace. Abram sighed in relief; it was over, and he was still standing.

Then Gary took a quick step back and pushed Abram hard, so that he lost his balance and fell onto his back in the gravel. His vision blurred, and when it cleared again, Gary was standing above him, his gun drawn and pointing between Abram's eyes. Shelly and Maggie were silent, eyes wide, standing stock still. Maggie had released Shelly, who had grabbed her sister's hand when she realized what was happening.

Nick was on the ground and Abram couldn't see his face, but as far as he knew, Nick was still unconscious. Corey had Rae Ann in his arms, her face pressed into his chest so that she couldn't see. Abram looked up into Gary's eyes, and he didn't know who he saw there, but it wasn't his friend.

The two things Nick realized upon regaining consciousness were that his head hurt like hell, and that there were too many people talking. Corey was calling for Nick to wake up, Shelly was screaming at Gary, and Maggie was yelling at her. All he really wanted was some quiet and for his head to stop hurting, but it was clear that wasn't going to happen.

He opened his eyes to take in the chaos. The world spun and then righted itself. Corey was at his side, holding Rae Ann; Maggie and Shelly were huddled at the fence; and Gary was landing punches on Abram's face and head at an alarming rate.

Nick struggled to get up, ignoring the way the ground tilted away from him.

"Dad, what are you doing?" Corey asked. "Stay down."

But, as Nick had anticipated, Gary was pulling a gun from the back of his pants and aiming it right at Abram's head.

The world had gone deathly quiet now, which was an improvement in Nick's mind, but the danger level was Defcon three. If Gary killed Abram, he would take charge of the compound, and Nick and his children would have to flee. He couldn't let that happen.

Nick got to his feet, out of view from Gary, who had his back to him. He pulled his own pistol from his waistband, grateful he had not returned it to the weapons room that morning.

"Gary," Nick said. "Don't do this." He started forward slowly, making as little sound as possible.

"Stay out of it, Nick," Gary said. "You don't belong here."

Nick gripped his pistol tighter. "Don't do it, man. You'll never forgive yourself."

"Shut up," Gary said.

Nick was close now, if he could only be sure Gary wouldn't pull the trigger. "Just hear me out."

"Say another word, and I'll kill you instead."

"Gary, wait a minute," Nick said, heart slamming in his chest.

"That's it—" Gary began to turn around.

Seizing the opportunity, Nick gripped his own firearm tighter, and slammed it down on Gary's head. Hard.

25

Nick watched as Gary slumped to the ground, and Abram struggled upward.

"Corey," Abram said, "run to the barn and bring back some baling twine. It's hanging on the wall inside the door."

Corey let go of his sister and ran. Nick held out a hand and helped Abram to his feet, as Shelly rushed over to see if he was okay. He brushed her off, even though his nose and lip were bleeding and his left eye was already swelling shut.

"I'm fine. Don't fuss," Abram said through swollen lips. He turned to Nick. "Thank you. I didn't know you had it in you."

"Neither did I," Nick said, trying to catch his breath.

Abram pursed his lips. "Okay. We don't have much time. Someone needs to bring the handcart up to the barn so we can load it with food."

"I'll go," Maggie said.

"No," Nick said, "here comes Corey with the twine. I'll send him and Rae Ann to get the cart so we can talk."

"Here, Dad." Corey handed his dad the baling twine.

"Go down to the garage, Corey, and bring the garden cart back to the barn, okay? Take Rae Ann with you." Nick placed his hand on Corey's shoulder. "I'll be fine; you two are not to worry about me. Okay?"

"Yeah, Dad, if you're sure."

"I am. Rae Ann, go with your brother."

Rae Ann nodded, although she still looked like she might burst into tears at any moment. The minute they were out of sight, Nick rolled Gary onto his stomach and tied his hands securely. He considered leaving Gary's feet free, so he could walk, but decided against it and tied them too.

Nick and Abram dragged Gary, his feet trailing, down the drive toward the upper barn. Once inside the barn, he'd begun groaning a little, and they propped him against the wall where he could breathe without inhaling dust and hay, which Nick thought was a kindness he didn't deserve.

"What are we going to do?" Nick asked Abram when the adults all joined them in the barn. "Give them everything they demand?"

"Half our food?" Shelly was incredulous. "I don't think so."

"How would they even know how much food would be half?" Maggie asked.

"No," Abram said, "we'll give them back what we stole, maybe a little more. We can stack empty boxes, or maybe boxes filled with dirt on the bottom level of the cart and put the food on top of that, so it looks like more than it is."

"What if they check it before they hand Emma over?" Shelly asked. "That could be fatal."

"There are no guarantees regardless of what we do. We don't have time to load up half our supplies even if I was willing to give them away. I'm betting what they really want is the man who killed Ron." Abram glanced at each of them in turn, as if gauging their reaction.

Nick caught sight of movement outside the door. It was Corey back with the cart.

But then Gary spoke. "Wait, Abram, you can't hand me over to them!"

"Oh, I can, and I will. You brought this down on your own head. Putting my family at risk, my daughter. You'd better believe I'm handing you over."

"Come on, man," Gary said, and Nick could see he was struggling against his bonds without being obvious about it. He wanted out.

"Nick," Abram said, "will you watch Gary while the women and I load the cart? I don't want him getting any ideas about leaving without us."

"Sure." He had no objections. As far as he was concerned, Gary could use a swift kick to the head.

Corey came through the barn door before Abram could leave. "I want to come too. I want to help rescue Emma."

"Corey," Nick said before Abram could agree, "I need you to stay here and protect Rae Ann. Shelly and Maggie are going to be preoccupied."

"Shelly says she's going, and I am too."

"That's not necessary, Corey," Abram said, "although I appreciate it. I have a plan, and it won't help me to have to worry about too many people. I need a small, tight group so we can get in and get out efficiently."

"Corey," Nick said. "Why don't you go help them load the cart? We'll need to leave soon to make the deadline."

"But, Dad..."

"Go on, Corey. This isn't up for discussion. Just do as I say."

Corey huffed in defeat and left through the barn door.

"Come on, Nick," Gary said once Corey was out of the building, "you know I don't deserve this. Let me go."

"Gary, I will never understand your disregard for life. And I will never forget watching that man die. You deserve whatever you get."

"He was weak. It's natural selection."

"He was merciful and understanding. Empathy does not make you weak." Nick turned and walked away from Gary into the middle of the room.

"I don't think you get what weakness is," Gary said.

Nick glared back at him. "And you don't understand strength. Bullies don't come from a place of strength, they come from fear." He turned and walked the rest of the way across the barn, so he wouldn't have to listen to Gary's poison anymore.

The floor beneath Emma's head was cold and unyielding. It smelled of damp and mildew and her clothes, where they touched the floor, felt wet. She couldn't see, a blindfold made sure of that, but she was pretty sure she was in a basement. She'd been here since they'd dragged her out of the forest; it must have been hours ago now. Her hands were numb from being tied too tightly behind her back, and her legs were bound from ankle to knee with duct tape. That was her own fault—she'd kicked out hard when they'd first snatched her and caught the man holding her feet in the mouth.

The thought he might be missing a tooth now gave her grim pleasure.

The flash of red that Corey had thought might've been a beer box had been the body of an emergency flashlight. From the conversation they'd had on the ride in the car back to town, she got the idea that they had been planning to wait until dark to breach the fence and exact revenge, but she'd made things ever so easy for them. Walking right into their hands. She felt stupid now.

They had asked her who the men were who had robbed the general store, but she honestly didn't know. When they asked who had killed Ron Hammel, she'd just shook her head. How would she know who had killed a man from town? She'd never even been to town. They'd tried pain only once, kicking her in the stomach when she said she didn't know, but the pain had made her vomit, and they didn't try that again. The woman made the man clean it up. She said it served him right for kicking a child.

The muscles in Emma's shoulders were starting to really burn now, and her wrists stung from where the rope had rubbed them raw. She couldn't feel her fingers, and the spot where her weight rested on her hip just plain hurt. She was afraid to roll to her other side for fear she'd get stuck on her stomach. That would be far worse. She wished she could pull her wrists further down so she could slide them over her butt. If she could get that far, she was confident she could slip them over her legs and have her arms in front of her. If she had use of her arms, she could get rid of the foul gag, the blindfold, and the tape wrapped around her legs.

There were footsteps overhead, on the floor above, and Emma strained to listen. Muffled voices were talking, but she couldn't hear what they were saying. She suddenly felt cold, and fear boiled up inside her. She tried to contain it, breathing through her nose in shaky gasps. But when the door opened, and she heard footsteps on the stairs, she couldn't help but scream, although the sound was muffled by the gag in her mouth and she started to retch.

"Loosen the gag," a woman's voice said from close by. "It's cruel."

"Can you hear yourself?" This was a man's voice. "Those people killed your husband, and you're worried about how tight we gag our hostage?"

"She's a child, not a murderer. There's no need to treat her cruelly."

Someone knelt beside her, and the woman spoke quietly. "Don't be afraid, I'm just going to loosen this a little, so you don't gag and vomit."

The woman's hands were gentle on Emma's head, and the pressure on her mouth lessened, though her lips were still cracked and dry.

"There," the woman said, "that's better."

"Why are you nice to her? Whether she lives or dies should not matter to you after what her people have done."

"I'm surprised at you, John. You didn't even like your brother. And you treat animals you are about to slaughter better than you've treated this child. You should be ashamed."

"This is war, Cindy, plain and simple. They came here, into your home, your space, and stole your provisions and killed your husband. Do you think the police are going to show up and take care of this? They have their hands full. There are groups of bandits now and they're tearing up and down the interstate getting off wherever they want. Killing, raping, and stealing everything in sight."

"You're unbelievable. There are no bandits driving up and down the interstate. Where would they get the gasoline?"

"I don't know. But the Andersons up the road saw them. There are bad people all around us now, and until law enforcement gets back online, we have to take care of it ourselves. And it annoys me to see you waste your time on her."

"Even in war, there are rules about how you treat prisoners," Cindy said. "This is America, not Honduras."

"Honey, it doesn't matter where we are, there is no law anymore—there are no rules. It's survival of the fittest, and this child will have to prove that she's fit if she's going to live." He kicked Emma in the foot, and she flinched.

"Listen to you talk, like you're some kind of big man. I'd like to see you survive for more than five minutes gagged and blindfolded with somebody kicking your guts in. This is my house and my store and my rules. We treat people with compassion, especially children."

"Weak." John spit the word at her.

"I'm smart, not weak. If we send this child back to her parents covered in bruises, what do you think they are going to do? They are going to come down here and kick the crap out of the guy who injured their child. And, if they are true to form, then they'll kill him. Kill you, as you're the one that thought that kicking her would be such a smart idea.

"I'm going to sit you up and give you some water, okay?" the woman's voice was in Emma's ear again.

Emma gave a nod, and she was propped up and leaned against the wall. The gag was pulled down, and the mouth of a bottle was touched to Emma's lips. She sucked the water into her mouth, and it tasted normal, so she swallowed. She grabbed the neck of the plastic bottle with her teeth and tipped her head back, drinking the entire bottle.

She said, "Thank you," before the gag was replaced gently in her mouth.

"It shouldn't be long now," Cindy said. "You just hang in there, okay?"

"Are you finally ready to go back upstairs?" John asked. "We need to be ready when they come."

There were footsteps on the stairs.

"Shut up, John," Cindy said. "We don't want to talk about that down here."

"Why not?" John asked. "To save her feelings?"

"You do realize we could be talking about her father or her brother? We don't know who exactly killed Ron." The door opened and closed, the key turned in the lock, and they were gone.

Tears burned in Emma's eyes. It wasn't her father who killed the man, she knew that, but they didn't. And what if it had been Corey's dad who'd done it? What would happen to Corey and Rae Ann if Nick was killed? The tears were absorbed by the blindfold, but her nose was running, and she couldn't wipe her face with her arms secured behind her back. She bent her legs and rubbed her nose on her jeans. It might have been gross, but it was better than gagging on her own snot.

26

WHEN THE GARDEN cart was full, Nick met with Abram, Shelly, and Maggie to figure out who would go into town with Abram. Nick felt strongly that he should go, as he was part of the original raid and should take some of the blame, but everyone had their own opinion.

"I need to be there when we get Emma back," Shelly said, but Abram was already shaking his head.

"We need one of us here," Abram said to Shelly. "I invited Gary here, and I need to take responsibility for that."

"I can't just sit here and wait."

Abram took her hand. "You need to stay here with Maggie and the kids. Keep this place safe."

Nick stepped forward. "I'll go. I was stupid enough to go with Gary, to begin with. If you want, Abram, I'll go alone. That reduces potential casualties down to one."

"Two, if you count Gary," Maggie said. "I mean, no one is talking about this, but we are surrendering a member of our community."

"Only because he put Emma at risk," Shelly said. "He brought this on himself."

"That may be, but it's still a life."

"Maggie's right," Nick said. "If we don't count him as a life then we are stooping to his level."

Shelly crossed her arms. "I think our community would be better off without him." She looked around. "I told you all along I didn't trust him."

"Then it's agreed. Nick and I will go into town and take care of this," Abram said.

Maggie shook her head.

"We can't keep a guy who's dangerous," Abram said. "Especially around the kids."

Nick inched back. "Let me say goodbye to Corey and Rae Ann. It will only take a minute."

Abram nodded, and Nick hurried into the storage room, where Corey and Rae Ann were sitting on a crate playing a clapping game. Nick was somewhat surprised—Corey hated those games. He was a good brother.

Nick sat down next to Rae Ann and wrapped his arm around her. "I'm leaving now, but I should be back in an hour or two. Corey, help Shelly and Maggie with Rae Ann, okay?" He wanted to say if he didn't come back, but couldn't bring himself to terrify his children.

"I should come with you, Dad," Corey said. "It's my fault they got Emma."

"It's not your fault, Corey."

"It is, Dad." Corey's voice was filled with despair.

"We're going to get her back." Nick placed his hand on Corey's shoulder. "But in order to do that, I need you to stay here."

Corey got up abruptly and walked out of the room.

"Corey!" Nick called, but the boy didn't come back.

Rae Ann threw her arms around Nick's neck and held him close. "Come back soon, Daddy. Louise will miss you."

"I wouldn't want to upset Louise." Nick rubbed the teddy bear on the head. "But I have to go. I made a mistake, and I have to help fix it."

"Okay, Daddy." Rae Ann pulled her head off his shoulder.

He gazed into her eyes, wishing he didn't have to leave her. But he did.

"I love you, sweetheart."

"Love you too, Daddy." She rested her head back on his shoulder and held him close.

"I'll be back soon," he said, hugging her back. Then he pulled her off his neck and set her on the dirt floor, placing a kiss on her forehead. She took his hand, and they walked out to where the others were standing, near the cart. He handed Rae Ann off to Maggie, who gave him a grim nod.

Nick turned and walked into the barn, where Gary was still sitting against the wall. He'd half expected him to have tried to escape, but he hadn't. Nick cut a length of baling twine about six feet long and attached it at Gary's wrists, still bound behind his back. He gripped Gary's new leash tightly, then cut the bindings from his ankles.

"I've got my pistol, so don't try anything," Nick said, voice firm. "I know they want you alive, but at the moment, I don't care much either way."

27

When he left his dad and Rae Ann in the supply room attached to the upper barn, Corey headed straight to the weapons shed near the shooting range. He pulled the pistol he used for target practice from the locker and pulled two magazines and a box of bullets from their drawers. Then he started opening drawers, cupboards, and cabinets looking for a holster that would fit him.

He found one in the locker that held Emma's gun, of course. She had pretty much the same size waist as Corey did and the holster, while not comfortable, fit well enough. He loaded the magazines and slipped one into the gun, holstering it on his right hip. The second magazine, he pushed into the belt as well.

He felt better now, ready to help protect the farm. And if anyone decided to surprise them while Dad, Abram, and Gary were on the way to town, they'd be in for a surprise themselves. He closed the lockers and drawers, made sure everything was back to normal, and made off out into the late afternoon.

His footsteps took him along the path, down toward the fence where Emma had gone over. It really hadn't been all that long ago. Less than two hours, he figured. Standing there, he replayed their conversation over in his mind. The bright red object that they had assumed was a beer or soda case was gone. It had been a flashlight, or at least that's what he thought he'd seen while chasing them through the forest. They'd meant to be here after dark.

He climbed the fence and went to look at the place where the intruders had been hiding. The undergrowth and grass had been flattened. He could see footprints and the place the large flashlight had rested on the ground. More like the shape of a lantern, really. Something metallic caught his eye, and he scrubbed the dirt with his toe, which dislodged something. He reached down and tugged, revealing a pair of bolt cutters. They'd been planning to cut through the fence, not go over it.

How were they to protect the farm from intruders with bolt cutters? Even if they installed razor wire all along the top of the fence, anyone could come along and cut their way through. What was Abram thinking? Of course, they'd have a night watch to check the perimeter, but there were acres and acres of land. They could come through anywhere.

Corey's face flushed, and he clenched his fists. No one here knew what they were doing. Abram and Dad couldn't protect them. They would need dozens of people to keep all this land secure. He took the bolt cutters and tossed them over the fence, so they were inside the property line. No point in leaving them out here where anyone could find them and use them to get in.

He had heard Emma yelling and crying as she was carried away out of the forest. She'd been terrified, probably still was scared. He struck out along the fence, moving toward the road, his hand resting on the holstered pistol. He decided he wasn't leaving this to Abram and his father. Emma's life was too important to risk it. They didn't know everything, that was damn certain. One set of bolt cutters could have breached their entire security system.

He broke into a jog, watching his footing and keeping to the fence. When he reached the road, he lengthened his stride into a lope. It was a pace he knew he could keep up for long distances. He had been a cross country runner at school. He didn't usually run in boots with a gun at his hip, but that was okay. Everyone had to adapt.

After a few minutes, Corey moved to the softer dirt at the side of the road. Dad, Abram, and Gary couldn't be that far in front of him, and he didn't want them to hear him coming up on them. When he reached the paved road, he'd have to run in the grass on the verge for them not to hear him, and meanwhile, he'd keep his eyes open. He didn't want to come around a bend and find them right in front of him.

He thought he heard voices ahead and slowed to a walk, keeping his eyes open for a sighting of the men.

As they came into Fenton, Abram scanned for signs of life. Not a soul could be found. Even though the rural town was small, there had usually been a few people out. Now, it was desolate.

Perhaps the townsfolk were hiding indoors, ensuring that they and their loved ones were safe from the unsavory people who were beginning to commit heinous acts. He set his gaze on Gary to see a prime example of such a person. Surely, there were more people like Gary—soon, he figured, the area might be overrun with them.

And then he thought of the tiny police station that was more than a mile outside of the town, between Fenton and a neighboring town. He remembered that he hadn't been able to find the chief nor his two officers the last time he was in town, shortly after they'd arrived to the compound. He'd figured they were kept busy elsewhere, but now realized that in light of the current situation, they were likely focused on ensuring their own families' safety. He couldn't blame them, if that were the case.

Motion off to his left caught Abram's attention.

A couple of teenaged boys rushed at them, with what Abram thought was the intent to steal their supplies. Abram's heart kicked into high gear, and he reached for his pistol, but before they came any closer, Nick drew his own firearm, and the boys ran off before a warning shot even needed to be fired. Gary looked at Nick with approval, but Nick ignored him, re-holstering his gun. Abram, on the other hand, pulled his out. He needed to be ready.

Nick seemed to realize what he'd done, and pulled the weapon from its holster, holding it ready in his right hand again. Abram wondered what was going through Nick's mind. Was he as worried as Abram was? They each were at risk; Abram knew this and appreciated Nick's courage. He had been conned into Gary's raid on the store, but he had volunteered to help rescue Emma. He didn't have to do that. Didn't have to herd Gary down to the general store. Abram could have handled both the cart and the man.

Now that they were here, he was having second

thoughts about sending Gary to his likely death, and he was formulating a plan that might be risky. What he needed was to get Emma free and clear, but give Gary the chance to get away. Was it even possible? He had to be sure—he couldn't take a chance of not getting Emma back, or of her being caught in any crossfire. He needed an infallible plan.

He thought about it while they skirted the green. He could make it work if he could trust Gary. Abram felt a cold rock in the pit of his stomach—Gary was his oldest friend in the world, and here he was wondering if he could trust him. What had gone wrong between them? Was it just the lawlessness speaking to Gary's need for freedom? Or was he like this all along and Abram just hadn't noticed?

They rounded the corner across from the green and Abram came to a halt. He motioned for Nick to come over, which he did, playing out the line he was using as a leash so that Gary couldn't hear what Abram had to say.

"I can't send a man to his death," Abram said.

"He did."

"I appreciate your straightforwardness, Nick, but I'm not sure I can have this on my conscience. I think there might be a way to do this so we don't have to sacrifice Gary."

"What's your plan?"

"I want to loosen the binds around Gary's hands. That will give him a fighting chance to get free. But it will have to look as if they are still tied—do you think you can do that?"

"I can, but can we trust Gary to keep it a secret until you have Emma back?"

Abram pursed his lips. "I think so."

"It's up to you, Abram. Emma's your daughter, and Gary is

your friend. I'm just not sure what we'll do with Gary afterward."

Abram considered his options. With time quickly running out, he had only moments to make up his mind.

They led Gary back around the corner, out of sight of the store, while Abram explained the plan. Nick looked around to see if anyone was watching, but he didn't see a single soul roaming the streets or sidewalks.

"Do you understand, Gary?" Abram asked, voice quiet.

"Yeah."

"If you try anything, or mess this up for Emma in any way, I won't hesitate to shoot you point blank where you stand."

"Trust me. I didn't mean for this to happen to Emma. I want to save her too. I swear, I won't mess this up."

Nick stood nearby, silent. He questioned Gary's commitment to go through with the whole thing, right up until Emma was in her father's arms. It was Gary who was ready to give up Emma when Nick and his family had arrived at the compound. Now, his about-face was somewhat unnerving.

"Okay, Nick," Abram said. "Do your thing."

Nick began to loosen the twine around Gary's hands so that when he held his arms crossed in front, it looked as if they were still tied together. Nick stepped away when he was finished and went to stand behind the cart. It wasn't that he was worried about someone stealing the supplies, but he wanted to appear to be doing something. He was nervous and wasn't sure what would happen in the next hour.

He let out a long sigh as he listened to Abram run

through the plan with Gary again. He wished that he and his children had stayed in Manchester. They would have been safe in their home—even if he'd had to travel to get food and water, they probably wouldn't have been facing the uncertainty of a hostage exchange. He had no confidence that it wouldn't go wrong.

And he had no desire to die in this tiny town in the Vermont backwoods. His children would grow up as orphans in a whole new world, and the thought terrified him. Sure, Maggie would take care of Corey and Rae Ann, he knew that, but he wasn't ready to die.

Emma needed to use the restroom. She tried calling out and then screaming until her throat was sore, but no one came. That's when she lay on her back and started pounding her feet against the wall. Her shoes made a decent amount of noise when she slammed her heels into it, and for a moment she was afraid her feet would go right through the wall. Then she decided she didn't care if they went through. It would serve them right for leaving her down here with no bathroom.

The basement door opened, and a pair of feet came quickly down the stairs.

"Stop that," Cindy said.

"I have to use the bathroom," Emma said through the gag.

There was a hand on her face, and the gag was pulled away. "What?"

"I have to use the bathroom," Emma repeated herself.

"That's a problem, isn't it? Stay here, and don't make any

more noise. I have to get something to cut the binds around your legs."

Emma was tempted to tell Cindy that it was pretty stupid to ask her to stay here when her lower legs were bound together, but she wanted to be on Cindy's good side, so she didn't. She rolled over on her side—her arms were killing her, tied behind her back and stuck under her body. A minute or two later, she heard Cindy's feet coming back down the stairs.

"Lie still," the woman said.

Emma felt a knife slide between her legs, front and back, and then Cindy was helping her to stand. She started to lead her toward the stairs, but Emma balked.

"I can't see to get up the stairs," Emma said.

"I can't take the blindfold off."

Cindy helped Emma climb the stairs, and it was slow-going. Once they were upstairs, Cindy opened the door into the hallway and directed Emma into the bathroom. The woman came in with her, and removed the blindfold, before stepping out again.

It was a windowless room, with no hidden exits, as far as Emma could see. It was like a service station bathroom, the old style where you had to go around the side or the back of the building. The sink and toilet were clean but stained, and the room itself was dingy.

She used the facilities the best she could with her hands still bound behind her back. When she was done, Cindy came in and replaced the blindfold back over her eyes before leading her back down the basement stairs.

"You don't have to do this, you know," Emma said. "The man who killed your husband wasn't even related to me."

"No, but I'm assuming your dad is bringing him to us because we have you to trade for him."

The sound of tape ripping from the roll echoed in the basement, and moments later, Emma felt the tape winding around her ankles.

"You could just let me go now," Emma said. "If they are almost here, then you'll have your man, and I'll be safe. Just let me go out the back."

"I can't do that. You are our bargaining chip."

Then the door opened at the top of the stairs.

"They're here," a man said. "It's showtime."

28

ABRAM, Nick, and Gary stopped on the far side of the street in front of the store. Abram wanted plenty of space between the people who had his daughter and his small group. There needed to be maneuvering room.

Three men appeared on the top step of the stairs up to the door, and when they stepped down, Abram could see a woman holding a bound, gagged, and blindfolded Emma.

His heart stood still a moment, then he reminded himself that she was alive and in one piece. And she didn't appear to be injured in any way, though who knew what they'd done to her mentally. He pushed the cart forward and motioned for Nick to send Gary ahead too.

"Here's what you asked for." Abram spoke loudly enough for them to hear him across the street. "Now let her go."

"No way in hell that's half your food—you're cheating us." The tall man appeared to be the spokesman of the group.

"It's what we could get together in the amount of time you gave us."

The tall man motioned to the cart. "Push the cart over here. I want to check what you brought."

Abram pushed the cart further into the street and backed away. This was where this could all go terribly wrong. The first two layers of boxes were fine, but if he opened either of the bottom layers, they were in trouble. He rested his hand on his pistol, ready to pull it from the holster. He wished Emma wasn't blindfolded. If gunfire broke out, she wouldn't be able to get out of the way.

The tall man opened the first box, then a second. The man then shuffled through the boxes and cans down to the bottom of the pile. When he reached for the third box, Abram's heart raced faster. He was sure the box in his hand was one that was filled with dirt. Nick tensed up next to him. He had to do something, and quick.

"Okay," Abram said before the man opened the third box. "You can see that we've held up our end of the bargain. Release my daughter."

The man opened the box, ignoring him. He paused, then glared up at him. "Oh, really?" He tipped the box upside down, allowing the dirt to fall to the ground.

"You cheat!" the stocky man said, reaching behind him. "She's dead."

"No," the woman yelled. "We can't."

"We can, and we will."

The stocky man pulled his gun and swung to aim it at Emma, but Abram was faster—he took his shot and a blossom appeared on the man's chest, his body falling forward down the steps, carried by his own momentum. The two men left alive on the steps scattered, Gary turned and rushed up the street, while Abram ducked behind a vehicle parked on the far side of the road. Nick too had retreated and was using an SUV as cover. Bullets were ricocheting off the cars, and the windshield of the pickup Abram was crouching behind was pockmarked with bullet holes.

Abram was having trouble seeing where the bullets were coming from; every time he raised his head, a shell pinged off the bed of the truck. He fired at what he hoped was the car shielding the tall man, and heard a window shatter.

He heard Emma yell, "Dad," and then a scream, and when he looked out around the side of the truck, she was gone.

When Cindy dashed back inside the store, Emma lost her balance and fell backward onto the top step. She hadn't been shot, but Cindy had been steadying her, and without her, Emma lost her equilibrium. She had her legs, but her arms were securely tied behind her back, and she couldn't see a thing. She felt herself falling but even stepping backward couldn't stop it.

She fell flat on her back, crushing her fingers and arms and banging her head hard. She blinked back tears and tried to think. If she stood, someone was bound to shoot her by mistake. Or on purpose—she'd heard a man threaten to kill her, and she didn't doubt he'd do it if he got the chance.

She rolled onto her side and, finding the railing with her foot, pushed her body in what she thought must've been the direction of the door. She wondered if she'd be able to open it with her feet and squirm her way through. A bullet hit the stairs, and something struck her face. It stung.

"Watch for Emma," her dad roared from the other side of the street.

Of course, they were shooting in this direction, so if one of her capturers didn't turn around and shoot her, the only bullets that would come her way would be her people's. That would be too bad, to be killed by the people who'd come to rescue her. She lay on her stomach as far from the steps as she could get, pressed up against the building, and of course, blocking the door she wanted to get through.

Lying helpless, she was still blindfolded and unable to use her arms. She might've been able to get to her feet, but if she did, she'd probably get shot before she could get away.

She rubbed the side of her face against the cement of the stoop and tried to dislodge the blindfold. The concrete was rough and hurt her skin, but she kept trying. The trouble was that the material rolled, and then when she raised her head to do it again, it unrolled right back down again. She grunted in frustration.

Footsteps came up the stairs, fast.

She cried out, "Dad!" but it wasn't her father. She was yanked to her feet, and a solid arm held her fast across the middle, shielding the man behind her. She screamed in frustration. She needed to be able to see. Her arms were trapped between their bodies, and pain seared her shoulders. He dragged her to the side, and then the door was open, and they were moving into the shop, away from her father. The only good thing was she wasn't as likely to be killed by friendly fire inside.

Then she realized that while she was safe from the firefight outside, the man dragging her inside probably had a gun too, and there would be no one in here who would care enough to stop him shooting her.

"Dad," she shouted through the gag. But it was no use—he couldn't hear her.

Abram glanced around the truck just in time to see one of the men dashing up the stairs toward where Emma was lying in front of the door to the general store. He raised his gun to fire, but a bullet hit the fender and caused him to jerk back. In the seconds it took him to recover and aim again, the man had grabbed Emma and was using her as a human shield. She was blocking his shot.

He watched in despair as she was dragged through the door backward, into the store and out of his reach. They would have to get inside if they were to rescue her. He spotted movement out of the corner of his eye and dropped to the ground just as a bullet hit the body of the truck where he'd been crouched. He rolled under the pickup and came out on the other side.

Now he was out of the range of the tall man's fire, but he also couldn't cover Nick without exposing his head to fire. He peeked over the hood, but Nick had drawn the man's attention, and they were shooting it out. They had to get out of here, find a way to escape before they were both dead. But he couldn't leave Emma alone here with these people.

What if he and Nick could escape across the green? Could they then find a way to ambush the store? Could they get there before Emma was killed? He wished he knew what was going on in there. He hadn't heard any shots from inside, so maybe she was still alive. He had to find out. If he went home without Emma, and he'd ended up sacrificing Emma for Gary, he'd never be able to live with himself.

Why had he been so foolish? Gary hadn't been himself since he'd gotten here. Gary had no great love for Emma that he would allow himself to be sacrificed for her. And yet Abram had tried to save him. Did save him, apparently, because Gary was long gone and only Nick had stayed to help Abram rescue Emma.

And now they were all going to fail. They would probably die, all three of them. He needed to think, to come up with a plan that would save them all. But those damn gunshots were like explosions in his brain, making thought difficult. It was impossible to come up with a plan. He tried the door of the truck, and it opened. He slid onto the seat, lying across the center console. It wasn't comfortable, but it felt safer, quieter. Maybe in here, isolated from the commotion outside, his brain would kick into gear and he would think of a plan to save Emma.

It was warmer in the truck than outside, and for some reason, it smelled of cinnamon. He wondered why that was. He noticed that the keys were still in the ignition, and he wondered if it had gas in it. Could he use it to ram the building? He doubted it would go up the stairs, and unless he could get through the doors or the boarded-up windows into the store, it wouldn't do him any good.

He wished there was a way to communicate with Nick. He needed his help. But he'd left Nick on the outside, battling it out with the tall man on the street. Nick seemed to be holding his own; as far as Abram knew, their adversary hadn't even winged him. But how much longer could this go on? How long until one of them was dead?

As Corey came into the outskirts of town, he noticed the birds had stopped singing. This caused him to approach even more cautiously than he had been. It wasn't something he would have registered back home in Manchester, whether the birds were singing or not, but here he knew it was significant. If the birds weren't singing, something was going on that they didn't like.

Maybe the birds in Manchester were just so used to cars and horns and other city noises that they didn't stop singing like this. Corey didn't remember them ever going quiet—they were usually squawking at some cat or larger bird, or driving the squirrels away from their feeders. He'd once seen a jay divebomb a cat that got too close to its nest of eggs. But here and now, the silence was creepy—it seemed unnatural.

He studied the houses as he walked, checking for signs of inhabitants. Everyone seemed to be hiding. No one relaxed on the porch, watching children play in their yards. No one washed windows or cars. Then again, they might not have water, and they probably couldn't mow their lawns, either. Still, it was so strange that there was no sign of human inhabitation. There were no kids on bikes or jumping rope—there were so many things children could do without electricity, and he knew there must've been children in this town.

A gunshot rang out from not too far away, and then a moment later, a volley of shots fired. He started to run, forgetting his caution. His heart pounded in his ears, and he had a lump of fear in his throat. What was happening? He hoped Emma was okay. His dad and Emma's dad too. Gary could die, for all he cared, if the others were still alive.

He rounded the corner onto the main street and came to a stop. A man on his side of the road was shooting at something across the road. As he watched, his father's head bobbed up and he took a shot at the man. Abram was nowhere in sight. It just seemed to be the man and his father caught in the battle. He stepped back around the corner and leaned against the wall of the building so he wouldn't distract his father. He needed to focus all his attention on the man with the gun.

Corey put his hand on his own gun. Should he shoot at the man? He didn't think he could kill a person. What if Corey tried and missed? Should he chance it? Something could go horribly wrong. But what could he do?

Corey lifted his gun, his heart pounding in his chest.

29

Nick was sitting on the ground, back against the SUV, his head pounding. *The shooter across the street must be reloading*, he thought. It had been at least ten seconds since a shot had been fired. He couldn't see how he was going to get out of this alive. Only one man was gunning for them at the moment, but there were more in the store, and Emma was in there too. How were they going to get out of this alive?

A car door slammed, which was kind of surprising—who would get in a car in the middle of a shootout? But then Abram ran across the gap between the truck he'd been hiding behind and the SUV Nick was using for cover. Abram touched his arm and said something, but Nick couldn't tell what it was. He just knew they were going to die here. He shook his head in incomprehension.

"Are you hurt?" Abram asked.

This time the words made it through.

"I'm fine," he said.

"We're going to end this now," Abram said. "We're going

to go in there and get Emma. But it's going to take two of us to get inside. Are you in?"

"How?"

"We are going to run right across the street and into the store. To get across in one piece, we are both going to have to shoot at the tall guy behind the car over there. If we both keep shooting, he should have to stay undercover, allowing us to get inside." Abram peered into Nick's eyes. "Are you with me here, Nick?"

"But what about the guy inside? He has a gun."

"We have to take our chances. Otherwise, we'll be stuck here for who knows how long."

"We'd be leaving ourselves wide open for the other guy. We need to be able to at least keep our eyes peeled for him. I can't do that and shoot at this guy." Nick pointed his thumb toward the tall man, who was loading his gun.

Abram let out a sharp breath. "We have to. There's no other way. I can look out for the guy inside, but you'll need to cover me, then."

Nick shook his head.

"For Emma."

Nick could hear a slight crack in Abram's voice as he said his daughter's name. He ran his hand through his hair and dropped his gaze. After a moment he met Abram's pleading glance. "Okay," he said, "but I think this is suicide."

Abram grabbed Nick by the shoulder in appreciation. "Put a fresh magazine in your pistol. We need all the ammo we can get."

Nick ejected the partially used magazine and pulled a fresh one from his holster, clicking it home. The task was a little more difficult with his hands shaking with fear. Or was it adrenaline? Maybe both. He looked up at Abram.

"On three," Abram said, and Nick nodded. "One..."

Just then, a gunshot came from another direction. Abram and Nick exchanged a quick glance, and Abram snuck a quick peek before yelling, "Go, go, go!"

Nick was confused but did as he was told. He stood up and ran as fast as he could toward the entry of the store. But when he went to shoot at the man, he noticed the man was firing his weapon in another direction, toward the source of the unknown gunman. Maybe Gary was back to help them—but where did he get a gun?

In less than ten seconds, they hurried up the few steps that lead to the store's entrance. Abram turned and fired one round into the tall man's head, and he collapsed.

Then, Abram grabbed Nick's arm and pulled him into the store. Shots rang out from the back of the store and Nick dived into one of the aisles. But someone had stacked a short wall of cans across the opening, and Nick tripped and fell. He struggled to get up, but the food was underfoot now, and he couldn't get purchase on the floor.

Footsteps sounded at the end of the aisle, and he looked up to see a figure, all dressed in black, coming at him from the other end of the row. He reached for his gun, but it was gone—he'd dropped it when he fell. He could see it, but it was out of reach. He relaxed onto the ground amidst the rolling cans and closed his eyes. He'd gotten Abram into the store, and now he was done.

A shot fired above him.

Abram heard Nick fall, the cans rolling along the floor and the scrabbling as he tried to get up again. He also listened for the steps of the gunman coming for him. He sent a covering shot down the length of the store and dashed across the gap so he could hide in front of the endcap of the aisle Nick was in. He risked a quick look to see Nick on his back on the floor, with a gunman who hadn't been outside bearing down on him.

Abram didn't even think; he aimed between the eyes and shot the gunman before he could kill Nick. The gunman fell with a thud, and Nick's eyes flew open. Abram gave him a hand up.

"We're even now," Abram said. He motioned toward the far end of the aisle to indicate they should go that way, and Nick nodded in agreement.

He wondered how many people were left in the store. At least one woman and one man. The woman who'd been holding Emma on the porch landing and the man who had dragged her inside. Plus, anyone else who might have been waiting inside for the transaction to take place. That number could be indefinite.

They made their way, stepping carefully and as quietly as they could down the aisle. These shelves were high, seven feet at least, Abram figured. Much higher than what was typically found in a small-town store, but it worked to their advantage as much as their disadvantage. He couldn't see the people in the store, but they couldn't see him either.

Nick stopped in front of him, and Abram came to stand beside him. He froze.

Emma was standing in the produce section, still blindfolded, still bound and gagged. But she was still in the clutches of the man who had dragged her through the door and was now holding a gun to her head. She was crying silently, the tears seeping out from under the cloth covering her eyes. He longed to talk to her, to tell her that everything was all right. That they'd have her out of here in a moment, but he was afraid to speak. Fearful that the smallest motion or sound would cause the finger on the trigger to twitch and put a bullet in her head.

Time stood still. The man seemed to be unsure of whose eye to catch, Abram's or Nick's. But he settled on Abram, perhaps seeing the panic that had welled up within him. They locked eyes, and Abram tried to take the measure of the man, but there was nothing there to tell him if his daughter would be shown mercy, or if he'd be willing to trade Abram's life for hers. There was nothing there at all, and Abram felt a chill run down his back.

On his way toward the front of the store, Corey saw the tall man sprawled out on the road behind the car, bullet hole in his head.

His stomach churned as he moved on to the stairs to the store. A shot rang out from inside and Corey raced up them, entering the building as silently as he could. He crept down the center aisle and couldn't see or hear anyone in the store, but he knew they had to be there. There'd been gunfire from in here just a moment ago.

He spotted Emma—blindfolded and gagged—and held his breath. The man holding her was looking the other way, focused on something out of Corey's line of sight. He'd have to be careful—Emma was so close to the man, but his aim was excellent now...he could aim for a spot behind the man's ear, then Emma should be okay. Her head only came to his shoulder.

He felt suddenly cold at the thought of killing a man at such close range, but the man had Emma, and if he were going to let her go, he would have done it by now. It was her or her captor, and Corey knew which one to choose. He didn't know what would happen to his immortal soul, or even if he had one, but he did know he couldn't stand by and let his best friend in the world be killed.

He raised his gun, stepping forward, and glass beneath his foot crunched. The man's head and gun hand whipped in Corey's direction as Corey pulled the trigger, and his bullet missed. The man was luckier; he squeezed his finger, again and again, the gun firing three times. The noise rang in Corey's ears, and a burning pain seared his side.

He dropped his gun and put his hand to his side, trying to stop the bleeding. He fell to his knees on the floor and then over onto his side, glass stinging his cheek. More gunfire echoed in the store, and he tried to cry out to Emma. But the world was going black, and nothing came out of his mouth.

The shot that was fired confused Abram—where had it come from? But the distraction was all he needed. The moment the man loosened his grip on Emma, he shot. A bubble of blood blossomed on the man's forehead as Emma jumped and screamed, and the man's body dropped.

Abram and Nick surged forward to grab her, Abram

wrapping his arms around his daughter. "It's me," he said and began to work the blindfold from her eyes. Movement caught his eye, and he saw the woman, who had been holding Emma outside, run for the door. He could take care of her later—for now, Emma needed him. The blindfold gone, he started to work on the gag as Emma stood sobbing and shaking.

"There's a boy down over here," Nick said.

"Can you help me with her wrists?" Abram asked, but Nick ran down the aisle, presumably in search of the boy.

Abram ignored Nick's distraction and pulled a Swiss army knife from his pocket. He carefully sawed at the rope around her wrists, careful not to cut Emma's skin. He felt hot anger at the condition of her arms where the cord had bit into her. She was rubbed raw, and there were bruises the size and shape of fingerprints. If the man hadn't already been dead, he would have shot him again. As it was, when he got his hands on that woman, she'd be dead too.

Come to think of it, he hadn't heard the door to the store open. Was she still in here, ready to die?

"Stay here with Nick," Abram said. "I have something to take care of before we head home."

Nick moved from Abram and Emma to see the teenager who was lying on the floor. His back was to Nick, and his shirt and hoody were soaked with blood. The boy looked familiar, but his hood was up, and Nick couldn't see his face. His clothes reminded him of Corey, but Corey was back at the house, safe on the farm. Not here with a bullet hole in his side.

But those were Corey's shoes, he was sure of it. He dove

for the boy, grabbing his hooded head, and turned his face so Nick could see.

"Corey!"

His boy's face was gray and bloodless.

"No, no, no," Nick cried, tears running down his cheeks.

He felt for a pulse, and held his breath, hoping one could be found.

Abram found the woman on her knees at the front of the store. She was staring through the window, her eyes on the man lying on the sidewalk, the first casualty of the gunfight, tears running down her face. Abram pulled his gun and aimed for her head, but Emma sucked in her breath behind him.

"Dad, don't," she said, the words coming out in a croak.

He stood a moment longer, the gun pointed at the back of the woman's head, knowing she was aware of him now. His hand began to shake, and he was ashamed of himself. There was a difference between killing someone in defense and shooting them point blank, execution style.

"Nobody else has to die." Emma's voice reached him as if through a fog.

Abram holstered the gun. She was right, but he couldn't leave the woman here—she knew where they lived. "Find me something to tie her with, Emma. We have to take her with us."

Emma disappeared and returned with a package of clothesline. He took the knife back out of his pocket, cut a length, and pulled the woman's arms behind her back. She didn't put up a fight, still distraught as she stared at the dead man outside. He quickly tied her hands behind her and said to the woman, "Stay here."

"Oh no," Emma cried, and dashed across the room. Abram turned to see what was happening, his hand straying to his holster once again. But it wasn't a threat...it was Corey, lying on the floor, his clothes soaked in his blood. It was Corey who shot at the man who was holding her, and he'd taken a bullet giving Abram a chance to kill the man.

A cold fear washed over him. Had Corey been killed?

"Corey! Corey, talk to me." Emma was across the room on her knees next to Nick, calling his name frantically, and Abram feared the worst. "Corey, wake up," she sobbed. Abram noticed Nick was crying as well.

Abram went to put a hand on Emma's shoulder to comfort her, but she shrugged it off.

"Corey," she cried again. And Abram felt helpless.

Corey heard someone calling his name from far, far away. He was lost in darkness and pain, but he could hear her, and so he tried to wake up. *I'm here*, he said, *I'm right here*, but no sound came out of his mouth.

Pain brought him to his senses, and he yelled.

"Easy, Corey," his dad said. "I'm packing your wound so we can get you back to the farm. I know it hurts."

But the pain was in his back, and his hands were pressed to the bullet hole in his side. He wanted to tell his father he was in the wrong place, but he was fading out again. He was awake again a moment later when they were working on the bullet hole. They'd pulled his hands away, and there was a searing pain, a burning that took his breath away.

"Emma, go out and empty the dirt boxes from the garden cart, and pile the food on either side. We want a channel in the middle for Corey. Do you understand?" This was Abram's voice.

"I can't put him in a fireman's lift," this was his dad, "because there might be a bullet..."

Corey was in the black again, the calm, painless black where nothing hurt. He wanted to stay here, to fall deeper into the cool darkness, but the pain kept pulling him back into the light. They were carrying him seated on their forearms. And just before his head lolled forward, he saw a figure holding the door open.

Something jarred his entire body, making the wound in his gut scream. There were trees and sky above, and he was being rattled along. He caught a glimpse of Emma, though she didn't seem real. Was he dreaming?

The tolling of the gate bell pulled him into consciousness. Someone was ringing and ringing the bell. Didn't Abram have the key? Corey was sure Abram had been with them. So why was the bell ringing? His head thudded with the metallic reverb. "You can stop now," he said, but no one heard him.

The Guinea hens and chickens squawked nearby, and the goats bleated, but Corey didn't open his eyes. His lids were too heavy. They had made it to the compound.

There was a rough patch where they carried him again, and it hurt so bad. He wanted to tell them to stop, to leave him in the grass, but he couldn't get any words to come out. Only groaning and sobbing, and he just wanted them to put him down.

Then, finally, he was still again, but on something hard. It was solid, but if he was still, he could go back into the dark, and he could stay in the dark where there was no pain.

"Corey." Something cold soothed his cheek. "Corey, open your eyes, I need to talk to you."

It was Maggie, and she was sprinkling something cold and wet on his face. Didn't she know he just wanted to sleep?

"Come on, Corey, I need you awake for this." It was Maggie's voice again.

He opened his eyes.

"There he is," Maggie said, looking down at him. "Corey, you've got a bullet in your side, and I need to get it out so I can sew you up. I don't have anything to put you under with, so I need you awake. You have to hold really still. Okay? It's going to hurt, but I want you to stay as still as you can. Do you understand?"

He nodded, but tears welled in his eyes. He didn't want her to know he was afraid. He held himself rigid so she wouldn't see his hands shake.

"That's right," she said, and then there was a horrible burning in his side.

30

Nick stood at the end of the kitchen table, watching Maggie work on his boy. He'd nearly broken down when tears had started dripping down Corey's face. The boy bit his lip and didn't say a word, but the tears still flowed.

Maggie cut back the shirt, cleaned the skin with disinfectant, and took a pair of hook-nosed tweezers from a sterile package. She felt along Corey's abdomen before plunging the instrument into the hole made by the bullet.

Corey let out a scream.

"Hold him down, Nick," Maggie said.

Nick held his boy's arms down, distraught at the amount of pain Corey was now in.

A few moments passed, though to Corey they must have felt like eternity, and then there was a clink as Maggie dropped the bullet into a kitchen saucer.

"Okay, now I'm going to irrigate this and stitch him up." She turned to Corey. "I'm going to pour some saline into the wound to flush it out, and then I'm going to stitch you up. It'll hurt, but not as bad as pulling out the bullet."

Corey nodded and scrunched his eyes shut.

"You're going to be fine, son." Nick took Corey's hand, his eyes welling up with tears.

Corey closed his eyes and grimaced when the saline was squirted into the bullet hole. As the stitches went in, he gritted his teeth, and when she was finished dressing the wound, Corey's face was gray again.

Nick lifted his son from the table and carried him to his bed. Emma, who was waiting in a chair by the bed, had pulled back the covers.

"Give us a few minutes, Emma, I'm going to put him in fresh clothes," Nick said.

She nodded and left, and Nick was left to remove blood-soaked clothes from his boy.

Emma found her father waiting in the living room, sitting with her mother and the woman who they'd brought back from the store. She could see Rae Ann sitting on the porch outside, hugging her stuffed bear. Her mother stood and wrapped her arms around Emma, holding her close. "I was so scared for you," her mother said.

"Me too," Emma said into her mother's shoulder. They stood that way a few minutes, Emma breathing in the scent of her mom, so thankful to be home. When they broke apart, Emma turned to her dad.

"Thanks for coming to get me, Dad."

Her dad stood up. "You don't have to thank me for that," he said and pulled her to him. He wrapped her in a tight hug and then let her go. "I'm so relieved to have you back in one piece. I've never been so afraid."

"Dad, I heard something while I was with those people. I think you should know."

"What's that?"

"There are bandits in pickup trucks raiding people. One of the men was talking about them. They sound awful."

"I'll look into it, Emma. But I don't want you to worry about it. Okay?"

"What happened to Gary? I saw him there."

"He ran away."

"Where do you think he went?"

"I'm not sure, but I imagine he'll come back sooner or later."

"If he comes back, are we going to let him stay?"

"I don't know." Her dad sat back down. "But as far as Nick and his family are concerned, they have a spot here for as long as they want. And we need them now more than ever—I didn't realize how many people it took to run a place this size."

"Yeah, and guarding the perimeter in case any of those bandits show up."

"Right. Why don't you go out and tell Rae Ann her brother is okay?"

Emma went out to sit with Rae Ann on the step in the fading light.

"Corey is going to be just fine," Emma said to Rae Ann, leaning closer to the girl.

"I know," Rae Ann said, playing with her stuffed bear, Louise. She held the bear to her chest again and shivered.

"You should come inside, Rae," Emma said. "You're cold."

"Can I see Corey now?" Rae Ann asked.

Emma stood up and put her hand out. "Come on, let's go see."

After a few hours, his dad let Rae Ann come in to see him. Corey tried to sit up a little so she wouldn't be worried, though he felt weak. Rae Ann stuck her head around the door, and when she saw him, she skipped in, smiling, and perched herself on the edge of his bed.

"Emma says you are going to be okay," Rae Ann said. "That's good."

"Yeah," Corey said, watching Emma sliding through the door to sit on the other bed.

"Does it hurt when you get shot?" Rae Ann was clutching Louise tightly to her chest.

"A little bit."

"Like getting stung by a bee?"

Corey chuckled, then stifled a wince as the pain coursed along his side. "Yeah, something like that."

"I've never been stung before, but I got a splinter once."

"I remember that. Splinters aren't fun either."

"Yeah, and Daddy said not to be afraid. He said that once Mister Tweezers got the splinter out of my finger, it would heal by itself, and the pain would go away. Did Mister Tweezers help you?"

Corey grinned. "Yeah, Mister Tweezers helped me too."

Rae Ann got up off the bed, and Corey noticed Emma still sitting on the other bed, observing.

"Where are you going, Rae Ann?" Corey asked.

"I'm going to see what Shelly is making for dinner now. Can we play cards later?"

"Sounds good to me, Rae."

Rae Ann shifted her gentle gaze to Emma. "You too?"

"Me too," Emma said.

"Good." Rae Ann turned and skipped from the room.

Emma came closer and sat on the bed. "Hey, how are you feeling?"

"Like I was shot."

Emma chuckled, then cleared her throat. "I'm sorry, Core."

"Don't be."

"But you got shot."

"I'd get shot a hundred times more if it would save you."

"I know." She leaned in to give him a hug, being careful not to lean on his injury. "I'm so glad you're okay. You really scared me." She kissed him on the cheek and sat back. "Remind me never to climb over the perimeter fence again." She made a face.

"I don't think you'll be able to. Dad says they are putting razor wire all around the top."

"Emma," Shelly said, poking her head around the door, "come and eat. Corey, your dad will bring you your dinner. Maggie says you aren't to get out of bed except to use the bathroom for a few days, while your body replenishes your blood supply."

"Yes, ma'am," Corey said.

He was glad when they left the room, and he could lay flat again. He didn't want to make a big deal of it, but he was tired and sore.

After dinner, Abram lumbered down to Gary's cabin with his food on a plate. Sure enough, Gary was there, sitting at his table in the lantern light, drinking vodka. Abram placed the plate in front of him.

"You should probably eat this if you are going to drink that," Abram said.

"You kicking me out?" Gary asked, a slight slur to his words.

"That's not a decision I can make by myself, you know that. We'll have to take a vote, and you should know, Nick and his family are full residents now, so Nick will get a vote too." Abram watched Gary's face.

"You know if it comes to a vote, I don't have a chance," Gary said.

"And whose fault is that? You make stupid choices, and you got my daughter kidnapped. If I didn't know you have a good heart under all that, I'd vote you out, too. But you and I have history, so I can't do it."

"What about the woman you brought back from town, you letting her stay?"

"I don't know yet. We'll have to talk about it. I'm afraid if we let her leave, she'll lead another raid against us."

"Can you convince the others to let me stay?"

"I'll try, but there are no guarantees. Eat your dinner, and I'll take your plate back with me."

Once Gary had finished his dinner, Abram grabbed his empty plate and headed back to the main house. There, he spotted Shelly washing the dishes. "He was there, just like I thought he would be," Abram said.

Shelly rinsed a dish with a jug of water. "Then tell him to go. We don't want him here."

"Shelly—"

"Abram," Shelly cut him off, slamming the jug on the counter. "That man almost got our child killed. He's reckless and stupid and a killer. I don't want him here." She began drying her hands with a towel.

"Shelly, you know sending him out into the world is the same as putting a bullet in his head. If we do that, we're as bad as he is."

"I don't care, Abram. Who has to die before you see the truth?"

"Trouble is coming. There are already groups of bandits forming. Emma heard about them in town, so I got on the ham radio and asked. It's true—young men that somehow have gasoline for their trucks are driving up and down the state, robbing and killing. You know Gary is good in those kinds of situations."

"I can't agree with you, Abram, not on this. I know that you think we'll need him, but I'm afraid he's going to get one of us killed."

"I understand," he said. But he worried. If bandits crashed through their gate with a truck, they'd need all the guns they could muster against a raid. Gary was a sharpshooter and fearless. He would be an asset in a fight. How to convince the others, though?

"What about the woman…Cindy?" Shelly asked. "Are you going to keep her here?"

"I don't know. It might not be a good idea to let her go—she could lead people to us. She knows what we have, and she has plenty of motive to retaliate against us."

Shelly nodded, but remained silent.

"We'll talk to the others about it," Abram said. "I've said Nick and the kids can stay, so Nick will have a vote, same as you and Maggie."

"Okay," Shelly said, her eyes now starting to water.

"Shelly," Abram said, his voice gentle. "What's wrong?"

Shelly inhaled a sniffle. "I just can't believe this is all happening," she said, her voice a mere whisper.

Abram wrapped his arms around Shelly, giving her a hug. He took a deep breath and closed his eyes. "Don't worry, Shelly. Whatever happens, I'll always be here for you and Emma. We'll get through this."

A few days later, Nick was coming off watch duty at breakfast time when he ran into Abram pulling the cart loaded with razor wire up toward the fence line.

"You're starting early, Abram," he said as they met in the drive.

"Trouble is coming, Nick. We need to be prepared."

"Have you heard something on the ham radio?"

"Nothing new, but there seems to be more and more young men joining the existing bandits. The draw appears to be the promise of food and safety for the men and their families. Apparently, they have compounds of their own in the south, near Bennington and Brattleboro. We're off the beaten track here, but people know where we are. I'm afraid your friend Joshua is unhappy enough with us that he'll tell them where we are. You were right; we should have let him join us."

"You weren't to know. Hindsight and all that." Nick motioned to the razor wire. "Do you want help with that?"

"No, this is not stuff you want to be messing with when you are tired, Nick. Anyway, I'm just hauling this up. It's time for me to go on watch. I'll see you later."

Nick nodded and strode down to the house, enjoying the fresh morning air. It would warm this afternoon; spring was progressing. He heard the laughter emanating from the kitchen before he even reached the porch, and he was smiling when he walked in. Corey, Rae Ann, Emma, and Maggie were playing a lively game of cards at the kitchen table. Rae Ann was hampered by Louise, who was clutched in one of her arms, but that didn't stop her from laughing as loudly as the rest.

"What are you playing?" Nick asked, grinning at their flushed faces.

"Nertz," Corey said.

"It's a game I saw people playing on some TV show I watched a few years ago," Maggie said. "It looked like fun, so I learned how to play it."

"You're not too tired, Corey?" Nick asked.

"I just got out of bed, Dad, and I've been there for three days. It will take more than a card game to tire me out." Corey grinned wide.

"And here I was, thinking you'd be missing the internet. Carry on." Nick waved his hand at the cards and went to see if Shelly had left him anything for breakfast before she'd gone out on watch with Abram. "Oh yeah, bacon sandwich," he said happily.

He stood at the counter, eating his sandwich and watching Maggie play with the kids. They seemed happy, and they were safe, for now. He hoped the bandits wouldn't come their way. Maybe they would never find them out here on a back road. That was another reason to let Gary stay: He wouldn't betray them if he were living here.

He pushed the thoughts of danger from his mind. For right now, today, they were healthy and happy, and that would have to be enough.

# # #

TO BE CONTINUED IN BOOK 2...

Thanks for reading! Want to help out?

Reviews are a big help for independent authors like us, so if you liked our book, **please consider leaving a review today.**

Thank you!

ALSO BY JJ HOLDEN

Dark New World (9 Book Series)

Dark New World
EMP Exodus
EMP Deadfall
EMP Backdraft
EMP Resurrection
EMP Retaliation
EMP Resurgence
EMP Retribution
EMP Redemption

** NOTE: The Dark New World series **contains strong language** and graphic depictions of violence **

ABOUT THE AUTHORS

J.J. Holden is the co-author of the EMP CRISIS and DARK NEW WORLD series. He lives in a secluded cabin and spends his days studying the past, enjoying the present, and pondering the future.

Mark J. Russell is the co-author of the EMP CRISIS series. An avid outdoorsman, he enjoys reading and writing stories of survival.

For updates, new release notifications, and more, please visit: www.jjholdenbooks.com

Get in touch: contact@jjholdenbooks.com

Made in United States
Troutdale, OR
01/03/2024